PRAISE FOR CAREY HARRISON'S WORK

'Fascinating, a superb analysis' *The New York Times*

'Essential reading' *The Financial Times*

'Bawdy, turbulent, rife with fiendish beauty'
The Atlanta Journal-Constitution

'Rivetingly entertaining' *The Daily Telegraph*

'Weirdly compelling, reminiscent of Jack Kerouac'
New Woman

'Fruity characterizations' *London Review of Books*

'A hypnotic novel, very clever, very imaginative, a breathtaking
attempt to get a handle on the entire human condition'
The Mail on Sunday

'Superb' *The Sunday Times*

'Astonishing, affecting, holds the reader spellbound'
Publishers Weekly

'A minor miracle, the way Harrison stitches together
the goonish and the gorgeous' *The London Times*

'Glorious, full of sensual exotica' *The Observer*

'Tremendous, a catapult of a novel' *The Kansas Star*

'As thorough an examination of postwar European
consciousness as Thomas Mann's The Magic Mountain
was of its era' *American Library Journal*

'Magnificent' *The Times*

JUSTICE

By the same author

FICTION

FREUD, A NOVEL
RICHARD'S FEET
CLEY
EGON

PLAYS

DANTE KAPUTT!
TWENTY-SIX EFFORTS
AT PORNOGRAPHY
IN A COTTAGE HOSPITAL
WEDDING NIGHT
LOVERS
SHAKESPEARE FAREWELL
MANOEUVRES (with Jeremy
Paul)
I NEVER KILLED MY
GERMAN
A SHORT WALK TO THE
STARS (with Jeremy Paul)
VISITORS (with Jeremy Paul)
A NIGHT ON THE TOR
A SUFFOLK TRILOGY: 3
PLAYS FOR RADIO
WHO'S PLAYING GOD?
I KILLED JACQUES BREL
FROM THE LION ROCK and
THE SEA VOYAGE TRILOGY
MR POPE'S TOILET
THE WATER-CURE
NEWTON IN LOVE
LAST THOUGHTS UPON
ST. PAULES

SELF-PORTRAIT WITH DOG
A WALK IN THE BOIS
THE EMPRESS WU,
THE CONCUBINE WANG
FOR A SON
A CALL FROM THE DEAD
THE PSYCHIATRIST'S TALE
EAST OF THE SUN
RICHARD'S FEET
HITLER IN THERAPY
A COOK'S TOUR OF
COMMUNISM
BREAKFAST WITH STALIN
SCENES FROM A
MISUNDERSTANDING
BAD BOY
MAGUS
MIDGET IN A CATSUIT
RECITING SPINOZA
HEDGEROW SPECIMEN
REX & REX
I WON'T BITE YOU:
AN INTERVIEW WITH THE
NOTORIOUS MONSTER,
DOROTHEA FARBER

CAREY HARRISON

JUSTICE

SKYSCRAPER

First published in the US by Dr. Cicero Books June 2013

This book is a work of fiction. Names, characters,
places and coincidences are a product of the author's mind
or are used fictitiously. Any resemblance to actual events,
locales, persons or animals, living or dead,
is entirely transcendental.

www.iwontbiteyou.com
www.drcicerobooks.com

Cover and design by Madeline Meckiffe
First UK Edition
Manufactured in the United Kingdom

ISBN-13: 978-0-9551810-2-3

For my mother

and for Chiara

In January we set out on foot my son and I starting in Budapest where Adolf Eichmann's achievement in deporting so many so fast makes other feats of racial house-cleaning seem sloppy

Maps revealed the cattle trucks' route out of Hungary across Slovakia into Poland and beside it roads that we might follow running beside the tracks

In the frozen haze of the plains only guard dogs stirred yapping behind suburban fences into the silence of the Carpathians where we walked along the rails through villages shuttered and sad as if still under a curse

Cattle trucks some of them disturbingly antique dating perhaps from 60 years ago rumbled slowly by so close we could reach out and touch them too late

The eldest of my mother's family to die in the camps was her grandfather whose grandfather watched Napoleon ride into Poznan and described it to his grandson who told my mother who told me who on the way to Poland told my son whom I had named for his great-great-grandfather

We walked in January the better to recall the cold when the Russians entered Poland and when on the death march out of the camp survivors froze shots rang out stragglers were killed

We also walked in memory of the SS our exemplars without whose obedience this camp laid bare before us would not be the capital of horror sacred to the human heart in all its heartlessness most desolate most human place on earth

–Jokubas Lissman
Seven Breaths Made Visible

PREFACE

AS I WRITE THIS, THE CONTESSA MIRI has recently celebrated her 80th birthday, surrounded by her many friends from the town, and by her sisters from England, her nieces and nephews, and two grand-nieces, very blond and very English.

I, alas, am a little bit older than Miri; but I managed the climb from the bus stop beside the little beach up to the Casa Rosa, to join the celebration, with the help of dear Pina, as sturdy a 70-year-old as I have ever known. Not for nothing are Ligurians the longest-lived of all Italians.

All that I've described, in the account that follows, happened a long time ago. It is now 1990 and Renzo Cipriano has been dead forty years and more, forty-two to be exact. No one remembers him except us. Miri and myself, that is. My wife has been dead fourteen years now; Serafina and Leandro are no longer with us; Giacomina died young, after twenty years at the Casa Rosa; young, but, as she knew, loved. Many of us, from the town I knew as I grew up in it, are gone. I spend as many days as my legs will permit – I go once a week, usually, when a fine day comes along – on the terrace of the Casa Rosa, gazing out with Miri at the view we have both studied for over sixty years, the arm of the bay as it sweeps south into the haze and melds the sky, the mountains and the sea, at last, into one colour. The lure of it is inexhaustible, and consumes all thought, all words. We are one person (I like to imagine) as we gaze at it.

Certainly, we have long since said all there is to be said about the past, although sometimes a memory will surge up, like the *beee-bahs* rising from the patient buses on the coast road, to make us laugh again at the peccadilloes of our longlost loved ones.

We still speak, from time to time, of going to visit Auschwitz together, but I think we both know we never will.

There's no need. We have a view of eternity from Miri's terrace, receding from us into greyish blue and drawing us towards the future we share with our beloved children, on whom the loneliness of age will never fall.

Much has changed. The fishing fleet goes out no more than once a month, and the night fishing, with the globular lamps like fallen planets dotting the bay, is a thing of the past. More and more the town is a resort, a tourist venue that dies in the winter (rests indoors, rather, in its yearly chrysalis) and flutters back into life in the spring. Nonetheless, the town prospers exceedingly, and there are more and more millionaires from Milan to be seen on the esplanade, moving proudly from their summer home to their yacht and back.

Are these the important things, though? Millionaires in place of fishermen? The question should be, Are we any kinder, wiser, more tolerant than we once were? (My shop sells many wise books, but what does that mean? The Germans, after all, were probably the best-read nation in the world when they embraced Adolf Hitler.) At my age, I am sceptical of human improvement. So what *is* important, then, in our town, in our life? As one gets older and lets go of certain hopes and ideals, some things still shine clearly. Beauty, for instance. I would say that, as I approach my ninetieth year, I'm still as much of a devotee of beauty as I ever was. (A propos, I like to think I spotted Miri Gottlieb's beauty even before *il Conte Piero* did. A few days before him, at any rate, because it was on the very day of her arrival in our town that the Berlins brought Miri and her family to browse in my bookshop, and I saw a gorgeous, shy, 18-year-old Jewish blue-stocking with spectacles and small, bruised-looking, pretty features in a pale round face, gazing very seriously at my bookshelves. She had not yet, I think, stepped onto the little beach and into Piero's empire. Thank goodness she did, since it has kept her here in our life, the life of the town and mine.) But in truth the beauty I intended to speak of, when I said I was still a devotee, declares itself on every fine day, as the sun draws the blue out of the sea and sends our eyes roving down the coast. As you stand on the esplanade, all earthly beauty is before you. If anyone could spoil this, that, I think, would be an important change.

(You should understand that in the Bay of Catania, my home town, all you can now see when you look out across the Ionian Sea, I'm told, are oil rigs.)

Whatever else has gone, by the time you read this narrative, including, more than likely, myself, and Miri too, I wish I could know for sure that the beauty will still be there. And I would love to know, as none of us can, while we live, how everything turns out.

Perhaps, if you tell me, I can hear. So, you who read this, kindly murmur the answers under your breath (or, if the thought embarrasses you, speak the answer in your mind, for I am surely there too, if you have read my story), and tell me: is the bay still bright with sailboats? Can you see Porto Venere on a clear morning in March, after a storm? And Africa? Can you still see Africa?

Have the fish returned, and with them the fishing fleet? Have the sea urchins returned? The jellyfish? The waterspouts?

Is Pina still alive and living at the Casa Rosa?

Is the *cancello* still open?

What has happened to the Vessinaro and its empty houses, in their bee-nuzzled cages of wistaria?

Do the *pinoli* still cluster on the sandy orange path?

Is Olimpio's *boccia* court still in use, above San Sebastiano?

Does anyone there remember the Contessa Miri?

Can you, on certain nights, hear my old friend Dario, long since gone, call his stumbling mules together on the goat track?

Are there still fireflies on the clifftop path?

Has anyone bought my cousin's farm?

YOU KILL HIM, SIGNORA CONTESSA. *WE'LL look the other way.*

The young police chief's words were already beginning to blur in Miri Gottlieb's mind as she emerged into the sunlight of the esplanade. Astonishing sunlight, after the shuttered penumbra of the police station. It was like jumping from one phase of a dream to another. And the words had been senseless, absurd. "We'll look after it," Andrea had said. *Ci occupiamo noi.* Not "We'll look the other way." But it came to the same thing. It was what he meant.

Ammazzalo lei, signora Contessa. You kill him.

CONTE, *COUNT*, WAS a title Piero had renounced long before they were married. Before Miri had even met him. But no one in the town or the neighbouring *terre* paid any attention. "*Si, signor Conte,*" tripped off their lips as readily, as naturally and unstoppably, as it had off the lips of their father and grandfather when addressing Piero's forebears. They liked saying "*Si, signor Conte.*" Miri had liked saying it too (wasn't there something pleasing about the syllables, and also something pleasing about the act of deference in itself – wasn't it consoling to have a title to nod to, regardless of its owner's worth?), and she had sometimes addressed her husband that way herself when he was being lovable, or when he was being impossible.

No, the deference was anachronistic and offensive, and the title itself was meaningless now, Piero had always insisted – rather loudly and dramatically, Miri always thought, for someone who really wanted to be done with aristocratic labels and be unobtrusively re-absorbed into the bosom of the *popolo, la gente*, people. Piero had been an ardent Communist, greatly vexed, it seemed to Miri when they first met, by his hereditary title. Later, it had come to seem to her that he enjoyed occupying both camps, exclaiming to all within earshot that he was plain 'Piero' but enjoying the feudal forelock-tugging of the peasantry, the obstinately subservient *contadini*.

Not only were titles themselves ridiculous, but his own in particular, Piero would say less loudly, was especially absurd. His grandfather Gian Carlo had been so inveterate and so inept a gambler that he had been obliged to sell all the family land, every last vineyard and property, to pay for his compulsion. Only the pride and kindness of his own *contadini* had spared him a life in a debtor's prison. They had banded together and raised the money to pay *il signor Conte*'s debts. "*I* should be bowing down to *them*," Piero very reasonably argued, mimicking it: "*Buon giorno, signore e signori contadini*. It's only thanks to them that we have a roof over our heads."

It wasn't even their roof. The house in the steep, narrow valley behind the little beach belonged (as did the beach) to a wealthy peasant farmer – he was especially obsequious in his "*signor Conte*"s – whose family had let both house and beach to Piero's family for three generations now, at a peppercorn rent.

They had met, she and Piero, when Miri Gottlieb came to Italy on holiday with her parents, who were intimates of the philosopher Isaiah Berlin, a British luminary with a summer residence in Liguria. The Berlins had invited the Gottliebs to stay in their villa across the valley from *il Conte* Piero's house. The villas straddled adjacent ridges. You could wave from the Berlins' *terrazza* to Piero's, as Miri and Piero soon discovered, across a plunging green abyss of pine and bramble and scrub. Miri was then 19 and entirely ready to fall in love with the astonishingly handsome and athletic young man Piero had been. To her it was as if he had leapt off a Greek vase or a classical fresco with his golden locks, bronzed supple limbs and soft skin. Miri had been sick with love for him on sight, and so amazed at the existence of such a being that she had stood simply staring at him and forgotten to take off her glasses and make 'the best of herself' in her mother's dispiriting phrase.

She first saw him on the little beach. Piero let anyone use it whom he knew and was inclined to like. This included the Berlin household. The beach was sandy, a rarity on this rocky, volcanic stretch of the Ligurian coastline, which was otherwise liable to tear at feet and legs and even arms and torsos with its sharp edges above and below water, and with its sea urchins, whose spines stabbed deep into human flesh and broke off there, to be picked at laboriously and painfully.

Every day, Piero was on the beach with his friends; better said, his acolytes. To Miri it seemed that Piero moved and spoke as if the word 'dashing' had been coined for him, and as if he were committed to incarnating it in every word and deed. He jumped up onto tables and sang (loudly, badly, but with maddening charm), dove spectacularly, and with an Olympian's skill, from the highest board, drove like a demon and danced like a god – so it appeared to Miri's besotted eyes.

And in truth there *are* such bewitching creatures. A beautiful, blond Italian! And interested in her, it seemed, of all impossible things. On their first date, Piero had demanded that Miri put her glasses back on. Standing back, he studied her. "Now I can see you better," he had said in English, smiling, delighted at his own joke.

A beautiful, blond Italian, so young and already a count, to boot – Piero's father Vittorio had died young at the wheel of his car, an aristocratic Italian death, it was generally agreed, and one whose likelihood Piero seemed eager to inherit along with the title. Miri had a father, something Piero's charm and title could not buy. She always thought it was her family Piero had fallen in love with, not her. Nonetheless, Piero had loved to show Miri off – the bespectacled, not especially pretty Jewish girl, as she felt herself to be – and had immediately flashed Miri under the noses of his racehorse-sleek Riviera girlfriends, as if Miri were the latest in socialist accoutrements. A plain, relatively poorly dressed – (well, *English*, so what could you expect? Miri felt) – Jew in glasses. Could you get much more left-wing that that? It was 1928, the year of the Sixth Communist International Congress, the year of Trotsky's exile from Russia. If a pedigree were required for Miri Gottlieb, her father Avram was not only a friend of Isaiah Berlin's and a real live Communist, but a celebrated one. Avram's book-length attacks on capitalist economics were known to all his friends, Piero claimed, though Miri saw no evidence of this. Piero was certainly excited to know Gottlieb's daughter; it was her father, specifically, with whom Piero had fallen in love, Miri suspected, not with Avram's small, stout, bearded person but with his fame and impeccable socialist credentials.

"We shall marry in Moscow and attend Karl Marx University together," Piero announced within a week of meeting Miri and before marriage had even entered Miri's most outrageous daydreams, as besotted with Piero as she was. Marry in Moscow? Karl Marx University? Was that in Moscow too? She was in ecstasy. As a suitor Piero was tireless and inventive (couldn't he see, Miri sometimes wondered, that he didn't have to be so industrious, or was he just doing it to glory in the role?). He brought her roses every single day, on foot and perspiring from the climb to the Berlins' eyrie, an entirely unnecessary pilgrimage since the Berlins had installed an elevator, at great expense, which rose through the mountain – visitors reached the foot of it via a tunnel at sea level, leading into the hillside from the coast road – to reach their lovely hilltop villa. But it was the unnecessariness, Piero would point out calmly, that was the whole appeal of it. He knew how to delight and surprise Miri, although for her he was miracle enough in himself; she would have loved him without bribery, without romantic paraphernalia. He arranged cruises for her, and underwater dives in search of sponges and oysters. There were no oysters in the bay, but Piero had reconstituted some restaurant oysters, inserted a pearl in each one, and paid the diving instructor to lead her to the spot where she would 'discover' them. He always owned up to such pranks (in this case he did so by putting a small emerald in one of the oysters), knowing he had more substantial cards in his hand. Playing the ace, he drove Miri to Milan, to a box at La Scala. There she saw Caruso's successor, Beniamino Gigli, as the Duke of Mantua in *Rigoletto*, her favourite opera. For Miri, who adored Verdi, it was one of the highlights of her life.

Three more years it took, nonetheless – years during which people around her and even Miri herself began to realize that far from being a plain girl, she was something of a beauty with her dark, bruised-looking eyes and small features in her pale, round face – and three more anguished summer visits to Liguria, as well as a great deal of letter writing, tears and parental finger-wagging to convince the Gottliebs that this wild Piero boy was serious. Not only the Berlins but the Berlins' cook, maid and gardener were suborned by Miri's parents in pursuit of local gossip (and there was always plenty) about Piero's goings-on when Miri was in England. But serious Piero was. He had been serious about Miri, if about little else in his life. And when Miri had literally shuddered, at times, during the years of courtship, in the presence of the 'racehorses', the groomed girls of Piero's set, Piero had always applied himself to reassuring her in his most focused, charmingly serious tone. They are painted shadows, *amore mia*, he had insisted. You are a person. A woman. I could never love one of them. Only you.

Was she a person? At 22, newly graduated from Oxford and newly engaged to be married, she was stuffed with books and book-learning, Miri knew. Nothing else had mattered much to her, until she met Piero, who seemed to have sprung from literature straight into life without pausing for any of the doubts or glooms in which most humans were baptized. Later she learnt about Piero's doubts and glooms. Later, after Vittorio was born.

THEY NEVER WENT to Moscow. The wedding had taken place in Muswell Hill, London. Miri's parents were no longer observant Jews, and their eldest daughter's wedding to an Italian gentile, a socialist (yet also, it was whispered, a Count), was, in theory, perfectly satisfactory. The Gottliebs had their doubts about Piero himself. Miri wept when Avram tried to discuss them with her, and Avram couldn't bear it when Miri wept.

Unknown to the wedding guests – even Miri herself didn't know for sure yet – Miri had been pregnant when she married Piero. The birth of their son before nine months were up embarrassed nobody, however. Since Miri and Piero were wed in England, the couple's Italian neighbours had only an inexact sense of the date, and the Gottlieb family was untroubled. These were sophisticated times. They were also perilous times, and Miri had been shocked to discover an Italy from which Piero had shielded her during three successive, idyllic summers. Like the country itself, cities and towns and often households too were divided against themselves as Fascism and *Il Duce* made steadily greater demands on loyalty.

As his *Contessa* (in the people's eyes), Piero assured her, Miri remained protected from such vexations. Everything in Italy, he liked to say, was a local matter. Sometimes he said this with wry pride (this was the *signor Conte* in him speaking), sometimes, speaking as a socialist and internationalist, with exasperation. The good news in this regard was that, at the administrative level, among the *Commendatore*s and *Dottore*s who seemed to inhabit the decision-making strata of local government, matters could be settled between personalities, between friends on either side of a political question; the bad news was the same aspect of local government life, but with enemies factored in, and, instead of tolerance, old enmities and feuds that had little to do with political allegiances at all. One such long-standing hostility was between Piero and a man called Cipriano, who became mayor, despite Piero's opposition, and later police chief, having been deposed as mayor by voters who found his Fascism too strenuous for their temperament, and a good deal more uncompromising than his campaigning for mayor had indicated. As *comandante di polizia* he could apply his military leanings to keeping down crime, the town hoped, and leave broader civic matters to others. But the town now found that they had understimated Cipriano, who as police chief turned out to regard himself as a kind of political commissar, working to make sure that the buddy-buddy world of local friendships and business connections, not to mention marriage connections, didn't obscure the ancient rot still haunting the foundations of the new Italy, a rot which had to be located, exposed, and rooted out. Jews, in other words. Jews and the network of Jewish finance that held the Western world to ransom. In this regard he was way ahead of Benito Mussolini, who had welcomed Jews into the Fascist Party. Cipriano was ready to bide his time, confident that *Il Duce* would eventually see sense.

Miri had never met Cipriano, although Piero once or twice pointed him out in the town, walking the streets, or sitting in a café, but Miri was never sure that she had identified the man Piero meant, since no sooner had she turned to locate him than Piero always hissed, "Don't look!" in an alarmed and alarming tone. Cipriano the Faceless (faceless to Miri, as he was to remain for nearly twenty years) was the subject of weekly, if not daily conversation among Piero's friends. The tension between Cipriano and Piero was not only ideological, since they stood at opposite extremes of what was then regarded as the political spectrum, from Communist to Fascist – neither would have been gratified to learn that the young Joseph Goebbels had reportedly flipped a coin to decide which party he would join, the Nazis or the Communists – but also personal. There was an old grievance at work. Piero himself had nothing to do with it, since its origins dated from before he was even born, rather than in any dealings between the middle-aged Cipriano and the youthful Piero, who was 25 when he married Miri.

When Cipriano had been a medical student, travelling every day to Genoa's San Martino hospital, he had regarded himself as unofficially engaged to a local girl named Rosanna Lanfranchi. Cipriano's studies left the lovely Rosanna perilously unattended, for weeks at a time, in their home town on the sea; Piero's father, Vittorio, had stepped in and won the day (with, as Cipriano understandably saw it, the title of *Contessa* as an egregious lure). Thirty years had passed, and now *Contessa madre* Rosanna, the dowager countess, was a widow of fixed and largely sedentary habits who occupied a set of second-floor apartments in the Casa Rosa. This was the pink-washed, bougainvillea-crowded house above the little beach, where Rosanna's son, Piero, had been raised and now lived with Miri and their child, named Vittorio in honour of Piero's late father. Had Cipriano been of a different temperament entirely, he might have regarded Piero as the son he never had, and even offered the boy an element of surrogate fatherhood after Vittorio senior's death at the wheel of his sports car. An idealistic speculation, perhaps; but there are such people... just as there are preternaturally beautiful young men, as Piero was – offensively beautiful, as he must have seemed to Cipriano.

A separate gravity attends provincial life, as if attaching lead to smalltown shoes. Events that, in a city, might be swiftly trampled and soon obliterated by life's traffic, resonate for a lifetime in a more tightknit community, and Cipriano, the embittered loser, made of his youthful betrayal by Rosanna and the treachery of Piero's father Vittorio, once Cipriano's friend, the cue for the rest of his days. Vittorio's death brought no appeasement to Cipriano, only a keener sense of their blighted lives, his and Rosanna's, and the waste of it all. Cipriano had never married, whether by spontaneous devotion to Rosanna or determination not to surrender the resentment around which he had coiled his life like a serpent guarding a treasure. Piero (whose features were the very image of his mother, rather than his father) was now indeed the son Cipriano would never have, a cruel and perpetual reminder of his barren domestic life.

This might have been the end of it. Cipriano might have subsided into decent obscurity. But Fate often seems to compensate with a measure of public success those whose hearth is cold – or perhaps it's simply that such men and women have more time and energy to devote to the public arena than those whose spirit is, in part, detained at home. And Cipriano thrived, both as a medical man renowned for the long hours he worked, and, for a while, as *sindaco*, the town's mayor.

He was never popular, although he was praised for his hard work as doctor and administrator; he was respected, and later, under Mussolini, he acquired a loyal following; but he let the shadow that he felt had fallen across his life fall on those around him. He held his grief before his face, distancing him from those he met, like a cross that not only he but they too must kiss. The very pains he took, the long hours, the unfailing punctuality, were a reproach to destiny for the way it had spurned him.

Cipriano's severity as a person hid years of patient intrigue. (The severity was not his choice; it was chosen for him, he would surely have said, if there was anyone who could have got close enough to him to elicit such intimate reflections, and in being faithful to his suffering he was a victim of the accidents of life itself rather than obeying the dictates of his character.) By espousing Fascism and,

in doing so, opposing the reck▮▮▮ erratic but much-loved Piero, as
Cipriano regularly did in ▮▮▮▮ers of public policy, he was already
putting himself in the w▮▮▮ where many inhabitants of the town and
the surrounding cou▮▮▮de were concerned. At the same time, there
was a core of obsti▮▮▮ly puritanical men and women who found Piero
and his cavalier ▮▮ys obnoxious, and rallied to Cipriano regardless of
the issue. Cipriano didn't especially want to be the rallying-point for
and leader of the resentful – or not of the resentful only. The problem
was that Piero had cornered not only the conservative element, since
in their eyes he was *il Conte* whether he liked it or not (and they
doubtless sensed that he did, no matter what he proclaimed), but the
left as well, by virtue of his Communist views and speeches. Cipriano
had to move carefully. Deference and, no less powerful, sentimental
attachment were at the young man's command. For many the Count
was the town, symbolically; his achievements were the town's – even
his glorious looks, his acrobatic dives and fast driving ennobled the
town, just as any failure of Piero's would disgrace it. He was their king.
This ran too deep, both historically and at an instinctual level, to be
easily overthrown. The town knew perfectly well that their *Contessa*
was a Jew. They said nothing and made nothing of it. Anything else
would be disloyalty to *il signor Conte*. And wasn't she a delightful
girl, kind, sober, polite, a loving mother to the *Contessino*, the future
Count? Besides, she was a foreigner, and that was a category that
overlapped and blurred some of the edges of the word 'Jew,' which
for many if not most Italians lacked the automatic stigma it evoked
elsewhere in Europe.

Not for every Italian, of course. Despite Mussolini's relative
benevolence towards the race (until at last *Il Duce* capitulated to
Hitler's urgings), for some, a Jew was a Jew, and *"Buon giorno,
signora Contessa"* came low and bitterly from their mouths. The fact
that Miri probably disdained the title, sharing her husband's views
(so people suspected, because of her diffidence, her gentle ways and
lack of aristocratic hauteur), was only an added irritant to those who
resented Piero's choice of bride.

Miri and young Vittorio were not the only people of Jewish blood
in the town. Baldini the bookseller was Jewish, although no one

knew this. (Except Cipriano, who made it his business to know such things.) Baldini had a cousin, too, who lived with his family in the hinterland, high up, overlooking the Mediterranean, where he kept goats, and grew peaches and figs, in idyllic seclusion. And then there was *il tedesco*, Enrico (originally Heinrich) Schmitz, 'the German', who was known to everyone for his poor Italian and his loving photographs of the town and its district, which he sold as postcards to the *tabacchi* and as individual enlarged prints to tourists on the esplanade, signed "Schmitz" with the "z" on its side and made into a bow-tie, with a smiling face and cat's whiskers above it – Schmitz's logo. Schmitz and his wife were thought to be yet another German couple on their *Italienreise*, the journey to Italy that had a place in the hearts of all Germans, who had fallen in love with the place and simply never gone home. *Sehnsucht nach Süden*, Schmitz would say to Miri, who had some German (it was her parents' native language): 'longing for the South.' Schmitz was as much a victim of it as any of his compatriots, but the truth was that he – wiser and earlier than most – had read *Mein Kampf* and decided that as a Jew he would not have children in Germany while Hitler was in power. Heinrich became Enrico. He and Hannelore, his wife, had found Liguria and with it the bay and the town and a coastline that never ceased to excite the eye.

How beautiful and how unusual it was, Piero's *paese*! A succession of little inlets led to a peninsular formation on the horizon, visible from the esplanade and from every ridge above the town, that looked as if a dinosaur had immersed itself in the Mediterranean, leaving only three conical flaps projecting from its incompletely submerged back, like a stegosaur taking a bath. These three pointed hillocks, Japanese in their triangular symmetry, reached out from the Italian coast towards Africa, each a little smaller than the other, as if they were land's last gasps. Northwards the coast stretched towards Genoa, beneath steep volcanic cliffs. The water at their foot was correspondingly deep, the deepest trench in the entire Mediterranean. Southwards, the bay of Rapallo swept round in an immense enfolding arm, recouped its geologic energy and unfurled a long succession of fishing ports in the direction of Rome and the

Campagna, past enchanted Porto Venere, past the Cinque Terre with its vineyards, La Spezia and its naval base, and, before Rome beckoned, Livorno, or Leghorn as the British had called it when Shelley took a fatal swim off its coastline.

Who could resist that sea and its loveliness? In those days of our youth, the *mer mère, mare nostrum,* the inland sea that had been the jewel of all waters since man's earliest sea travels, the Great Green as the Egyptians had called it, was full of fish and darting squid, and *ricci di mare* or 'sea hedgehogs,' the sea urchins whose shells reached the size of little pumpkins, fine as lace (fine as the parchment-coloured lace spun by a dozen pairs of elderly hands, on our esplanade), in a dozen hues, red, yellow, purple, green and brown and all gradations in between. Jelly-fish, too, sometimes huge and sometimes tiny, invaded the bay, blown across from Africa. Waterspouts danced on the waters like sailing ships, leaning and swirling past each other as if in battle – a sea battle recast as a deadly water ballet. At night the fishing fleet, now long a feature of the past, went out with their great globe lights, to draw the schools of fish up from the depths, *dentice, branzino, orata.* What culinary genius, or what accident first devised *orata al cartoccio*, sea bass cooked in a paper bag (slathered first with herbs from the hillsides about the town)? Only in Liguria, where pasta itself was born, could such a delicacy be conceived. All night the fleet's huge round lanterns bobbed in the bay like fallen planets. Dawn brought the slow, thudding engines of the concerted fleet's return, a team of giant snails chugging back together into port, their course plotted directly to the quayside, to the housewives and to those who, like Ettore, the Berlins' gardener, and Piero's man, Leandro, were sent out by the housewives to meet the night's catch on the dock. This was the heartbeat of the town; its nightly breath, in and out. Without the fishing fleet, the town's lungs, what would the town be? How would it live? On pebbly slipways in small, cavernous inlets along the coast the great brown fishing nets hung like a stage set for Ulrica's cave in *Un Ballo in Maschera* (another favourite of Miri's). Who would take these triumphal curtains down? It was unimaginable then.

The hills of the hinterland, in any case, would never change. Their savage smell of hot earth, pine, dry herbs and salt had been there long before the first fishing net was woven, and nothing, not even the forest fires that blackened the hills every summer, could alter it. Wild fruits grew there, wild blackberries the size of plums, pine nuts, aniseed amid the wild garlic, the wild sweet peas and the foaming umbellifers. At night the fireflies massed like drunken starfire. "*A-ooo*," came the hoarse cry of Dario the muleteer, echoing from ridge to ridge in those bygone days, as he marshalled his beasts, driving them home into the hills.

MIRI LOVED IT beyond anything she could ever have imagined even in the days when she had fallen for Piero, when she saw him, perfect, barefoot, running furiously across the little beach pursued like Pentheus by a horde of Bacchants; Piero hard and aggressive, tough-sinewed, his feet like cured camel-skin, Piero soft and golden, his smooth cheeks unmarked, as if the gods had chosen him to be their darling.

It had all been about Piero then. The background had been obligatory, but incidental. You couldn't picture Piero in a different setting – (in truth, he'd looked less glorious in Muswell Hill; no less pretty, but smaller, less at ease and as a result less compelling a presence) – and so the town, the sea and the hills had also been Piero. The little beach was not a beach but Piero, even when his figure was absent.

Gradually the outline of Piero detached itself from the landscape, and the landscape assumed an identity that didn't speak of Piero or require Piero in it (as the little beach, when empty, had heretofore been a question: *Piero dov'è?* – where's Piero?), and finally acquired a character all its own.

Miri was aware of this process, and was given to wondering whether it would have happened if Piero himself had not detached himself from his own identity, at any rate from his bachelor identity, and become the restless spouse he had perhaps always been destined to become. He was gone for days, often without warning. Rosanna, Miri's mother-in-law, shrugged tolerantly (no doubt, Miri thought, her Vittorio had been the same). It was nothing to be wondered at,

Piero's friends assured Miri if she betrayed any sign of impatience or distress. He was becoming his father. Didn't they all? He was in Rome, perhaps; more likely Genoa, at the club. Miri had been mildly startled to find that Northern Italian aristocrats had clubs, British in décor as well as in conception, to which they repaired like the drones in 19th century novels, and sat in panelled rooms in dark leather armchairs, under portraits of racehorses, wearing blazers (she had extracted these details from Piero one by one, in disbelief, while he stared in puzzlement at her mixture of amusement and contempt) and toasting 'the ladies' in imported Scotch. It was such a far cry from dolphin-Piero, barefoot running Piero on the beach, that she wondered whether she'd ever have fallen for him if she'd met him in a blazer.

Why was he in Genoa, at the club? Or in Rome, without taking her there? Was there something she was failing to supply, at home? Piero laughed at the question, genuinely amused. She had the child; he had his pastimes, as he expressed it.

Can't I come? Miri asked. Rosanna would look after Vittorio for the day.

Come to the track, *amore mia*? You'd be so bored. You wouldn't like it. And even if you did, Piero said quickly, where would you go afterwards? Women were not allowed in the club.

It mattered less and less, Miri was a little shocked to find. At first it had seemed to her a kind of falling out of love, the way the landscape outside her window, both the seascape and the warm, green terraced hillsides, were increasingly no longer Piero. She still loved Piero, and his presence in her arms continued to fill her quite literally with wonder at the sense that such a being could ever have allowed itself to submit to her embrace, like a tame puma. But the place and Piero were no longer one. Perhaps they didn't need to be, any longer. Or rather, perhaps the landscape had to become its own thing now that Piero was so much less frequently in it, silhouetted against it; *of* it. And what had felt at first like a loss, something being slowly torn out of her – the union of Piero and the very colours and temperature of the day – made way, created a space, for a new, separate passion for her new home, as intense as her feelings for Piero and, in its differing forms, more diverse.

Their variety gave her room, and choice – a different spot, and view, according to her mood. She walked, with Vittorio strapped to her, and later with his toddling form beside her, hand in hand, through the hills, each walk a landscape as distinct as if it were a different country. Some she named for the country they evoked. There was a Switzerland of open, grassy slopes with rounded boulders, a Scotland of shaded ravines with rushing streams, and an Africa of umbrella pines and harsh, uninhabitable and unfarmable slopes where the volcanic cliffs became a precipice over the sea.

She felt herself to be fully at home in each of these countrysides, as though she had dreamed them beforehand, as a child. Now they had adopted her as much as she them. Their inhabitants too, the *contadini*, had adopted her; they were telling her she belonged there, in every way they could. Yet the appellation, the *signora Contessa*, stood between her and them, and made her feel distinct once more.

The friends she made were largely outsiders like herself, of one sort or another. She visited the Berlins once a week or more, while they were in residence; she saw the Schmitzes more often than anyone else, partly because she liked their tireless bohemianism and the way that she could share with them her delight in so many details of the landscape and the ever-changing sea and sky, as she could not with a native (to whom it would have seemed absurdly *turistico* to go into ecstasies about Nature), and also because their little son was barely six months older than Vittorio. Tancredi was his name, a perfectly absurd choice despite (or perhaps because of) its literary forebears, including a Lampedusa character and Rossini's opera of the same name; perhaps it would have fitted well with a more glamorous surname, but Tancredi Schmitz, as a combination, brought to Miri's mind an undergraduate she had known at Oxford, with the unfortunate name of Endymion Pratt. Still, it was typical Schmitz; their fearless, unselfconscious love of all things Italian was precisely what she enjoyed in them.

There were townspeople she might have seen more of, had their children been of the right age for Vittorio, like the bookseller, Baldini, a sympathetic soul who followed her perhaps a little too eagerly with his eyes, when she visited his bookstore. In any case, Baldini's younger boy was six years older than Vittorio.

Miri's parents visited at least once a year, and both of her younger sisters visited regularly, hoping to land another Piero. But there was only one Piero, and only one *signor Conte*.

Much of Miri's day was spent in Serafina's kitchen. In Muswell Hill, in her mother's kitchen, Miri had always been in the way. Bustling, wheezing Serafina, a prey to asthma, seemed to like having Miri there, and gave her things to do, chopping, salting, decanting, while Serafina worked. She seemed proud to have the *Contessa* watching, and she was a patient, forbearing teacher, silent but smiling a huge toothy smile of genuine delight when Miri showed how well she'd learned. Miri might never learn to make pastry as perfect as Serafina's, or to tease out the pasta until the newspaper that lay between it and the stone table beneath could be read through the pasta, as Serafina required. But by sheer persistence Miri learned to make a passable imitation of many of Serafina's dishes, the veal pounded within an inch of its life before being breaded, the *ossobuco*, the *gnocchi*, the *arrosto*. In Serafina's kitchen Miri learned not only how to cook but also the rudiments of the Genoese dialect that she heard among the *contadini* in the hills, and which had so far been a mystery to her. It was a plangent, more French-sounding tongue (descendant, indeed, of *Languedoc* and *Langue d'oeil*), often quite different from Italian in its forms, as when Serafina would say *zeen*, a word and sound unknown to Miri, as in the insult regularly applied to the town's interfering bureaucrats, *che gondoni che sono!* – what contraceptives they are! – which came out *che gondooon che zeen!*

Manya, fijeu! – (*Mangia, figlio*, eat, boy, it would have been in 'educated' Italian) – Serafina would say to little Vittorio as she handed him an offcut from her meal in progress, for the boy was always there with Miri, growing up in the cramped, steaming, kitchen, while Serafina wheezed and bellowed at her daughter Pina, rested briefly, gasping, to catch her breath, cursed her utensils and imperfect food, appealed to the gods, apologized to Miri, and sent her husband scuttling out fcdor more and better victuals.

Serafina was Miri's standby, telling her where to buy the best and least expensive items, comforting her if Piero hadn't returned from Genoa as promised – she had been in service with Piero's father, knew the family ways, and had known Piero since he was a *fijeu* himself, underfoot in her kitchen like little Vittorio – and advising Miri on birthday gifts for her mother-in-law.

There was really no one else, no one native to the town or the hills that Miri became close to. But to have been lonely, during those years, even for an instant, was inconceivable. She had Vittorio.

Miri hadn't quite known what to expect of motherhood. It was distantly terrifying, the idea that a great love and a great certainty would simply arrive with a baby, like a set of instructions in a box. It was hard to imagine a reservoir of dormant instinct being switched on like a light in what seemed to Miri the already well-appointed house of her soul, a house in which she had been living (and tidying dutifully, and filling with knick-knacks where there was room) quite unaware that there was a huge suite of apartments in it to which she'd never been introduced. And would she step into them now to find they'd been perfectly prepared, like Vittorio's nursery, but in her sleep, without her knowing it? Or would she find, behind a locked, reluctant, creaking door, bare mouldy rooms without furniture, with rotting floorboards and peeling walls, staring back at her and saying, What are you doing here?

It seemed like a terrible lottery. You became pregnant, for the first time, without the faintest idea whether you would be at home in the role of mother, yet with the burden of everybody's expectation – history's expectation, even – that you would. What if, after all the pain, the creature you clasped to your bosom felt like alien meat (it was the very reddish pinkness of the imagined baby that seemed to radiate all her alarm), and not a beloved person, your child, at all? What if you had to spend the infant's entire childhood pretending to be its mother?

And whom could she tell about these fears? She'd never felt herself to be a coward before. She had known fear, but it had never cowed her. Her mother, who had borne three daughters, seemed to recognize no possibility of psychic distress (unless, Miri wondered, she knew it all too well herself but was afraid, as a parent, to confess to such frailty – this would fit, Miri thought, with her mother's personality, her firm, bold front), and perhaps deliberately seemed to misunderstand Miri's timid questioning as referring only to the physical ordeal. None of Miri's London friends had babies yet; there was no one she could write to; and who was there, in the small Ligurian town where she now lived, that she could possibly engage in such a conversation, with her still faulty Italian? Piero, as she knew from the expression on his face when she expressed even the faintest hint of anxiety, was the last person in the world who could minister to her fears. Hilde Schmitz had experienced nothing but bliss, she proclaimed to all and sundry, during her home delivery of Tancredi in the rear of a fruit and vegetable truck travelling between Siena and Assisi. It sounded most unlikely to Miri. Did everyone simply lie about the terrors of oncoming motherhood – or forget, thanks to an autonomic function accompanying the event, as the body itself was said to forget the extremities of pain involved?

Turning tentatively to her mother-in-law for advice, or simply for a measure of womanly comfort, Miri was distressed to find Rosanna evidently ill at ease with the subject, and couldn't fathom why. Had Piero's birth been traumatic? (It had not, as Serafina was able to tell Miri.) Was it inappropriate, in aristocratic circles, to discuss such things, even between a mother-in-law and a daughter-in-law whose own mother was far away? On this score, as on the whole matter of Rosanna's evasiveness, it would be many years before Miri came to understand Piero's mother.

In the end it was Serafina who saw in Miri's pallor and haunted eyes the full extent of her fear, and took Miri into her own small shuttered bedroom (a room which was never troubled by the light of day), hot as an oven, with its bed and giant bolster that seemed to fill the room like an enormous, swelling soufflé, sat Miri down and talked her through it, holding Miri's hands in her own, huge, sweaty ones.

The birth itself, in Genoa's San Martino hospital, where Piero's nemesis Cipriano had been trained, brought a volume of pain for which, as Serafina had warned Miri, neither words nor imagination could have prepared her. Serafina hadn't mentioned the anger that would accompany the fear. Lying there, powerless to do more than help increase the pain, her fury at the excessive violence of it (why did Nature demand that a human offspring be ripped out?) felt more like a summoning of her spirit, of a capacity to endure this experience and survive it, than the rage it mimicked. Unkindly, but needing an image on which to focus the blind desire for retribution – and not wanting to make it Piero, who was nonetheless the proximate cause – Miri focused on Hilda Schmitz and her promises of 'blissful' birthgiving. Let her next one be a baby rhino, Miri muttered, knowing she'd be able to forgive herself, and Hilda, in time. Vittorio was big – of this Serafina had warned her, telling her they were all "born big, in this family." Serafina had been in no doubt that it would be a boy.

But what astonished Miri the most was Vittorio's beauty. Surely it wasn't a maternal illusion, though of course she would have loved him regardless (and once he was lying on her breast, it was impossible to even imagine any longer what some unfortunate women had felt – she knew it was true and it had fed her fears – who found themselves indifferent to their baby, or even appalled). But he was so far from the wailing pink meat she had tried hard not to conjure in her mind, that the image now seemed laughable. She had always pictured a tiny Piero; but the baby looked nothing like Piero. He was a tiny replica of her father, only with hair, lots and lots of hair, and with her father's sweet soulful eyes in a face whose pouches, for the first few weeks, were evocative of Avram Gottlieb in old age. She was breastfeeding her father. It was dizzying, yet somehow not at all incongruous. What she had been through, it seemed to her now, was not the gruesome ripping out of a child from her flesh, but the overwhelming pain of passing from one world to another, giving birth to the past as the future, an extruding of the insides of time – because here in her arms was the past, her heritage (born so evidently a Jew, as if all of Toranic wisdom and Hebraic suffering were encoded in his dark stare), which without knowing it she had been carrying in her body. No wonder it had hurt so much to pull all of that out of her! She had given birth to Israel. And now it was breathing, panting, stretching on her breast, unimaginably precious, as if she held the whole consequence of Jewry, its future, in her arms.

And what she had never expected – could never have dreamed – was the extent of the companionship she felt with Vittorio, from the moment their eyes met. While he was small, Miri continued to wonder whether this sense that she knew his inmost heart and mind (because, in fact, they were hers, indistinguishable from her) was a fond illusion bred of her love, of blind maternal attachment, and even of the way he *looked* so familiar, as she always said. (She had seen him before. Was it just the resemblance to her father?) Could it really be true that one person could see so deeply and infallibly into another? Wasn't it just a story she was telling herself, while the child was too young to deny or disprove it?

Miri had never known this experience before, or anything close to it. In fact, it made her realize how much her defining sense of life had been her feeling of difference from others. No one had been like her, ever, not her mother or father (though he was certainly the nearest thing to a soulmate she had known), not her friends, and certainly not Piero, whose gift to Miri was the surrender to her of his impossibly alien soul and personality. Precisely this, until now, had seemed the glory of her existence, for Miri: that someone at whom she could only wonder, whose thoughts she could only dimly guess at and whose very physical movements seemed to have been bred on another planet, in a different gravity, could lie in her arms and be hers.

What Miri had discovered now, from her first moments with her son, was a universe so new that she could only dread finding that it was a mirage. In Vittorio it was as if she had been cloned. She knew that most parents had no such experience – neither her own nor her friends' nor even Hilda Schmitz with her blissful birth, who was forever screaming at the gleefully disobedient Tancredi. Miri told no one, in case they mocked her, or simply disbelieved her, or were somehow able to expose to her the error under which she was living. Yet there was no need to tell anyone; everyone could see their extraordinary affinity for each other, this mother and child. It was not only in the way she looked at him, the look of adoration everyone expected to see; it was his answering look, a quality of trust – later of shared humour – that you might expect to see in a little child, but less often in a growing boy. They were each other's witness, in the world. They spoke and thought for each other. It wasn't only that they saw things the same way, were amused or disheartened by the very same events. They woke in the same way, hid their feelings in the same way, ate the same way – it was unnatural, Piero often complained (this was his son, the future *Conte*, and did he, Piero, have no share in him? Did the boy have no character of his own?), they suffered the same way, grew tired at the same instant, required the same amount of water, loved even the ugliest animals – (bugs, even! Serafina would remark in disbelief) – and fell asleep the same way. This is what it means, Miri thought, to experience your own immortality. After I die, I will still be alive just as fully as I am now, in him.

It *was* unnatural. It was utterly uncommon, at any rate, and other parents often resented it in Miri and Vittorio, seeing before them a kind of twinship (not entirely healthy, they suggested) that they had not only never experienced but genuinely did not envy. It would be exhausting, claustrophobic. It would take up all their time. Miri, who was entirely happy that it took up all her time, could sympathize nonetheless with people's doubts and distaste. Hitherto, intense companionship was something which Miri had always experienced as faintly threatening, after a certain time; even Piero's beloved presence could become cloying, as irritating as a clammy, neighbouring body under too many blankets. As a child she had been known for her love of solitude, and for her constant reading, although she had known her chief impulsion for this was not a love of books but the need to get away from her noisy, overly playful younger sisters, who were closer to each other in age than Miri was to either of them. Now she found herself blessedly closeted with a being from whom she could hardly bear to be separated for a minute in any given twenty-four hours. Those who loved to see and to be with Miri and Vittorio were always offering to give her a rest – and regardless of this altruism they naturally wanted to hold little Vittorio for a while themselves – but even to them she rarely acceded for more than the shortest time that courtesy permitted. The one exception to this was Serafina, in whose ample bosom

Miri saw a version of what she herself felt that she had become, the abstractly maternal. She and Serafina were one continuous bosom, to Miri, and to little Vittorio too, who seemed equally at ease on either manifestation.

He grew up bilingual (trilingual, if you count Genoese, as you should, as a separate tongue), seemingly without any sense of which language he was speaking or thinking in, fluent in all of them. This meant, perhaps, that there were in him a Piero, a Serafina and a Miri, linguistically and with the temperament appropriate to each, rhetorical, trenchant and discriminating by turns. But when you looked at him, he was all Miri – all Avram, if you knew Avram, and even for those who didn't the eyes and above all the eyebrows certainly evoked Sephardic origins. Yet Vittorio also looked entirely at home in the gallery of his comrades and contemporaries of the town. He lacked even a hint of his father's open, golden looks, his wavy blond hair and pale eyes, and as a result you could easily have thought him more Italian-looking than Piero. He evoked some Byzantine icon (those caterpillar eyebrows!), with his long face and long nose. He was entirely Mediterranean in appearance, though hardly in temperament.

Vittorio's manner was what Piero called, with wry amusement (since after all he'd married into it, and what did he expect?) *piuttosto inglese*, English rather than Italian. Like Miri he spoke little, and then carefully. It pleased Piero to say that the boy had refused to speak until he finally uttered a string of words "as long and as perfect as a sentence from Charles Dickens." The sentence Piero usually cited (he had several, all invented) was, "Excuse me, Papa, but would you kindly pass me the bread?" Miri knew well how Vittorio hated, as she did, to speak until he knew what he would say and how he would say it, and she tolerated Piero's mockery as a loving, irritated tribute to herself.

She was not volatile enough for Piero, she knew. It was one of the things he had loved in her at first. Her reserve. But in time, when she would not rise to his sallies, his arias, his operatic rebukes, he began to suspect that this reserve was actually a form of resentment. There was no way to heal this misunderstanding, since nothing could move Miri to the outcries Piero needed. (He got them, daily, from Serafina, whose wails of *"La fine del mondo, signore!"* announced the end of the world as manifested in the absence of Milanese salami at the butcher.) Now poor Piero had two *Inglesi* in his household, sitting on their hands, zipping their mouths, and exchanging meaningful looks. *Porca miseria!*

Miri and Vittorio talked a great deal, in truth. But they preferred to do it on their long walks through the hillsides.

An hour's walk from the Casa Rosa stood a hill (part of the land Miri called Africa) where the coastline turned and its cliff-fortress journey eastwards from Genoa abruptly yielded, stopping dead as if in sudden amazement at its own monumental resolve. The high promontory where it reared up and halted resembled an act of consciousness, the coastline itself reflecting on its journey like a momentarily puzzled giant. Then it reached back, making the huge scoop of the bay where Piero's town lay cradled, before continuing to the south-east, resolute once more. The promontory, with the view it afforded, was one of Miri and Vittorio's favourite haunts. A stand of huge old umbrella pines gave shade to the earthen track beaten flat by generations of clifftop farmers' feet. Fallen *pinoli*, pine nuts, buff–coloured with their distinctive little smudge of black as if hastily marked by a charcoal pencil, clustered, awaiting Miri and Vittorio. No one seemed to want to gather them, or perhaps, seeing Miri picking them up with such care and delight, they left them there for *la signora Contessa* and the *Contessino*. Together, Miri and the child would sit in the shade of the pines and prise open their tender fruit, the fresh, tiny morsel somehow too delicate to be properly called a nut; it was almost halfway to a seed, yet thick and juicy, at once supremely modest and explosive on the palate, like a blueberry, filling every crevice of the mouth with taste. How could these tender buttery-coloured slivers, so pale and vulnerable, contain the lifeblood of the rugged giants waving above them, these kings of the promontory with their craggy aggressive bark and rich green needles? Each pine nut was sacred to her. Each one was a Vittorio awaiting her, soft and trusting and entirely unprotected, a Moses in the tiny canoe of its opened shell.

There were small houses on both sides of the path, where the pines stood and the nuts littered the earth, unusually solid, stucco houses, unlike the ramshackle farmhouses farther along the ridge. They were, Miri supposed, holiday homes. Many rich Milanese bought such properties on the coast, and might visit them no more often than a weekend or two a year. Yet what a waste, Miri thought, of the promontory view, saturnine in one direction where the steep slope of the *vallone* plummeted to the sea and an outcrop of rock – Vessinaro Point was its name, *Punto Vessinaro* – and where only the occasional merchant ship or cruise liner broke the severity of the immense horizon (but, beyond it, Africa!), while in the other direction, where the bay of Rapallo curved back and around, the astonished eye was met by a crowded, joyous panorama, protected from the wind, dotted with houses, villages, distant sailboats like so many butterflies – a land of milk and honey, Miri called it in her mind, feeling like a pilgrim each time she returned along the ridge and caught her first glimpse of it again. But the walk was long up to the windblown Vessinaro promontory where the stucco houses were, an hour and a half at least of steep climb, and no doubt the citified owners of these houses found that the charm of such an expedition quickly faded when you were carrying several days' worth of provisions.

One day Miri had felt a presence, a watcher, as she and Vittorio sat by the wayside nibbling their prizes. (How perfectly Vittorio-sized they were, the *pinoli*!) Yet the windows she could see, over the tall hedges – two were cypress, and another was a dense mass of laurel – were shuttered and blank. Miri decided she was merely imagining a spy, out of residual guilt at scooping up the pine nuts. (Were they anybody's in particular, the parent umbrella pines, was she stealing from them, or was she perhaps exercising some ancient seigneurial right over the pine nuts?) But, over succeeding months, the sense of watching eyes materialized into faint scuffling noises, behind the laurel hedge. A dog? If so, a very quiet dog – and who fed it? Neighbours, perhaps?

When Miri finally plucked up the courage – the gall, she felt it was (*forgive me: I am your Contessa!*) – to approach the laurel hedge and try and pierce its dense wall of waxy green and yellow leaves, she could see nothing, and retreated, puzzled.

Then one day there was a pair of eyes, unmistakably human eyes, at a child's head height, between the laurel leaves. Dark eyes, heavy eyebrows on pale skin – that was all Miri could see. *Buon giorno!* Miri exclaimed, as if in explanation of her presence on the path outside the house. But no answer came, and the unblinking eyes disappeared without a sound.

Despite the heavy eyebrows, Miri had felt sure it was a female presence she had seen and sensed, and each fresh sighting, always as brief and inconclusive, reinforced this hunch. Who was she then, and why was she so secretive, refusing to answer greetings? *La prigionniera*, Miri called her in her mind, the prisoner, as if the mystery girl, or woman, belonged to a 19th century romance. No one in the town seemed to know who it was that Miri might be referring to, when she enquired about the house with the laurel hedge; neither Piero nor Rosanna, his mother, nor Serafina could imagine who this personage might be. Mightn't she like to come out and play? Miri had tried calling, and ringing the bell at the laurel-hedge house, without reply. Once or twice an adjacent, cypress-sentinel holiday home was inhabited by its vacationing Milanese family, but although they were delighted to answer Miri's questions, and invite her and Vittorio in for a cup of very English (and very Milanese) tea, they knew nothing of their neighbours, let alone a *prigionniera*. Was she a phantom, perhaps, summoned – as Miri had felt in the first place – by Miri's pine nut theft, was she the *pinoli*-loving ghost of some earlier owner of the umbrella pines? Eventually Miri became comfortable with the guardian eyes that studied her and Vittorio through the screen of laurel (Vittorio himself never seemed in the least perturbed), and over time the mystery became a harmless, familiar feature, for Miri, of her visits to the Vessinaro.

YEARS WENT BY. Despite clamorous events in the world beyond the town, as Hitler rose to power and Mussolini increasingly allowed his Nazi admirer to influence his own agenda, little changed in Miri's life, it seemed to her, compared to the miracle of Vittorio's steady growth into a striking, slim, intelligent boy, one who continued to intuit her thoughts and her moods as promptly as she did his. He was a gift for which she never failed to thank Providence every day.

Wrapped up in the unanticipated magic that linked her both to her son and to the landscape they patrolled whenever Vittorio wasn't in school, a familiar sight to the contadini to whom Miri brought provisions and, where necessary, medicines, Miri paid as little mind to local politics as she did to international news. Even the locally notorious *Guerra del Cancello* passed her by, although its outcome might be said to have determined the rest of her life, or at any rate helped to do so. Ligurians heard about this 'War of the Gate' as far away as Genoa, where a journalist reported on it for the *Secolo* with some amusement, as though it were an illustration of the quaint absurdities of provincial Italian life.

For the inhabitants of the town it was as great a preoccupation and a disturbance as the larger events reported in the newspapers and supposedly shaping the course of the nation. In the eye of this local storm sat an orderly process, the re-election of Cipriano as mayor – or the election of a new mayor in his stead.

The election had turned, not on national issues, let alone international ones, but, as local elections do, on personalities and matters of minuscule but intense concern. In this case it was the *cancello*, the gate. This gate stood on the lower slopes of one of the most desirable mountains overlooking the bay, a mountain that was a magnet for wealthy blow-ins looking for a second home with a majestic view. They could not build on the mountain, which belonged, somewhat surprisingly, to the Vatican. Of the monastery whose lands these were, not a trace remained, but the Pope still collected rent (at medieval rates) from its farmers, and held a veto on any further development. The existing farms and peasant homes were vulnerable to purchase, nonetheless, and the lower slopes of the mountain were already inhabited, for at least part of the year, by some of the richest and most famous families in Italy. (Their offspring were precisely the sleek 'racehorses', Piero's friends, who had so intimidated Miri when they were courting.) The gate in question, the notorious *cancello*, had originally protected the monastery lands, and the mountain itself, from unmonitored entry. It had been locked, however, for centuries. So it was said. Foot passage was afforded by a gap the width of a man, between one of the gate's gigantic pillars and the still inhabited hovel which must once have served as a gatehouse. This, the hovel, was almost derelict – a sequence of migrant families had lived in it – and crouched beside the anachronistically magnificent gate like a starving mongrel beside a nobleman. The sight reminded Miri of 18th century prints, at the dawn of archaeology, showing classical temples now fallen into desuetude, with shacks built against a remaining wall, and urchins playing among the fallen pillars.

Had the gate really been locked for centuries? For generations, certainly; no one knew how long. The farmers who lived above the *cancello* descended to the town to do their shopping by slipping through the man-sized gap between pillar and hovel, as did the servants of the great families who lived on the mountain. The gap, which had two steps in it, had turned its own distinct colour, a weary grey-brown, from the rubbing of so many bodies against wall and pillar, over the centuries. When the modern grandees arrived from Milan, for the weekend or for the summer, in their splendid open cars, they parked below the *cancello*. Then they too stepped delicately up the steps and through the gap ("Give me your hand, Adalberto!") and walked on up the steep, winding goat track to their palatial houses, while their servants, the ones in permanent residence in the grandees' holiday home, who had been dozing in the shadow of the gate while waiting for their masters – alerted as to the likely, though never the precise, hour when the *signore e signori* would arrive – climbed after them, carrying the luggage. Seeing this procession, you felt transported to the 19th century, or the 18th, perhaps, or even the Middle Ages. The goat track above the *cancello* functioned as a kind of penance, in its abominable steepness, so great at times that even Dario's mules were obliged to descend sideways. Yet it was good, the *signore e signori* insisted, to get out of the Bugatti and be obliged to suffer the reality of the goat track, and to work a little for the joy of the view to come.

Of course, the grand houses were all on the lower mountain, requiring no great climb. Higher up, the track steadily narrowed until it wound its way across ridges, and then down into the corresponding valley, and up to the next ridge, and down again and up again until at last it reached the Vessinaro promontory and became a single Indian-file clifftop path above the sea and across the mountains to Genoa. Inhabitants of the distant farms in the hinterland would walk two hours down to the *cancello*, and another half an hour into the town; they and their forbears had always done so; the return journey, heavily laden with whatever they needed or wanted but could not grow themselves, would take a little longer.

The stones of the goat track, many of them huge and polished by a thousand years of variously bare and sandaled feet, seemed to belong to some ancient causeway built by and for a race of giants. They evoked ancient pilgrimage, to the monastery that no longer was (there was even argument as to its location), that had been abandoned and finally pillaged, little by little, so that now it existed piece-meal, incongruously incorporated into the tumble-down farms of the hinterland – you could see a section of stonework here, a slab or a pilaster there – yet still proclaiming its serviceable after-life.

The grandees wanted the *cancello* opened, so that access could be provided, and a road built, not for them, they protested, since they were happy enough to walk the short distance to where their car was parked below the great gate, but for their friends, who longed to join them on the mountain. These friends would have to purchase, and 'renovate' (transform) peasant houses farther up the track, less easily accessible to the elderly. If it wasn't for the *cancello*, these desirable families were ready and waiting to join the community, bringing not only the glory of their family name and the beauty of their offspring, but their money to enrich the peasants who, the grandees proclaimed, were prepared to sell up (and live so much more comfortably, surely, in the town, where their windfall would buy them ample premises), indeed to enrich the whole town, where the new grandees would spend the money, and provide construction work on the interminable improvements they would make to their houses. They would bring many new jobs in their train, inside and outside their brand-new palazzos.

But the town council, the *commune*, had always rejected these arguments. Willingness to walk up the goat track as far as was necessary to reach your house, the *commune* seemed to be saying, was an index of your preparedness to become part of the community, and not merely an old custom or a tax on lordliness. But the aged grandmother, the advocates of gate-opening pleaded, and the arthritic patriarch! What of them? In truth, as both sides knew, the issue wasn't physical fitness to be admitted to the world of the town. It was a matter of the integrity of the *paese*. Open the *cancello*, so long a marker delimiting those above the salt and those below, and a flood-tide of *stranieri, forestieri, sconosciuti*, strangers and foreigners of every kind, would dilute the very nature of the town. The mountain would become its own fortress state, a pleasure dome full of the capering rich, through whose domains the last obstinate mountain men and women would thread their way like worms through silk. And wasn't this silk, the very beauty of the mountain, theirs to guard and embroider as they wished? Wasn't it they, silkworms that they were, who had clothed the mountain, fashioned its terraces, olive groves and vineyards? As for what the interlopers could bring to the town, what of it? The town had money and work and fish enough already; let be.

But the rich had heard a rumour that the new mayor, Renzo Cipriano, was open to argument on the question of the gate. And so began *la guerra del cancello*, the war of the gate. As so often where bitter local quarrels are concerned, you could imagine the main combatants taking diametrically opposite positions to the ones they so passionately held. You could picture them exchanging sides even during the run-up to the election. The Mayor Cipriano who was prepared to consider the merits of opening the gate could so easily, Miri thought, have been the same Mayor Cipriano justifying the contrary view, insisting with restrained but puritanical dignity upon the town's historic privileges and their limits. Piero could have been leading his friends – a parade, as Miri pictured it, of clubmen in striped British blazers – in support of opening the Great Gate to the Bugatti brigades, rather than campaigning against it.

So how had they chosen their seemingly inflexible line on the issue? As Miri envisioned it, both her husband and Cipriano would have heard rumours of the other's leanings – rumours false or true, who knows? – and hastened to strike an opposing stance. Piero, it seemed to her, was the first to pick up the distant tune and find the counterpoint. Was Cipriano weakening over the inviolability of the *cancello*, and had he been seen dining with old man Agnelli, one of the millionaire proponents of opening up the ancient monastery lands? If so, Piero would dust off his socialist credentials and rally the troops of the poor against any charter for the invading rich. He was their Count, the town's Count, not an aristocratic voice for hire. He knew where his duty and his allegiance lay.

Miri now had to listen to a good many impromptu speeches along these lines, over the dinner table, and she could see how torn her husband was. Piero was proud to exercise his socialist and populist muscles. Yet he knew, of course, that the money his friends and their friends would bring to the town would precisely benefit, as they themselves argued, the poorest inhabitants and those seeking employment. It was, Piero declaimed, the old blackmail: let the rich in, to make you a little less poor. Let them in, or starve. But they wouldn't starve, not in this land of milk and honey – of homegrown olives and peaches and wine! Besides, who could weigh the nourishment of pride, of ancient continence preserved? How ashamed would we be, Piero repeatedly asked Miri, Rosanna, little Vittorio and the dining room walls of the Casa Rosa, when we found that we had sold our patrimony for a new refrigerator?

It could have been a difficult political channel for Piero to negotiate. For some years, as the campaign grew more heated, he was shunned as a traitor by some of his rich friends on the mountain. On the other hand, the local populace praised and loved him as never before, for putting their history before his social connections. They were proud of him – this was how *il signor Conte* should behave, he should be heedless of any ties, whether of amity or blood, other than his ties to the people. The town should come first, for him. Yet at the same time, they didn't feel unthinkingly obliged to agree with Piero (it was important that he should stand up for the town's traditions and its ancient honour, but not that they should follow his lead – he represented their past, but the future was theirs), and as it became clear that a vote for Cipriano would be a vote for opening the Great Gate if the austere doctor were granted a second term as *sindaco*, many local shopkeepers contemplated the advantages of a *montagna aperta*, a mountain open to the Bugatti world, and found them more pressing than the claims of history. As regards the rich themselves, the inhabitants of the town very sensibly judged them as individuals, case by case and household by household; neither unthinking deference, though this certainly coloured their feelings, nor automatic resentment, though this too simmered under the surface, was decisive. Ultimately, on this case-by-case basis – the sober view of a peasant culture – it was *il sindaco dottore* Cipriano versus *il Conte* Piero, or more precisely the restaurant-owner Prospero Velo, Piero's surrogate. It came down to the wire. Cipriano seemed to be drawing ahead, gossip maintained. But abruptly, in the final lunges of the race, it turned out that Cipriano had overestimated peasant greed and underestimated the tug of hereditary loyalties.

What no one knew at the time was that *il sindaco* owned property on the mountain, way up on the Vessinaro, where Cipriano himself was never seen. To reveal this would have been to invite the suggestion that he, the spirit of rectitude (to a fault, to the very edge of stiff-necked disdain for ordinary people), had an interest in increasing the value of his property by opening the mountainside to a new road and new purchasers.

To be exact, *almost* no one knew. Piero knew of the existence, though not the precise location, of Cipriano's Vessinaro property. He knew it as he knew all the secrets of the town – both because it was in his nature, in his tireless curiosity, to know them, and because it lay in his role. As *Conte* he not only gossiped in the restaurants, he also squatted for hours in his haunches beside the soccer players at practice on the dusty soccer field in the mountains, stripped of every blade of grass by mid-September. It was his feudal duty. Everybody told him what was happening in the town; they told Piero about the sick and the recovering and who was sleeping with whom and who was secretly in love with whom and who had inherited money from a distant relative. This was his function, as *Conte*, to be a second confessional (more ribald, more shameless than their disclosures to the priest) and a repository of the town's private life. It would enable him to exploit and manipulate his subjects, it was true; but in a just lord, it would allow him to act with informed impartiality.

And now Piero showed a remarkable aspect of his character (well beyond the demands of impartiality). During the war of the *cancello*, Piero never divulged the fact that Dr. Cipriano had an interest in unlocking the gate. (Piero himself had no such interest, since the Casa Rosa had its own little track, largely composed of steps cut into the hillside, too far from the goat track above the cancello to be affected by having the gate opened.) Piero kept Cipriano's secret, which if divulged would surely have sunk the doctor's hopes of re-election, and he kept it not only out of an exalted sense of fair play but for several further reasons. Certainly, Piero prided himself in a seigneurial sense of justice (and claimed it for socialism) which disdained the dissemination of rumours, true or false. (He could certainly have managed to detonate a rumour, had he been so inclined, without fear of its origin being traced to him.) But there was more: his heritage, as he understood it, also demanded that he put himself at the service of the people without regard to his own interests. He loved his town and wanted its people to make the decision about the *cancello*, about the future of the mountain and of their community, on their own, independently and without regard to himself or Cipriano.

Also – shall we be a little cynical? – perhaps there was a part of him that would have been glad to lose to Cipriano, see the gate opened, and a fresh horde of his friends arrive for year-round frolics. He would have taken the honourable, losing part. And then won, since Cipriano's victory and the opening of the *cancello* would guarantee a prompt reconciliation with the families in whose homes he had become unwelcome during the campaign. If, on the other hand, he won the election – which is to say, if the anti-Cipriano faction won and a new, Piero-sponsored mayor was installed in Cipriano's place, forbidding the opening of the Great Gate – it would be some while before Piero was forgiven in all quarters.

So it seemed to Piero that this period, that of the War of the *Cancello*, was the most lordly, the most perfect of his public life.

He couldn't lose. Whoever won, Piero gained. This was what it was, he thought, truly to be *il Conte* – above politics, loving only the will of the people. But also using the *Conte's* role as the spider at the heart of the gossip-web to advance his own interests.

And then, on the eve of the election, and perhaps lulled by this deep sense of fulfilment that the campaign had brought him, Piero made a fatal error. Its consequences were to go far beyond those that ensued from his election victory – a period of constricted relations (soon enough forgiven and forgotten) with the rich families of the mountain; they went so far beyond these short-term repercussions that it's fair to say that Piero could never have foreseen them. But what he did was reckless, nonetheless, quixotic in the very mould that had attracted Miri to his dashing youthful self. And, in the long term, disastrous.

Piero invited Cipriano to dinner – not at the Casa Rosa where Cipriano and Rosanna, Piero's mother, might have come face to face, but at Prospero Velo's restaurant in the Piazza Mazzini, on more neutral ground. The offer was made in a spirit of may-the-best-man-win conciliation, and Cipriano accepted it with his usual polite reserve.

That night, over *gamberi*, the prawns that were Prospero's speciality, Piero revealed that he knew about Cipriano's Vessinaro property, and had always known about it. In disclosing this, Piero's intentions were good – they were for the best: he wanted Cipriano to know that he, Piero, honoured the old doctor, his father's enemy, sufficiently to refrain from underhand tactics, even when these were easily justified. Indeed, who could have blamed Piero for pointing out that Cipriano had an undeclared interest in the election? But it didn't follow, Piero said, glorying in his own chivalrous argument, that because Cipriano had an interest, the mayor didn't genuinely believe in the value to others, indeed to the whole town, of opening the gate to the mountain. Piero himself could see the force of that argument. So of course Piero had not informed the electorate about Cipriano's secret incentive. It was the issue itself that mattered; on that and that alone, the electorate should judge.

Piero genuinely believed that his gesture could at last draw the sting out of the long resentment in the Cipriano's heart, and permit the two of them to breathe freely in each other's company. He even hoped, perhaps, that on the morrow it would happen that Cipriano would win the election and confirm Piero's action, in silent complicity between the two men, as one of generous reconciliation.

As always Piero was more ardent than canny. He liked to think of himself as knowledgeable, sly, even devious; yet perhaps it was a fundamental innocence and unworldliness in him that encouraged the townspeople to love and trust Piero, and that encouraged Miri, who was equally unworldly, to do the same. Lordliness and the common touch, both of which Piero possessed, were one thing (and had perhaps presided at his cradle, as part of his inheritance); politics was quite another, as was shrewdness when it came to people. TheCiprianos of the world not only regard an enemy's gifts with the utmost suspicion, but dread being patronized by the gift itself. Why couldn't the wretched boy – so over-eager, so intense, his blue eyes staring – keep his gallantry to himself? That capacity for restraint, Cipriano thought, he might have respected. So Piero had helped Cipriano's cause in the campaign, or at any rate refrained from damaging it. Now what would he expect in return? What further part of Cipriano's soul did this boy now own? Cipriano had never hated Piero with so pure a passion as he did at the moment when Piero unveiled his largesse.

And then came Cipriano's defeat at the polls, narrow enough but still conclusive. Piero had, in effect, tipped him from office, from the one seat that offered some compensation for his ruined life – and then deigned to seal this with a kiss? There would be time, now, to hatch a plan, and to return that lordly, condescending kiss with poisonous interest.

FOR PATIENT CIPRIANO, the opportunity came to press home his revenge, but not before the war was well under way, and a number of the town's sons had been lost, fighting for the Axis powers in North Africa, in Russia, even, and finally, after Anzio, defending their own land, in tandem with the Germans. The old petty feuds and local concerns had been re-valued, for most people, by personal tragedy. Not for Cipriano, who had no children to lose. There was no one in the town who didn't know a dozen bereaved families; Cipriano, now as chief of police and self-appointed Fascist commissar, knew them all, but kept his eyes on his own private war.

Meanwhile, Piero's world was changing. For some years now it had been darkening from the inside as well as the outside, as Europe slid towards war and Fascism slid towards racism, even though most of Mussolini's supporters were luke-warm at best about this. Piero's hopes for Italy had turned sour; yet what he saw in the bathroom mirror was the face of a man disappointed in more than his political dreams. He was growing old. The bounce had gone from his step. Piero was one of those men whose springtime is their best time, far better even than their summer. Barefoot Piero was the real Piero (indeed, this was how he felt about it himself). All through his youth he had been masquerading, he felt, when he put on slacks and a blazer – he was a juvenile delinquent graced with a title and pretending, on occasion, to be a grown-up. (He was a *condottiere*, someone with a romantic imagination might have said, transplanted from his natural habitat in the Middle Ages, where he would have died gloriously or ingloriously but, in either case, early.) The slacks and blazer, too, the fun of dressing up, he had loved. But now when he looked in the mirror he saw the face of a man whose beauty had faded too quickly, an aging boy whose almost feminine features were beginning to look pinched. He could no longer leap into a pick-up soccer game in the hills or in the town, as he used to, instantly becoming the star player on the field, fearless, rough (aggressive even), speedy and acrobatic. Now, if he tried it, the teenagers beat him to the ball (where was their respect?) and he wound up in the dust. They were as he had once been; as he still was, in his head. But to them he was already an old fart, and he knew better than to go on contesting this. It was a fact.

His domestic life, too, was leaving him – or so it felt. Miri and Vittorio were more than mother and child, they were a clan. A separate faction within the household. Not that they intrigued against him – why would they? They simply didn't need him in the least. This too was an unavoidable fact. He had married a woman who had transferred her affections to her child. It was hardly unusual. Many if not most women did that, his friends confirmed. And the ones who didn't were whores. (Secretly, he toyed with the fantasy of having married just such a whore, an upper-class whore, still mad for his body and indifferent to their children, whom she left to the servants, as an upper class wife should.) It was as if Miri had returned to England, but left her body behind. Worse, it was as if Muswell Hill, that hostile place (he had smiled through his wedding but he had read the clannishness in the eyes around him) was here in the Casa Rosa, in a parallel house within the walls, or behind a door he couldn't find, and the woman had kidnapped his son and taken him there.

Or perhaps she hadn't kidnapped him at all. Perhaps Vittorio had gone of his own accord – lured by his own blood, which after all was hers as well as his. He had no heir, then. In his place sat a silent upstart English boy who answered to Piero's father's name.

In the life of the town Piero had become largely redundant, he felt, a figurehead and little more, ever since Cipriano had taken over the police force and made the town itself into a docile supporter of *il Duce*. Resistance was up in the hills to the north, out of sight. Refusing, as he put it, to 'suit up' for the German imperial venture, Piero had declared himself a conscientious objector. These were rare under Fascism, and many – already gaoled since the early years of the war – were Jehovah's Witnesses, whose sense of their sacred mission placed them above history and forbade them to salute Mussolini or his deputies; by and large it was a local matter, as Piero liked to say; *obiettori di coscienza* were mostly left alone, provided they didn't take up arms against the Germans, and Piero was loath to put not only his family but his whole town at risk of reprisals by doing so. *Il Conte*, ever the charming eccentric and now, of all things, an objector to the war – it was his contrarian nature, most people agreed – was left alone. Cipriano may have felt that he benefited more by the opprobrium a freely circulating, non-combatant Piero received, in some quarters, than by the halo Piero might have acquired by being incarcerated. Regardless of this, the town divided along the usual lines. Some thought Piero the same showboating playboy as his father; others said you couldn't possibly accuse the *Conte* Piero, of all people, of cowardice, and that conscientious objection was one of the highest forms of civic courage. But the principled stand for which his supporters lauded Piero wasn't a form of courage that gladdened his heart, and finally, when Vittorio turned 13 and was ready (or should be ready, Piero felt, and would be ready if his mother hadn't coddled him all his life), to take more than a child's part in the running of the household, and even to stand in for him in certain ceremonial aspects of town life, Piero volunteered for the ambulance service and was sent at once where this was most urgently needed, on the battlefields south of Rome.

By this time, Miri was back in England.

UNIMAGINABLE, TO MIRI, to be away from Vittorio. In reality, she wasn't; only her body was in England, much as Piero had supposed her soul to be, when Miri's body was in Italy; her entire spirit was with Vittorio from morning till night and even when he slept. She felt sure he knew it.

But the choice had been stark. Stay with her son another day and it would be her last day with him. Her last day ever with him, not just her last day in the *paese*. By 1943 the rumours were unambiguous. Deportees – Jews and insurrectionists of various stamps – would not be returning alive.

She had begged Piero to be allowed to take Vittorio, when word came that Cipriano had prepared a list of those to be sent to Modena, where the transit camp was, en route to Poland, and that she was on the list. She, but not Vittorio. Had Piero struck a secret deal with Cipriano? It was too awful a thought and Miri didn't dare ask. On her knees, hugging his body, she had begged him to be allowed to take her son to England with her.

Vittorio would be safe, Piero had insisted. He had Cipriano's word. And the fellow was, if nothing else, a man of his word. Miri too would be safe – Piero had procured her a passage from Genoa, on board ship to Barcelona. From there she would reach England, and return as soon as the hostilities were over. Soon, soon! The war couldn't last, now that the Americans were in Europe. A year at most, no more, and they would all be reunited.

Miri refused to go. It didn't matter how graphic Piero's descriptions were of what would happen if she stayed and was deported and murdered. What use would she be to Vittorio then? he insisted. What did her love mean if she volunteered for death, when she could live and return within the year?

Still Miri refused, until Vittorio himself, speechless with tears, implored her. *Un anno solo, mamma,* he repeated. Just a year. *Un anno solo.*

I WOULD SAY, from what I know, that she never forgave herself for leaving. I say 'from what I know,' and I say 'I', because I can no longer sustain the pretence of anonymity, the convenient mantle of the philosophizing Pirandellian observer, an urbane chap like Lamberto Laudisi, say, in *Così È,* who knows the town and its secrets just as well as, if not better than, our Piero did.

I can hardly write at all, for tears, even now, and I cannot hide who I am while at the same time setting down the words I will shortly have to write. I had not expected this, but the disguise of the nameless, god-like narrator suddenly feels base. Perhaps I had forgotten that in the story I had set out to tell, we would reach a place where to be God Himself would feel base. In any case, I feel an imperative to come clean: my name is Angelo Baldini; I am – I was – the aforementioned Baldini, bookseller in the town and one of the Jews whose origins only Cipriano knew.

Enough, for now.

As I say, I believe that Miri Gottlieb never forgave herself for leaving Vittorio. Leaving him was her best hope, perhaps her only hope, of seeing Vittorio again, of being with him again. And still she couldn't forgive herself, because of what happened next.

She would undoubtedly – and here there isn't the shadow of a doubt in my mind – have elected to die with him rather than survive him, if that had been the choice with which she had been presented.

TO ALL OF us, I think, it seemed as if we had slumbered through a hundred years before the war broke out, and then lived through another hundred, but condensed into a sharp, terrible succession of shocks, during the next seven, as if a crazy driver had taken the wheel of our life.

Within twenty-four hours of the news of Piero's death during the retreat from Monte Cassino – he was one of seventeen ambulancemen killed in the terrible, protracted struggle later called the Battle for Rome – Cipriano gathered his men and issued the long-prepared instructions.

The next day, at dawn, Vittorio was rounded up, along with Enrico, Hilde and Tancredi Schmitz, the Baldini boys, Abramo and Beniamino, and their cousins, who were brought down at gunpoint from the hills beyond the Vessinaro, in case they ran away into the hills. My wife and I would have been with them when they were loaded into a police bus; we were on the list; but, unknown to Cipriano, and in ignorance of what was about to happen, we had left at five a.m. that morning on the bus to Tortona to visit my wife's sister and her husband, the Rietis, both of them inconsolable over the deportation to Poland of their eldest boy, who lived in Rome and had fallen into the German net.

The irony of this reason for our journey has always seemed to us the cruellest of all God's jokes (if, God forbid, there is a God) on our family. Out of consideration we'd decided not to take our children – Beniamino, the younger, had just turned 18 – to visit their aunt and uncle, as we normally would have, because we feared to remind the Rietis of their loss. By going at all, to grieve with my in-laws over their deported son, my wife and I evaded deportation, yet by leaving our own children behind, to respect the Rietis' grief, we doomed our boys.

The news reached us in Tortona, where my wife's relatives kept us hidden until the liberation.

Our children, like their cousins, like Miri and Piero's Vittorio and the Schmitz family, were taken to the infamous transit camp at Fossoli di Carpi, near Modena, which served as one of the departure points for Auschwitz. They were all put on trains for the death camp on June 2nd, 1944.

None survived, not one from our little *paese*.

HOW MANY OF us in the town really approved of those deportations, I wonder? How many would have voted for them, if it had been put to the vote? How many would have voted for them in their heart?

I doubt if there were more than a handful of passionately convinced anti-Semites in the town, people who truly believed that Jews were polluted by collective responsibility for the death of Jesus, and polluted everyone else with their guilt, or who believed that Jews were forever conspiring to infiltrate and manipulate Christian institutions. But were there ever more than a handful of racist believers, convinced and committed believers, anywhere and at any time? Wasn't that all it took, anywhere and at any time, to inflame a crowd of malcontents eager for a scapegoat?

(Perhaps I am too optimistic, despite everything, perhaps I of all people still refuse to recognize how deeply the virus has invaded the hearts of men.)

As soon as the war ended, you couldn't find a soul in the town who spoke of Cipriano – and by implication, the deportations that were his most flagrant act as police chief – with anything but disgust and shame, if they spoke of him at all. But then of course the war was over, Hitler and Mussolini were dead, the death camps were no longer only a rumour, and not even the most passionate racist would have stood up for Cipriano's creed. We go with the tide, most of us, in and out as the times decree.

All of which makes it hard to know, looking back at that October day when the Jews were rounded up and no one made an outcry or even a single gesture in protest, how much the act itself can be said to have spoken for the town. The town permitted it. Perhaps that's all that matters and all one can say. We stood by. (I say 'we'; I cannot say 'they'.) How many of us believed that the Nazis and German rule were doomed and that history would very soon bring in a verdict on the Ciprianos of the world? Did anyone really believe that Italy would be a German province forever? But such questions shrivel in the shadow of a larger one: what does 'belief' mean, in relation to the future? In retrospect, everyone now says they knew that Greater Germany was over-stretched, undermanned, unpopular and untenable. But in truth wasn't that what we hoped rather than what we 'knew'? Did we truly know for certain that they were overstretched? There were few of them, certainly, the Germans. Most of us had never spoken to one, and some of us had never even seen one. It's said that occupied France was ruled by a couple of hundred German officials, backed of course by troops – and this is said as though to show the cravenness and complicity of the occupied nation. But how many Roman administrators had it taken, in each province of the Empire, to sustain it for hundreds of years? No more than the modest number that the Germans deployed, surely. It will be objected that, unlike the Nazis, the Romans famously sanctioned local ways and local worship, and that this was the very basis of their survival as overlords. But who's to say that National Socialism, if it had held the line against outside attack, wouldn't have learned similar flexibility and acquired local colourations? It seems an absurd thought – but how tolerant were the Romans while their invading forces were still embattled?

So, yes, we hoped, rather than knew, that the Germans would be defeated; at the same time others of us hoped, rather than knew, that fascism would win. Many, surely, didn't care, so long as they and their loved ones survived and were able to feed and clothe themselves. And all of us, when the contest was over, united to despise the losers and proclaim that we had hated them all along and known all along that they would lose.

Even then, as we celebrated our liberation, followed by the collapse of Germany, we didn't care enough, as a nation, to prosecute, let alone summarily depose the local fascists whom the times, and in some places the newly despised Germans themselves, had put into power. Fascist mayors, many of them, were replaced by Communist mayors, but fascist police chiefs were not ousted. This carried a quite specific message, and it was not one of forgiveness for these individuals or their cause, nor of a lingering element of loyalty to either. The message we were sending to each other was simply this: we will move on, in a way that seals the door against the past, that annihilates the past by incorporating it, rather than, by expelling its representatives, creating a nest of resentful pariahs who will keep the past alive as a cause betrayed. We will retain the same masters, under a new name. That was not intended as a lazy or cynical proceeding, but as the safest, wisest, quickest way to move forwards.

There were exceptions. Our town was one. We wanted nothing more of Cipriano, though not because he had been a convinced Fascist. (As everyone said of retribution, *la retribuzione*, "If you start down that path, where will it end?" – these were the words on everybody's lips, for several years.) We hated Cipriano because he had acted not only on ideological grounds – the grounds on which an unspoken amnesty had now been declared – but on personal ones. Weren't these the very grounds by which we had all tacitly agreed to abide, in the world of smalltown politics? The grounds upon which we safely based our choices by personality rather than by creed? Ah yes, indeed; but now, thanks to Cipriano, we had no *Conte*. The line was ended. We were decapitated, now and forever. Some were glad; we were now a little republic, without a monarch, and about time too. But everyone agreed on one thing. No one had mandated Cipriano to create this firebreak between the town's past, a dozen centuries of it, and its present. And no one approved of his having done so in the name of revenge.

Miri's Vittorio had been *il Conte* for less than a day when the rumour of his father's death was confirmed and Cipriano issued the deportation order. Cipriano must have known in his heart, before he even issued the order, that now, if Fascism fell, he would fall with it. When it did, he resigned before the town could depose him, and young Andrea Capodimonte, who had no connection with Cipriano and his minions, and who was to be our police chief for the next thirty years, swiftly took his place. Cipriano pled illness as the reason for his resignation. We knew better, we thought. We didn't know then that he was indeed ill. We simply never wanted to see his face again. Talk surged up briefly, proposing that we rename the Piazza Mazzini and call it Piazzi dei Martiri, after the victims of the deportation, or even call it after Vittorio, our last Count. But the former suggestion seemed, though we would not have admitted it to each other, to situate the Jews at the heart of our community in a manner that was – shall we say – a little excessive in its remorseful tribute; and then someone pointed out that the latter suggestion, to name the Piazza after Vittorio, would forever raise the spectre of Cipriano himself, without whom we would hardly be naming our main square after one of his victims. Why not go the whole hog and rename it Piazza Cipriano, argued this cynic (it was not me but Vanna Fiore, a fine and fearless woman at odds with bureaucratic cant all her life), and with her discomfiting point the whole matter of publicly commemorating the victims of the deportations sank without a trace.

This, then, was the state of mind of the town to which Miri Gottlieb, *Contessa* Miri as she still was and as everyone would forever call her, returned when the war was over, looking to find out what the town – well, why beat about the bush? Looking for justice.

"*IF YOU START DOWN THAT PATH, WHERE* will it end?"

The first time Miri Gottlieb heard these words were from the lips of Andrea Capodimonte, whom she had known as a boy playing on Piero's little beach, a boy a good deal older than Vittorio but always gentle, kind, indulging her son. (Because he's the future Count, a voice had always said in her mind, when people went out of their way to be nice to Vittorio.) And now here was tall thin myopic Andrea, grown like a weed, Miri's mother would say, sitting before Miri in ridiculous epaulettes, too thin for his uniform or for any uniform on earth, Andrea the bespectacled police chief seated behind his desk in the penumbra of his shuttered office. It made her feel impossibly old.

When he said she should kill Cipriano herself, she hardly took it in, except as some kind of foolish, helpless joke. What was she going to do, take a gun and put it to the old man's head? Perhaps Andrea had some sort of war psychosis, to talk this way about killing. But his steady stare, through his crude wartime glasses, was clearly intended to tell her he meant every word of it.

She hadn't come all this way for such nonsense.

"*IF HE WAS* over-zealous in the execution of his orders," Cefalù, formerly Piero's lawyer and his father's, paused and sighed dramatically, "there is no legal provision, so far as I know – "

"Over-*zealous*?"

They stared at each other. Cefalù was an old Communist, an amiable, careful man, bald, jowly, small and plump, his white shirt always immaculately pressed. He had lost no one in the war (certainly not whoever it was that pressed his shirts), to the best of Miri's information, but seemed to be grieving abstractly, to make up for this. Or was it just that everyone seemed tired, more so now that the war was over, it struck Miri, as if the strain of wartime were hitting them at last?

"*Signora Contessa*," he began miserably. Miri could hear in his voice that he was about to tell her again how much he deplored her tragic loss, how much the town deplored it.

"What orders?" Miri asked. "How do you know he had orders?"

"*Signora Contessa*, there were standing orders. Everybody knows it."

"Show them to me."

She was surprised at the icy firmness of her tone.

"Find them. Show them to me," she repeated. It wasn't her own forcefulness that startled Miri, but the fact that there was so much life in her voice. She had come to think of herself as of one dead, and often, to her own ears, her voice sounded like it. "There were standing orders to arrest Jews, but most police chiefs ignored them. I know all this," Miri said. "I want to see the exact wording of these orders. I want to *see* them."

"I will speak to the *comandante di polizia, signora Contessa.*"

"I've already spoken to him, *signor* Cefalù. Andrea says he doesn't know where the orders are. He's lying."

Miri held Cefalù's gaze until at last he gave the smallest of shrugs.

"I want to see them," Miri said again. "I want to know just how much Cipriano acted on his own initiative, do you understand?"

"*Signora Contessa*, many documents have been burned."

"Been *burned*? By whom?"

"In the celebrations, *signora Contessa*. Flags were burned, uniforms, papers."

"Why papers? Didn't they understand that some things would be needed?"

"People burned everything they could put their hands on, *signora Contessa*. They would have burned *il Duce* himself if they could, and Cipriano too, if he'd shown his face." The lawyer hesitated, studying Miri. "You have to understand, there is a moment for such things, and then the moment passes."

CELEBRATION HAD DISGUSTED Miri when it came to London, as it did in waves of rumour, and at last, given official license, on VE-day and again on VJ-day as if people couldn't get enough of it. How much clearer did it have to be, that death was the only victor? If you looked around, as the guns fell silent, and found that your comrades were mostly dead, would your impulse be to cheer? It was obscene.

She had heard of Piero's death and Vittorio's deportation in separate letters that arrived on the same day, June 7th, 1944. That week had seemed to bring the longed-for up-swing at last, with the fall of Rome and the Normandy landings, promising a rapid end to the war. It had been another false dawn.

June the seventh. The blackest day of her life until confirmation of Vittorio's death supervened.

That had no date, no accompanying letter. It blackened all calendars.

And it also had no date because it was her family who heard the news first, before she did. Miri never knew when exactly. They had kept it from her, because of 'her state,' as it was called, until they felt she could take it in. That was how Miri's mother put it. And then they weren't sure Miri *had* taken it in, because of the calm with which she received the news.

From the way Miri had reacted, her father said – or rather from the way she hadn't reacted, that day, or in the weeks and months that followed – they had begun to worry, Avram said, that she would never come back to them.

Why couldn't her father understand? Miri wondered. He had always known her heart.

But he had never known loss like this, Miri reminded herself. They had known loss, her family, but not like this.

Yet why couldn't they understand that she had been readier for the worst this time, had not cushioned herself with false hopes and prayerful thoughts as she had, during her London years, until the twin horrors arrived, Piero's death and Vittorio's deportation, on the seventh of June?

WHEN MIRI FIRST reached London she had followed her sister Hannah's lead by throwing herself into nursing, six months at nursing school in Roehampton and then full-time at the Middlesex. The fuller the better. If she could have gone entirely without sleep, she would have. As long as she was at her mindless work (rather, her mindful work, since mindfulness was not only in its nature but was its very purpose, for her), Piero and Vittorio were safe in the Casa Rosa, in Serafina's kitchen, watching her roll the pasta out over the newspaper, obliterating the news.

Miri hadn't prepared herself for Vittorio's deportation any more than she had for Piero's death, and afterwards she wondered at her blitheness. Being separated from Vittorio was purgatorial enough – had that been the cause of her failure to prepare herself? To imagine anything worse than she was already suffering would have been wanton, she must have felt; so she had fallen back, no doubt, on her belief that under Piero's protection Vittorio was untouchable, and that Piero's stance against the war guaranteed that he himself was going nowhere.

Why in God's name had he changed his mind, regardless of his choice of a non-combatant's role on the battlefield? Why risk his life, and Vittorio's with it?

She couldn't fathom the meaning of Piero's behaviour. The fact that by its outcome, by leaving Vittorio exposed, he had not only removed their child from the world and from Miri, leaving nothing of her worth inhabiting, but also torn out of her life the page that came before Vittorio, the page filled with the image of Piero and who he was, as she had understood him – this hole, this riddle now awaited Miri in some impossibly distant place, beyond the loss of Vittorio. She couldn't imagine ever reaching that place in her lifetime.

AFTER THE NEWS came, confirming that the camps had swallowed him (this was as close as she would allow herself to get, in picturing it), that he was dead, she had been with Vittorio all the time.

She was with him not in his death, not in the nightmare he had had to suffer, alone and crying out for her – Miri had refused to clothe this in its gruesome rags, she had avoided all images, all newspaper reports and all newsreels devoted to the death camps – but in their past together, where he now safely was. He was there entirely now. She was there with him whenever she could be, which was still a great deal of the day.

This had, Miri knew quite well, been her way of preparing herself for the worst. The first shock, the double-barrelled shock of Piero's death and Vittorio's deportation, had caught her by surprise, amidships, as the wartime word was, and she was not going to be caught that way again. Until that June morning she had lived through each day as though she was living it with Vittorio, rising with him, eating breakfast together in Serafina's kitchen, heading off down the hill with the boy, to school. This routine had not cancelled fear, let alone the sense of certainty that had descended on her in Genoa harbour as the ship, amid the deep, throbbing turmoil of its reversing engines, pulled away from the quay and from Vittorio, beside Piero, the certainty that she would never see them again. But she had called that certainty no more than an effect of fear, and done her best to relegate it accordingly.

There was bound to be fear; but as long as she could picture Vittorio's day, by the hour, the fear crouched obediently in its habitual place at the base of her throat. If she looked carefully enough she thought she could see it, in the mirror. It must be visible to others, she suspected, a pouch of terror bulging out where her throat met the thin bones of her chest. Was it visible even through her nurse's uniform? In public she often covered this area with her right hand, in case it was so.

Then after June 7, after the letters and the news, more drastic measures were needed, fiercer magic. Piero was gone; the town had betrayed them, letting Vittorio be taken – why couldn't they have hidden him, somewhere up in the hills? Was it because of the foreign blood he carried, her blood, that they hadn't bothered? Cipriano's treachery was to be expected, but what of the town that had bowed to her, murmuring her name, every day of her married life?

Italy itself had turned malignant, and she had to protect Vittorio from it.

Now she drew him into her own world every day, instead of entering his. He had been deported, yes, but the war would be over within a matter of weeks, everyone said so. In her mind, she had collected him and brought him back to Muswell Hill and introduced him to his Englishness. Now, instead of Miri being in Italy in her head all day, she was in London with her eyes open to her surroundings again. Instead of going everywhere with Vittorio, he went everywhere with her and she explained it all to him. Even the hospital.

It was no longer the Middlesex; this was a quite different kind of hospital, in Hemel Hempstead, and she was no longer a nurse but a patient now ("Nurses make the *worst* patients," her Roehampton tutor had liked to say) in this hospital, or so-called 'home'. Asylum was its real name, a pleasant one if you thought about its sense as sanctuary. You sought asylum from your pursuers, from politics, from persecution.

IT WAS EXHAUSTION that had brought her here, Miri knew. No one doubted her sanity. If she was mad – and she had every reason to be, surely – they would have kept her in Muswell Hill, her father said, smiling, where she would be indistinguishable from the rest of the family. Thank goodness he could still make her laugh. Avram's remarks reminded her that it was his sense of humour Vittorio carried, through her.

It was true that the family was in disarray. Miri's younger sister Hannah was also a war widow, and she too had thrown herself into her nursing with a dedication that was sometimes dreadful to see, as though self-punishment were its primary purpose. The sly, mobile, wicked child's face, the Hannah-face Miri had known when she was growing up, had closed its doors and become a mask of unforgiving anger. Rivkie, almost two years older than Hannah, now looked the younger of the two. Rivkie too had lost someone and still mourned him – the limbs of her long, angular body seemed to declare it – even though she had recently married and was supposed to be 'the happy one,' as she all too well knew. Rivkie's chatter and her small face with its pointed features, lifted in smiles, adopted the role willingly, but her drooping body told a different story.

Miri watched Rivkie at her bedside as she watched the others. They seemed like well-meaning people who were visiting the wrong patient. Try the next bed, she wanted to suggest. Had she ever truly been part of this family?

All her life, it seemed to Miri now, she had floated somewhere above and to the side of her family, bathed in her father's evident favouritism, for which her mother had dutifully tried to cut her down to size. Hadn't they all looked at her as though she were – what? At last she had a chance to assess it. Not an intruder exactly, but more like some kind of award from the state, a very studious, self-contained nanny, perhaps, or a school prefect donated to them as a boarder. She had certainly filled both roles in relation to Hannah and Rivkie when they were small. And it was surely how they saw her. Miss Prim, who'd bagged a Count and gone away.

Throughout her Muswell Hill years, her childhood and her youth, she had been holding herself in, preparing herself for something quite different. There had been no disguising it from her family; they had known, and in some measure resented it (what's the matter with *us*?) all along. She had been preparing herself for *this*.

Was it really for this?

Hadn't she been – as she had thought all through her marriage – keeping herself in readiness for Piero, for the *signora Contessa* in her, for Vittorio? For the hills, for the Vessinaro? Surely for the hills.

No.

Strangely, and now that the war had taken all of that from her, she understood that it was *this* she had been preparing for: lying here in the asylum, deprived of everything, without family. Gathering her strength. She had no idea what for, yet.

The hills, the Vessinaro, the *pinoli*. They were still there and still, notionally, hers. But hardly in the same way. They were a portion of the past that you could walk through in your mind, and one day, perhaps, in the flesh, it would look and smell the same.

But what was happening now, inside her: this was what she had been saving herself for, it seemed. Absurd as it was – shuffling in slippers to the window, strolling in the little park (hardly a park, although they called it that, dwarf trees and pebbled paths) – it felt more like the beginning of her real life than anything she had known before. It was in her body that she knew it. A person's body knew its future – this thought had come to her one day with such force that she had had to repeat it to the Ward Sister, and again to Dr. Hogg, her therapist. It had taught her a lesson. Some things don't change, and even in this brave new life of hers there were clearly thoughts that one should keep to oneself. It had always been like that, in Muswell Hill with her family. With Piero. With everyone, really, except Vittorio.

SHE DIDN'T EVEN know when it was that they had told her Vittorio was dead.

Apparently she had replied, and continued to insist – though to whom? Nurses, doctors? Her family? All of them? – that no, Vittorio was at the Casa Rosa, waiting for her. She had maintained this repeatedly, it seemed. And they would keep her here, at the 'home,' until she acknowledged that it wasn't so. Had she been told this, or simply intuited it? It was a perfect arrangement – she could stay and shuffle to the window, eat her food and take a walk, for as long as she wanted. Forever. All she had to do was say, *Vittorio's at the Casa Rosa.*

Every time she thought about this, every time she remembered that this was why she was living here, in the euphemistically-called Recovery Ward, where many of her fellow patients had even forgotten what it was they were hoping to recover from, she wanted to laugh. In all likelihood, she *had* laughed, a good deal, and it had confirmed their diagnosis. *Not ready yet.* What kind of a woman would laugh, long and hearty perhaps (a big eruption of a laugh, Miri knew that, from her slight body – she had never laughed in such an unhampered way before), who had lost her husband to the fighting and her child to the death camps? And laughed? Not an entirely sane one. Not ready yet. *Non ancora, signora!* Bulging-eyed Serafina would cry if Miri tried to pluck the *torta*, or the even more fragile *deliziosa*, out of the oven too early. Not quite fully cooked yet.

But she had to laugh – it was too funny. It was hilarious. All she had to do was tell them the truth, and they would allow her to stay here, in perfect safety. The truth: because after all Vittorio *was* in the Casa Rosa if he was anywhere. The doctor looked at her as if to say, *You* think you're playing a game with us, but actually we're playing a game with you. We're waiting you out. We can sit at the entrance to your burrow as long as you need, as long as is necessary. Time is no concern. When you feel like coming out...

And feel ready to acknowledge that Vittorio is dead, that's what he meant but wouldn't say. He couldn't say it. No prompting. In an asylum you have to remember your lines without help.

That's when she would laugh. Of course she knew Vittorio was dead. But to say so, to join them in their utter misapprehension as to what that meant – that *would* be death, not only Vittorio's but hers. (The same thing.) That would be to consent to madness, to enter the world of the mad where death was death and death only. *That* would be playing a crazy game, and she wasn't going to *play* at all any more. It was time for truth. She was gathering her strength and then it would be time.

And Vittorio *was* at the Casa Rosa. He was waiting to be taken to the Vessinaro, if she, Miri, *mamma*, would consent to forgive Italy and return. *Tu moé*, Serafina would say to him in Genoese, your mother, pointing at Miri, and she would get Vittorio to repeat it, *moé*, to her amusement, as if she were teaching the *signorino Conte* a subversive tongue, the language of the people. *Tu poé, tu moé.* Father, mother. *Poé, moé.* Along with the food, which somehow lay inside Serafina fully formed and issued from her hands like pottery from the wheel, wheezing fat Serafina contained another thing, an ancient language, older than Italian. Serafina was what lay beneath, under the murderous feuds. Once again she would help Miri to see it.

ALL THESE THINGS I learnt from Miri later.

As you may perhaps have guessed, I was the one who informed Miri's family that Vittorio had not survived.

It had also been I, in May of '44, who wrote to Miri the two dreadful letters informing her of Piero's death and Vittorio's deportation. (I've never known whether to regret that they arrived on the same day, or whether to be grateful on Miri's behalf that she didn't have to experience, as I feared she would, the hammer blows on successive days.)

Piero himself had entrusted me with an address in Spain, that of a friend who would post letters on, ensuring their delivery in an Allied country as we could not, if we tried to send them directly from our German-governed state. He and Vittorio had been using this friendly 'postbox' himself, Piero said, and he had left the address with Rosanna, his mother. But to guard against all eventualities, he said, it made more sense also to let someone else, someone trustworthy, share the secret and use the address if necessary. I was surprised and flattered that *il Conte Piero* chose me. We had always been cordial but never close. I didn't ask him, as perhaps I should have done, whether he knew that I was Jewish by descent. As I've mentioned, it was not something that was known in the town, nor was it something I advertised, and since neither my wife nor I had been raised within the religion – my grandparents had adopted a secular life, as had my wife's parents – there was little reason for anyone to guess our origins. I had no idea that Cipriano, his curiosity perhaps aroused by some of the books in my store, written by Jewish radicals (famous ones, Trotsky and Emma Goldman included), had investigated my background, and knew.

When Piero handed me the address, written in a defiant flourish on Casa Rosa notepaper, it flashed through my mind that he perhaps knew that I was Jewish – though how? How could he know? Angelo Baldini: was there a more Italian name? For an instant I wondered whether more people knew than I had ever realized. I hesitated, about to speak, about to ask him whether as a person who was himself vulnerable to arrest I was the right person to serve as back-up to the *Contessa madre,* his mother, in order for Piero to be sure that, in his absence, any urgent news would be sure to reach the *Contessa* in England. We had not discussed what such news might consist of, nor did this subject ever come up.

But at the moment when I was going to speak – and I may have hesitated because the characteristic daring with which Piero had written the address so openly on headed notepaper (it was so very different from what one might have expected, an address scribbled on a scrap of newspaper) held my attention for an instant – Piero gave one of his enormous, white-toothed smiles, the film star smile whose charm had won him the adoration of men and women, and the enmity of some. "Angelo," he said, "find a book in your shop which no one will ever want to buy, or read, and put this inside it." And in that instant, as he spoke and pushed the note towards me, I knew that this was why he had chosen me as its repository. He had pictured it inside a book on a high shelf. It was a romantic hiding place. The fact that his wife's ancestors and mine had shared a religion was a coincidence of which he was, it seemed to me now, quite unaware.

And I let the moment pass. Truthfully, I was too flattered to want to spoil it by pointing to a disqualifying factor. I admired the *Contessa* Miri, and had always done so. I was delighted to be made a conduit to her, and to have some responsibility for her state of soul, if only by transmitting information. And, perhaps most foolishly and culpably of all, I didn't believe Cipriano would move against the Jews – if he even knew who they were – in the town. The idea of Cipriano arresting Vittorio had never even entered my mind. What's more, I could never have imagined the event that made this possible: Piero's death. Nobody who knew *il Conte* Piero could ever have imagined him dead. It was easier to picture him marching uphill into a hail of bullets and emerging unscathed. There are some people who have that aura, and Piero was one. All our life, it seemed, we had known him leaping from windows, dancing along tables and balustrades, sometimes taking what looked like terrible falls only to jump up laughing. No one should have survived the car crashes from which he stepped unscathed, or even from the ones he somehow managed to prevent from being an accident at all. His grace, as infallible as his luck, was supernatural. Once or twice he turned out for the town's soccer team (mostly when they were in danger of relegation from their division) and scored numerous goals. He refused to play regularly because, he boasted, it would be unfair to the town's opponents. He was right. We urged him to enter for the Olympics, if not as a diver then as a skier (at which he was certainly of Olympic standard) and, if not that, then at least in an event favoured by gilded amateurs, like the bobsleigh. He would just smile and let his golden lids droop a little over his pale eyes, like a lizard. I think everyone knew what he meant by this. There *was* an event – this was before he met Miri – at which he had already won numerous golds, although it wasn't yet on the Olympic roster. Compared to these conquests, all other sporting events were simply a way of celebrating his achievements as a lover. And celebrations should not be treated as competitions, surely.

So I took the note with the address on it, and put it in an edition of Hegel's *Phenomenology of Mind* with footnotes by Azem Harxhi of the Albanian Academy of Sciences, one of the least sought-after books I possess.

When news came of Piero's death, I took the Hegel down, took out the note and stared at it, wondering whether this was really any of my business. Wouldn't Rosanna, Piero's mother, inform her daughter-in-law? But what if Piero hadn't been so sure of this connection, what if he'd given me this commission for a reason? I could have visited the Casa Rosa and conferred with the *Contessa madre*. Some anxious instinct – I could even call it a Jewish instinct – or demon held me back. What would the *Contessa madre* think of Piero's having chosen a back-up at all, and what place would I now seem to have held in her son's life? The Casa Rosa, though not as imposing as many a millionaire's mansion on the mountain above the *cancello*, was still precisely the kind of grand house I dreaded entering.

I decided I'd just do as the late Count had instructed me, and write to his wife.

"*Gentilissima signora Contessa,*

"As you may perhaps have heard already, and please forgive me if I am adding a cruel echo to what must have already been…"

And then, within twenty-four hours, came the deportations, which we only discovered when we got back from Tortona (by sheer luck we ran into none of Cipriano's men on the way home from the bus station) to find an empty house. Alerted by neighbours, we packed swiftly, and fled once more.

Now I had a second letter to write.

In her brief, answering note, which reached us in Tortona almost a month later, the *Contessa* Miri had asked me to inform her promptly of any further news. A London phone number was attached.

Fifteen dreadful months passed, filled with rumours and futile Embassy visits. Occasionally, people returned. Manfredo Viti, a huge fellow who had been a fisherman before the war, and now sells wine (although I believe he drinks more than he sells), arrived from Russia, where he had been captured on the battlefield and spent two years in a Siberian prisoner-of-war camp. Early in '45, Manfredo had escaped, and made his way home to Liguria. Eight months it had taken him, walking every step of the way.

But we had no news from Poland. At last, when I heard that a man had reached home in neighbouring Chiavari, an Auschwitz survivor, I hurried south along the coast to find him – my wife and I still had no news of our boys – and heard from his lips the terrible truth that neither our children nor Miri's child had survived.

In the midst of our grief I debated what to do about the *Contessa* Miri. Should I phone? Could I – and should I? – bring myself to tell her the news over the phone? Perhaps she already knew that Vittorio was dead, either from other survivors or by public information we ourselves had been unable to locate. This was in fact unlikely, though we didn't know it at the time. After its first, carefully documented years as a death camp, as we were to discover later, the sheer volume of murder outpaced bureaucracy, and Auschwitz ceased to keep exact records of those who went directly from the train to the gas chambers.

Even if the *Contessa* Miri didn't know yet, I speculated, would anything be served by telling her at once over the phone, by bringing her the harsher annunciation of spoken doom, compared to the more cushioned shock of a letter? Yet was that right? Was a human voice harsher than written words? I wasn't sure. In the end I phoned, and was told by a family member – one of the *Contessa* Miri's sisters, though to this day I don't know which, since Miri herself never discovered – that Miri was "not at home right now."

She was, of course, in the asylum in Hemel Hempstead, since the exhaustion that brought her there had overtaken her before the actual news she dreaded, news of which she was by now – nine months after the liberation of the camps – only awaiting the confirmation.

I'm ashamed to say I was relieved to be able to tell the *Contessa* Miri's sister the news and not Miri herself. I gave my address and telephone number in case, I said, I could be of any use.

Also, if it had been Miri at the other end of the phone, she would have asked about the other deportees. And I was glad not to have to oblige my voice to speak the answer.

So I was the one, the messenger. Appointed by *il Conte* Piero; doing his bidding.

What if I had protested? What if I had turned down the commission? *Io no, signor Conte. Mi spiace.* My life, infinitely the poorer for it if I had done so, would not, I think, be what it is now.

THE TURNING POINT for Miri, more than a year later, was a letter from Serafina, although Miri didn't read the letter until many months after it was delivered to her. She opened the envelope and took out the pages, and because she took the pages everywhere with her – they were her most precious possession, it seemed – everyone thought she must have read it, indeed read it repeatedly.

Miri had looked at the letter, often. Many times a day. But she hadn't read it. It was written on two small rectangular pages torn from a block of graph paper, with its grid of pale blue lines forming a background of tiny squares to Serafina's barely legible scrawl, as it always had when Serafina wrote her shopping list for her husband or her daughter or on occasion for Miri herself to carry out in the town. I had sometimes seen her myself, in the town, studying the little blue rectangle and trying to decipher the handwriting on it. Those shopping lists, and Serafina's looping, erratic hand, were so familiar to Miri that there were times, holding them idly in her hand, or laying them out on the bed, in Hemel Hempstead, when they were all she needed to take her back to the kitchen at the Casa Rosa. It was as if she had pulled a shopping list out of her dreams. In imagination she could walk around the town from store to store, making her purchases, greeting – and forgiving – each passer-by in turn, each street, each shop. There was no end to the task of forgiveness.

Miri hadn't dared to enter the town, in her mind, until Serafina's letter, her tiny pages with their scrawly, mercifully baffling script, took her there. She had been up in the hills all this time, hiding Vittorio. There were so many places to hide, even as close as the Vessinaro. As she pictured it, they had made friends with *la prigionniera*, the dark-eyed girl behind the laurel hedge, and she allowed them to stay there, in her house, behind the shutters, as long as they liked.

Now, with Vittorio at her side, she shopped for Serafina in her mind, taking each of Serafina's dishes in turn, one a day: *cotolette, orata, ossobuco, maiale, dentice, gnocchi,* and on Sunday *arrosto* – seven days, seven meals, and then begin again with Monday's *cotolette*, buying the meat and the vegetables and a *contorno*, a salad, maybe, or some *gamberi* as a starter. String shopping bag in hand, Miri descended the little steps, over a hundred of them, down from Serafina's kitchen doorway to the road, steps no more than two feet wide and overgrown with weeds, and twisting side to side amid the terraces where several dozen generations had confirmed their shape and placing (children running, leaping two or three at a time, farmers and monks descending, slowly, trying to cushion aging knees – they were all around her, in her mind, overtaking her or slowing her down without apology until they turned to see her. Then they stepped back with a bow. *Avanti, signora Contessa! Signor Contessino!*). In three places she had to skirt along the walls and then down more steps and downhill through the yard of a tiny, dirty farmhouse, the first of three, where each time the chickens fled her angrily as if she'd come to steal their scattered grain, and the dog raged madly on its rope, barking and slavering, trying to reach her. Three farmhouses, three dogs, each madder than the one before, because already alerted by the first. And always another brief set of mossy steps, another wall to skirt, along a vineyard raised above her head, and then more tiny steps, at a new angle, carving a path through the descending terraces, sheltered by figs and olives – and the smell! The sweet, rotting smell of odorous Italian paths in the shade, her vile, beloved hillside paths. Crushed figs mingled with dogshit.

And at last, emerging at sea level almost at a run along the final, sloping, sandy stretch between houses, to brush past the bougainvillea that covered the house-front on either side, both creepers riotous and stretching out as if to clasp each other and mate the slightly faded orange variety, on the left, to the brazen purple on the right, then there she was, at the road, with the little beach right in front of her where she had first glimpsed Piero, where in due course she had first introduced Vittorio to sea and sand.

She took the bus, as she had in the past, from the little beach into the town, the hooting, pooting bus that had to stop and honk its horn, *beee-bah, beee-bah*, always twice, before every single corner of the narrow road that hugged the coast like a map-making hand meticulously tracing every tiny twist and inlet, with never more than fifty foot of road before the next *beee-bah beee-bah*. You could hear the bus across the bay as far away as Chiavari, *beee-bah beee-bah*, and way up in the hills, where you tried to judge by sound where exactly the bus was on its slow way as you ran down the huge slippery giant's causeway stones of the goat track, to know whether you'd missed it already.

IT WAS A full day, in the asylum. She had to descend the terraced hillside to the bus stop, catch the bus, do the shopping, pausing in every shop to discuss town affairs and enquire about the storekeeper's family, both in the town and elsewhere, and return with the shopping, by *beee-bah*, and get off at the stop by the little beach. She didn't have to alert the driver, since there was no such thing as a bus driver who didn't know where the *Contessa* Miri's stop was and who wouldn't call to the passengers to kindly make way for the *Contessa* with her shopping, and her son.

Then came the long, laborious climb back up to the Casa Rosa, she and Vittorio both laden with shopping, while the chickens ran for their lives and the crazy dogs began the mad hillside routine in turn all over again, raging and straining at the end of their ragged, dirty rope as though they'd never seen Miri in their life. And once more, in her nostrils, the rich putrescent smell of the shady path as it skirted a vineyard, under the fig trees.

And the day's work had barely begun. With Serafina she would unpack the shopping, and Serafina would cluck over it – *ossignor!* – if it wasn't up to standard, and Miri would assure her it was the best she could find (her assurances convinced neither Serafina nor herself), and they would start the day-long process of cooking, stage by stage, item by item.

When Miri looked back at her Hemel Hempstead days (and it was always shocking to remind herself that she was there, in the home, for nearly two years), it never failed to strike her that what she was doing, in her head, was exactly what she would have been doing – or trying to do – in a concentration camp, if she'd been deported with Vittorio.

Together they'd be imagining their home routine, stage by stage, and it would surely, Miri thought, have been precisely this ritual that would have kept them alive. It would have been stronger than any punishment, any deprivation. They could have walked every step of the way together, down from the Casa Rosa, remarking on the state of the grapes and the olives, stealing a peach, perhaps, pacing out each yard of the journey; they would have made similar journeys round the town, enumerating every shop and inventing gossip for every shop assistant. Shall we go by Piazza Cavour today? We haven't greeted *la nonna* Giuseppina, the old seamstress, in a while, or asked after her eyes, and her asthma. Shall we? *'Diamo.* And they would have taken every walk into the hills together, noting every landmark, every turn and tree.

Now, instead, she shopped and cooked, each day of the week a separate shopping list and a separate meal to cook. No one, while she was consumed by her routine, could possibly intervene to torture her.

She never read Serafina's letter. It was more precious as a shopping list. More to the point, she knew what it contained. Others had written to her quite recently again, Cefalù, the family lawyer, and well-meaning people from the town (including Baldini the bookseller) to tell her that her mother-in-law Rosanna had also passed away. The *Contessa madre* never fully recovered from Piero's death, each one of her correspondents had said, as if quoting the official town word. No doubt it was true; but Miri, who had known Rosanna's distant, kindly, ghostly spirit, knew quite well that it was her husband's death from which Rosanna had never recovered. The Rosanna whom Miri believed she had fathomed (and as I've mentioned, there were shocks in store for Miri in this regard, as there are for all of us who are offered a belated, secret entrance into the life of a person we believed we knew) spent her time reading historical novels of the most romantic kind, and it was only of them that Rosanna ever wanted to speak. Piero's death had no doubt been the *coup de grâce*, but Rosanna had not been entirely alive while Miri knew her. She had been a decorous ghost, and little more. Would it be more true to say that not only Piero's death but the conjunction of Piero's and then young Vittorio's had between them sapped her will to live? But why lie, now, after so much suffering? Surely the best way to honour so terrible a past was to tell the truth, now and always, and in truth Rosanna had never entirely focused on her grandson.

Had this been Miri's fault for monopolizing the boy too much? Rosanna had always been willing to take Vittorio out for an ice cream, even on a visit to the cinema, and performed the duty fondly. Yet they all knew, Rosanna included, that the greater part of Rosanna was in exile, unable to understand why her life had been taken from her. She was, Miri often thought (but hardly dared say), Cipriano's double, by a cruel irony. Her life, too, had stopped, years ago, though Rosanna had turned the sting of it inwards, to spare others. To the best of Miri's understanding, Rosanna had blamed no one.

THE CHANGE CAME when Dr. Jeffries arrived at Hemel Hempstead like a wind blowing through an ancient ballroom and shaking out billowing curtains, dustcovers, and stale perfume. John Jeffries was young, red-faced, choleric. To everyone's amazement

– the staff's far more than the patients' – he marched through the wards, announcing, "There will be no more sponging on the State! The Welfare State is here to see to your welfare, *not* to pay you to *vegetate*! Malingerers *out*!"

"So," he said to Miri, "you're the one I've heard about, with the precious letter. Now, you see, I don't speak Italian. I want *you* to tell *me* what it says, please."

He made Miri read Serafina's letter.

NOI LE ASPETTIAMO. The placing of the "*noi*" said it all.

"*Le aspettiamo*," Serafina could have written. "We're waiting for you." Expecting you. Or "*Le aspettiamo noi*," indicating, "Don't worry, we're here, waiting for you." But *Noi le aspettiamo* – –

(Miri only realized she was crying when she heard, somewhere – was he close, or far? She couldn't tell – the red-faced man's voice, "*That's* it. Now that's good. Heavens above. Two years of mooning around, and at last some progress!")

– *Noi le aspettiamo* meant *we, we* are waiting, no one else may give a damn but *we*'re waiting for you here, till hell freezes over.

To Jeffries' nods of approval, Miri began to wail.

"You see?" he said to the assembled staff. "And you told me you hadn't seen a single sign of emotion from her."

Miri wailed until her throat was raw, until long after Dr. Jeffries had passed on and completed his inaugural rounds, and even after the day nurse, appointed to keep an eye on Miri, had gone to help distribute lunch. They noticed Miri again when they found her running through the building, searching for something on every surface, like a madwoman. The available staff banded together to restrain her, afraid that she was looking for something with which to do herself harm. It was natural enough, it struck Miri later, that they would think that somehow the reality of the letter, released at last, had pierced her all-pervasive denial, and that with it the loss of her husband and the horror of her son's death had come flooding in.

What Miri was looking for was a newspaper.

When at last she was able to control her throat and her voice enough to ask for one, she stared at it and then ran off down the corridor again, chased by nurses.

This time what she wanted were her clothes.

Serafina's letter, hard as it was to decipher (but *noi le aspettiamo* said all she needed to know), had a date in the top right-hand corner, and that date, she now realized, was four months ago. The letter told of Rosanna's death, too – *ancora giovane*, Serafina had written. Still young. Miri had no idea what her mother-in-law's age would have been, since Rosanna had always drawn a veil over the subject. But perhaps Serafina knew. Serafina knew everything. What this all meant – what *noi le aspettiamo* meant – was that Serafina and her family were determined to hold on there in the house, waiting for Miri, or rather that they *had* been determined to hold on, even though the rent would now have become due four times since Serafina wrote the letter, with no one from Piero's family to pay it, and the *Contessa* in a madhouse in far-off England. Would the owners of the Casa Rosa, would the town itself, have taken pity? Not hearing from Miri, would Serafina have given up?

What about Rosanna's will? For that matter, no one had told her anything about Piero's will. No one here – here in the home, or indeed here in England – would be able to tell her. None of this could be sorted out at a distance. She had to see Cefalù immediately. (Later it astonished her, even when she was told that this was far more common than a gradual recovery, that she could have lingered in her trance so long, and come out of it so fast and with a sense of urgency and energy that felt as if she was drawing – as she was – on months and months of dormant accumulation. Almost two years of it!) There was nothing for it but to go – at once.

This was all slightly more than John Jeffries had had in mind, in the way of instant rehabilitation. He wasn't at all sure whether Miri would provide a bracing example for the rest of the "malingerers," as he'd called them, perhaps inadvisedly, he now thought. If they all picked up their beds and walked, so to speak, if they all dashed out into the street, following the crazed Italian letter woman, he might – instead of the brisk wind he had hoped to introduce – reap the whirlwind. Perhaps this lady (what was her name, again?) should be encouraged to return to her ward, and rest, and think about the future a little more soberly, after consultation with the staff. Her name was what? Miriam who? Would somebody please fetch her file? And do *not* give this Miriam Gottlieb her clothes.

But Miri had never been sectioned, it turned out. No paperwork pertaining to her situation had been filed. No one could stop her. She even had enough money in her purse, she discovered when the day nurse handed her her bag, to pay for a taxi to Muswell Hill.

THE NEWS OF HER RETURN SPREAD SO fast that Miri didn't even have a chance to surprise Serafina and her family in the way that she'd anticipated so many times, walking softly in imagination round the Casa Rosa to look in at Serafina's ever-open kitchen door, perhaps finding the three of them at their lunch, squabbling, around the little square stone table with its cracked marble table-top – Pina would see her first, and gasp, and seize Serafina's enormous arm. *Varda, mamma!* Instead they were already tumbling down the steps towards the bus stop when Miri arrived, with Leandro and Pina trying to slow pop-eyed Serafina down, fearing an asthma attack.

People, some of whom she scarcely remembered, poured out of the houses that clustered around the little beach, to swell the tearful embraces, to touch her or simply see her, as if she truly was the spirit of the town, returned to life, as she had felt when the embraces had begun in the town itself, on the esplanade. Returned from the dead. This was how it must feel, how it *did* feel.

And voices in the throng kept asking, where was Vittorio?

It was the very question she kept asking herself, not in bitterness but like a dowser, in patient enquiry: was he closer, now, as she retraced their steps? Was he further away, simply because, having been so close when she imagined them together, here, during her years of exile, he was suddenly falling away from her, falling into the reality of the climb to the Casa Rosa, where he of course was not. Neither on the climb with them nor waiting in the house. It was hard to take in, since surely he was just a step away, outside the door.

This too was something she had never anticipated, the number of people in the town who asked her about Vittorio, and here again at the bus stop, amid the embraces of strangers and Pina's tears and Serafina's, and old Leandro too, whom she had never seen with red-rimmed eyes – the number of people who said: *Vittorio dov'è?* Where is he? But had they really not heard? Had they not heard because they'd taken no interest and had hidden from the war altogether, or because Miri's return itself seemed so supernatural that perhaps the assumption of Vittorio's death had been mistaken? – yes, after all, surely that was it, because when you live in a world of rumours, confirmed and unconfirmed, what was there that might not, at last, turn out to be untrue? If Miri could return so abruptly, out of the blue, why not the *Contessino* too?

The climb to the Casa Rosa brought no calm. This was perhaps the longest it had ever taken her to reach the house, even on a hot day in the past, carrying shopping and resting every few minutes. The *gente* from the beach had wanted to escort her, to carry her things, to keep her in sight a little longer. As if in triumphal procession – all they needed were the trumpets from *Aida* – they had formed an ever-growing line reduced to single file by the narrow flights of steps, with the children scrambling up the terraces beside them like outriders. Now, as the news spread, the hill-dwellers arrived from all across the mountain, to swell the numbers. At each little farmhouse, as their procession climbed, there was a crazy dog to be shushed or shut away where the barking was muffled – shut away! this was a whole new experience to add to Miri's fifteen years of climbing the hill – but the chickens were just as outraged as ever. At last the crowd stood back as they reached the house. Pina had hurried on ahead under Serafina's orders, made the *signora Contessa*'s bed ready, and now appeared again shyly at the front door to welcome her in.

Shaking now with emotion, and still, in her mind, calling on Vittorio for help – but he wouldn't come, *no, mamma*, this is *your* return – Miri turned back at the door and, as she feared they would, the assembled *contadini* burst into cheers and applause.

She had no memory of actually entering the house, of walking down the corridor, past Vittorio's room. Would she have looked into it as she went past? Had she done so? Or been too afraid of his absence, Miri wondered when she woke, still fully clothed, on her bed. The sensation of it, of her room, the sights and smells and even Dario's evening cries resounding now as the mules stumbled reluctantly up the goat track, were too much for tears. She felt as if she might levitate at any minute. She wished she'd never come. How on earth would she manage here, among these memories crowding her head, among these people treating her like a madonna returned to earth?

This wasn't what she'd anticipated at all. Her imaginings had always been about privacy and secrecy, she'd been a ghost in all her fantasies of coming home, she realized now, free to move, walking through walls, a listener, a witness.

What had happened to the new, brisk self she'd woken to in Hemel Hempstead? Would she ever get that person back?

And yet no more than 48 hours had passed, when she added it up. Not even that.

WHEN MIRI HAD arrived in Muswell Hill, in the taxi, it was the middle of the day and only her mother was home. Mrs Gottlieb had been alerted by Dr. Jeffries that Miri was on the way, since he had no legal means to keep her at her institution against her will, and she had promptly phoned Miri's father, who had been brought out of the seminar he was teaching, and was on his way to Muswell Hill. Not quickly enough, as it turned out. Neither of Miri's parents had anticipated how speedily Miri intended to move on. To them, whatever this Dr. Jeffries might say (who had in any case only known Miri for less than a day!), she was a child miraculously restored to them, but surely still in precarious mental and spiritual health. She would not be going anywhere for a while yet. Miri explained that she was going to Italy without delay, requiring only money to make this possible; it was a matter of the utmost urgency, since Serafina and her family could be obliged to decamp from the Casa Rosa unless she made her presence felt at once. To her mother, Miri's manner bespoke acute distraction. She assured Miri that the Gottliebs – or at any rate as many of them as Miri wished – would accompany her, when she was truly ready to go to Italy. Miri then made herself clear, in the brusque manner which was to startle not only those who knew her both in England and in Italy, but which rather astonished

Miri herself: she not only wished none of them to come with her, she told her mother, but she would tolerate no company, until she requested it, and no interference. She had returned to Muswell Hill to pack a suitcase, that was all. There was a chequebook in her bag, she would now take a further taxi to the bank, and from there to London Airport.

And despite frantic pleas from her mother to wait at least until Avram returned so that her father could see her so wonderfully well – as crazy as a cuckoo was in fact how Miri's mother described Miri to her father, Miri discovered later – Miri preferred not to wait to have a double dose of parental concern and well-intentioned restraint. She had been a child, in effect a ward of the state, for the past two years, and had a great deal of unhampered living to do, to make up for it.

How sane, how rational and responsible was she really? It was a question she asked herself frequently, both at the time and in the weeks and months to come. She didn't feel – she would have said to anyone she really trusted, of whom there were none in her immediate environ-ment – entirely real. Or perhaps what she felt was the imperfectly awake sensation of one who has slept too long. As a feature of consciousness it was a little disturbing. But she could see no reason to mistrust the direction in which her mind and her emotions were leading her. Her judgement seemed unimpaired, her priorities, as best she could assess them, correct. She felt a little slow, that was all. And the worst part was the worry that the relative clear-headedness and sense of purpose in which she was steeped would not last, that a cloud would cover the sun, she would feel faint or dizzy or confused, and would wake up back in Hemel Hempstead, having been found wandering a street, or an airport, in a daze.

At first she was afraid to sleep, for the same reason, and had to force herself to let go of wakefulness. She was afraid that her sense of who she was and what she had to do would be gone again when she awoke, and she wouldn't even know it. She would return to whatever her dream-state had been, her trance, her sleep-walking (she couldn't even recall it clearly now, and didn't want to) through the past, through imaginary presents and imaginary futures, with Vittorio, who was dead.

That at least, was magnetic north on her compass. He was dead. She would not be introducing him to Muswell Hill, to London, or to England generally; she would not be walking with him in the hills above the Vessinaro, except in the intimacy of memory that would always be inseparable from the paths they had shared.

All she remembered of her time in Hemel Hempstead (later she remembered a great deal more) was the presence of people who had not been and could not have been there. Now she seemed capable of looking around and seeing exactly who was there and who was not. It was this she wanted to hang onto. And it was this that made it imperative to act on her impulses at once, before they blurred.

And then there was her tone of voice, one that she heard emerging from her without having the least idea where it came from. She had never been imperious. Her mother was imperious. Had she become her mother, while under some kind of sedation in Hemel Hempstead? (And had she been sedated? At this point, she had no idea, but her suspicions were quite correct. She had been fed an ample dose of soporifics, and part of her sensation of unreality may well have been the result of going without them after two years.) Had this firm, quietly bossy voice been inside her all her life? Or had she8 been speaking this way for some time – forever, perhaps – while hearing instead a soft, submissive Miri-purr that no one else heard? It was mystifying. Nor did she set out to be brusque with people. She was just tired, tired to her bones, of beating about the bush. Perhaps she had never known what it was that she wanted before – perhaps that was it; now that she knew, it was easy to be firm, and boring to be a supplicant.

What had she ever known that she wanted? Only Piero. But he had picked her out and she hadn't had to fight, or to be firm, let alone imperious, to get him. That had been the miracle of it. Vittorio, of course – except that she hadn't known she wanted him, because until he was there she'd had no idea that such a being existed, a person carved out of the same material as herself. So he too had been a miracle for which she hadn't had to cut through foolishness and confusion. Perhaps this was her first experience of breasting the tide of benevolent human obstructiveness. The things she wanted – and she didn't even know all of them yet, just the immediate ones right in front of her – had to be obtained by making them clear to people who could help her and to people who might get in the way. This, perhaps, was how life was for most people. You had to speak clearly and distinctly, and brook no argument.

The surprise was that she was rather good at it.

But after all, she was 35 years old, it came to her when she did the sums, baffled and alarmed to realise that she didn't know exactly how old she was, for the first time in her life, without doing the mathematics. She was 35, and if she wasn't able to be commanding when she needed to be, at this age, when would she be? There were probably people who never were commanding, even once in their lives, but clearly, Miri thought, this wasn't her.

EVEN BEFORE HER bus-stop ordeal, with people fighting to touch her as though she were the Pope or Jesus brought to life, Miri's arrival in the town was like nothing she had ever known in her life. It had brought her to tears, and this itself was distressing. She had returned armed against Italy, the murderer. Now it seemed that the burden of her asylum-rage, as she now called it (knowing that Hemel Hempstead was no more than a convenient scapegoat), her long-meditated sense that Italy and the town had betrayed her, was ready to fall away like rotten bandaging, no longer needed.

When she had imagined going back into the town, walking along the esplanade beneath the palm trees, past the hotels, the bars, the restaurants where she knew every waiter, she had battled to forgive every one of them. Not always successfully. They had let Cipriano take Vittorio; they hadn't ever truly regarded him as one of theirs, let alone as their *Contessino*. Only in words, only on the surface, when nothing was at stake. One day before the war a carnival troupe had brought to town a host of miniature cars, battery-driven, slow and clumsy yet big enough for children to drive as if they were full-sized racing cars – each child pretending he was an Ascari or a Tazio

Nuvolari – around a circuit improvised on the esplanade, and lined with tires and bales of straw. How the crowd had cheered for Vittorio that day! *Vai! Vai!* Faster, faster, drive like *tu poé!* (But not like your namesake, many murmured to each other, your grandfather, dead at the wheel precisely because he tried too hard to be Alberto Ascari!) Vittorio had loved the racing, but had been too cautious by nature to be among the winners. Still, the town had long known by looking at Vittorio that he was no Piero. This was a quiet, serious, studious boy, *bello*, yes, but handsome in a different way, with a look of piety about him, like a romantic priest. Already at 12, he had fluttered a few hearts, not only of girls but of women who would have been glad of a chance to confess their sins to the *Contessino*.

Impossible now to walk along the esplanade without recalling their cheers for Vittorio, as he drove cautiously round the giant lorry tires that outlined the course, far too cautiously and with his caterpillar brows furrowed in dreadful intensity. *Forza, Contessino!* Did you hear them cheering for you? Miri had asked. Vittorio, grinning, had shaken his head. I was having too much fun, *mamma.*

And where had those cheers gone to? – this was what she had imagined herself feeling, with overwhelming bitterness, if she could ever bring herself to return to the curving esplanade – where had all the *Forza Contessino* gone when it was needed?

Yet in the flesh it was different. Perhaps, she reflected, it had indeed been the asylum-poison at work, misleading her. To *be* here, among the old friends crying, and running to her, and holding her, holding Miri as if they would never let her go again, was to know the place as it had always been (the buildings, the light on the dusty *trompe l'oeil* windows, the streets with their beeping horns and their rushing motorized bicycles, their *beee-bahs*), to know the love for her that had never changed, and the love for the town that burst from her again along with the tears. It had been there all along; there had never been another place she loved.

IT WAS WHEN she began thinking about Vittorio again, lying on her own bed in the Casa Rosa, thinking about him as opposed to feeling his presence, which was something that could never go away and that no possible experience could knife out of her without taking her identity with it, that it struck Miri as strange – for the first time, since it hadn't even entered her mind before – that she wasn't going to Auschwitz, to the camps, to see and know and understand what he had gone through.

But was there anything there to see? Had it all been burned down and trampled by the war, or blown up deliberately, razed to the ground so that no one should have to contemplate what human beings did to each other? It made no difference. It would be a place of pilgrimage, regardless.

And yet something quailed in her, still.

Whether or not she would ever be ready to go, she would know when that time was, because the question – was she ready yet? – was with her day and night. It was a part of her sanity. It was a part of knowing that Vittorio was dead.

AND THAT, IN turn, was how she got her anger back.

She had known all along that Vittorio was dead and that someone must be punished, yet since Vittorio was still alive, was with her every day at Hemel Hempstead, this itself was her revenge. The anger she had felt could be assuaged by taking Vittorio away from them, taking their *Contessino* away from the town and keeping him with her in London. That would be their punishment.

But now that she had come home, Vittorio was gone from her. Not in her heart, but in reality. His absence was all around her. His absence was what she felt as she walked through the Casa Rosa. His murder was what she felt, as if she were seeing it in front of her, the first time she re-entered his bedroom.

Take everything out, she told a startled Pina, take his toys, his pictures, his clothes, even his bedspread, and tell Leandro to give them away in the town. All of it. Discreetly.

(Yet how? Discreetly how? How would people fail to see in

Leandro's offerings a host of relics, the body of their *Contessino* distributed to the public? No, it was impossible.)

Better still, bring it all out, at the back, behind the kitchen. We'll have a bonfire.

Dismayed, Pina shook her head and refused to take part, studying her employer in disbelief. Was she seeing confirmation, Miri wondered, of rumours that the *Contessa* Miri had lost her reason and had been languishing in hospital in England? Such rumours would at least have helped to explain her absence. The townspeople might also have asked themselves what was left for her here, in the town, to come back for. But those who knew her would have known she would be back, and that the town itself, the bay, the Vessinaro and the hilltop ridges beyond it, all had an irreplaceable claim on her heart.

As Pina brought the news of the mad *Contessa*'s instructions to Serafina, in a shocked undertone, Miri stood in the silence of Vittorio's room. From the window she could see Leandro scuttling away into the sanctuary of the vineyard. Forced to do the job herself, Miri partly recanted, making a pile of precious items to be saved, yet nonetheless assembling the rest outside the kitchen door and, with Leandro's reluctant help, setting fire to it. Pina refused to watch. Serafina stood inside the kitchen, back from the doorway, watching and weeping as books and toys went up in flames.

It was the first, all-important step.

Afterwards she wondered she'd found the strength to do it and decided that she *had* still been a little mad, thank God

His murder. It had taken three years to achieve the word, and now she understood why. It sent grief packing, and she had not been ready, till now, to let go of grief.

THEN, IN QUICK succession, came the series of absurd, discomfiting, discouraging meetings with Andrea Capodimonte, the young police chief, with Cefalù, the lawyer, and with Giorgio Massone, the local Communist leader.

Pity. They all spoke about pity. That would always be available for the victims of Fascism. Pity, and monuments. The time had passed for an accounting, the plump, elderly lawyer had made it clear, yet as for criminal proceedings, the legal statutes were insufficient and documents were missing. Young Andrea was more honest. He told her bluntly that there never had been a moment for an accounting. It was irrelevant that years had passed (two, now, but soon it would be three), because no one had wanted war trials then or now. Drawn-out judicial acts would not heal the country's wounds.

And monuments would? Miri asked. Andrea had held Miri's gaze. It was the same boy she had known when he was a child on the beach, her beach, the same calm, composed gaze. A police chief. Yes, perhaps he always had that in him, despite his slender frame. Revenge, he now said – not in so many words, but close enough, was another matter, and a respected tradition. Retribution: he spoke it gently but with a certainty she could scarcely fathom, as if he had enrolled in early youth in a fraternity whose rites she would never discover. *Ammazzalo lei.* You kill him. The words amazed her, coming from this thin, bespectacled boy, the very spirit of the new, suffering, earnest Italy, one whose hands were clean. Miri had the feeling that if she'd asked him for a gun he would have lent her one.

But this wasn't a Western frontier town, for goodness sake, and she wasn't *La Fanciulla del West.*

Invitations came, many invitations, to dinner, to lunch, to cruises. Miri turned them all down, politely, trusting that the rich families who'd issued the invitations would understand that she was grateful but still grieving, still withdrawn. She wondered, too, whether they wouldn't be happier that she had said no. They'd done their duty by asking her; after the first few commiserations and questions, did they really want a death's head at their feast? Miri could foresee a time when she would be a person no one wanted at their dinner table, unless she perked up and became a merry widow with a tragic past.

She marched into the headquarters of the town's Communist Party and demanded a word with Giorgio Massone, the local party leader and once a staunch ally of Piero's. The audience was swiftly granted. Giorgio, a gaunt man with the pained eyes of a recovering addict – though Miri had never heard of any addiction on Massone's part – was gracious, and his sad expression told her that she too, like Andrea Capodimonte, appeared to have joined a club. Hers was the association of those in perpetual mourning. It occurred to Miri for the first time, talking to Massone, how much that prospect repelled her.

The problem with *la retribuzione legale*, legally enforced retribution, lay in a consideration neither Andrea nor Cefalù seemed to have explained to her, Massone said. (When Miri tried to shift the issue to one of "justice," Massone spread his hands wide and threw a glance heavenwards, more like a priest than the elegant, pale grey-suited atheist Miri had to presume he was, as a Communist. Justice, he seemed to be saying, was in the gift of a higher power.) He himself had lost close friends, Massone said, and also relatives. He understood. The real obstacle to the prosecution of war crimes, he explained, was neither the passage of time nor documentation nor the lack of public interest. It was the forthcoming election. The Communists, he said, were going to sweep to power – (Massone was wrong, but not by much) – and why? Not only because of their record as the focus of resistance to Fascism but, more pertinently, since there were plenty of foolish voters still nostalgic for *il Duce*, their overwhelmingly popular resistance to the Germans; yes, not only because they were the best organized and clearly the most plausible alternative to the muddling and corrupt Christian Democrats; above all, it was because they had stolen the Christian Democrats' platform of Christian forgiveness. Fascinated by Massone's suffering-addict eyes, a bored and distracted Miri realized that Massone reminded her of several Hemel Hempstead patients she had known. Dottie in particular, a girl whose resourcefulness enabled her escape from the asylum for frequent doses of what she called her 'medicine.' Miri had to force herself back to the reality of Massone's office, stacked with papers and lined with photographs of Communist heroes. What was the man saying? Communists too could be forgiving! What, then, Massone asked her, did that leave for the *Cristiani Democratici Uniti*? It left them nothing, and nowhere to go. Forgiveness, then, was the high ground everyone was fighting for. Perhaps, once the Communists were in power, he said with an expression that attached as little confidence to his offer as it was possible for the human face to convey, they could talk again about the matter of *la retribuzione*.

Sitting in Serafina's kitchen, watching her make miniature, single-portion evocations of the meals Miri had loved so well and conjured so meticulously during her incarceration, as she now thought of it, in the Hemel Hempstead 'home,' Miri could feel her spirits drying up and shrinking like the absurdly reduced versions Serafina was making of their feasts of old. This, the filleted, *signora Contessa*-sized menu, she would not be able to endure, she knew. A handful of *gnocchi*, two sticks of *uccellini scappati*. It was as if someone had conjured up a Versailles sampler in a dozen mouthfuls. It only mocked the past.

Serafina and her family would hate it, they would hate it for a long time, but Miri was going to command them to let her eat with them at the square, marbled-topped little kitchen table, and share their food. They would come to accept it, eventually; or rather they would never entirely accept it (they would never tell anyone that *la signora Contessa* ate with them, or allow anyone to witness it), but they would learn to tolerate it. There would have to be a lot of changes made, and Miri would have to learn to pay the price in Serafina-sulks, she knew, for getting her way.

While she watched Serafina cook, knowing that this, at least, lulled both of them with its nostalgic rhythms, Miri contemplated her next move.

Were there any? There had to be.

Miri watched Serafina cut the pasta into fine, *linguine*-wide strips with the deftness and certainty of a master.

She would continue to pursue legal redress. But the process would be slow, and probably disheartening; what was essential was not to get bogged down, not to relinquish her impetus. It was time to go to the Vessinaro, where the demon lived.

SO LITTLE SEEMED to have changed during Miri's years of absence that it was possible for her to feel that she herself, by sheer conviction, had been holding the town in suspension during that time. But gradually, one by one, she had to face the changes. They were there in the absences she hadn't yet noticed, losses that she hadn't heard about. Cefalù, the lawyer, had lost a son on the Eastern front, Miri was ashamed to discover – ashamed because in her intentness on her quest, her prey, she never asked, and only discovered Cefalù's loss at the door of his office as she was leaving and the lawyer once more offered his condolences. He added that he too had lost a beloved boy. In Russia. Buried there, Cefalù said. He hoped to go one day. And even this harmless remark once more blinded Miri with emotion, as she was upset to remember later: it had blinded her not with sympathy for Cefalù but with the absurd desire to say that she, Miri, would not be making a similar pilgrimage, in her case to Auschwitz, because Vittorio's grave was all around her. His grave was the town. Its inscription, she wanted to say, to fling in the lawyer's face, was written on the face of every person in the town who had stood by as Vittorio was dragged from his bed and down the hill and into town to be held in its flimsy apology for a gaol and finally dispatched to the transit camp at Fossoli di Carpi. Her loss was not Cefalù's loss! She wanted to throw it at him. It was not the loss of a fully-grown man – the lawyer's son, whom Miri recalled quite clearly, plump like his father, had been in his late twenties, a man who had decided to enrol in a vile, monstrous adventure, of his own accord.

Such thoughts were raging in her mind while she walked back through the town from Cefalù's office at the end of Corso Cavour, but she knew they were harsh and out of kilter. Could she find no pity to spare for Cefalù? And she remembered too, that she hadn't yet visited Baldini, the bookseller, who had troubled to write to her with the bad news (a messenger's wages, she reflected, to be shunned for bringing it), and who had also lost his boys to Fossoli di Carpi and then to Auschwitz. *Fossoli.* The word, so close to *fossili*, fossils, never failed to evoke, for Miri, the mummified bodies of those going to their death. Words too waited in ambush, dagger in hand. 'Mummified' itself – it was the shadow behind Fossoli, bringing the boiling nausea to her chest that she had come to recognize as the seething pot on the hob of tears, ready to overflow.

Miri dreaded visiting Baldini, where the tears would stream down once more, his as well as hers. There was no healing in the tears, she knew that by now. It was time for the tears to stop. She had not come into town to do more crying.

She would visit Baldini another day. They would talk about their boys, and the cousins, and the Schmitzes, whose memory would at least make them smile before they cried some more.

That day, as on other visits to the town, Miri was intent only on getting home to the Casa Rosa and taking a walk in the hills to get her anger under control – did people really think she was simply another war widow, and that Vittorio's death had been just another tragic accident of war? She stormed up the steps from the little beach, past the raging dogs whose spirit now invoked hers, not minding what the faces peeping from the farmhouse windows thought of her evident but mystifying fury. *La pazza!* The mad *Contessa*!

It was only when she glimpsed Pina beating a carpet in the garden of the Casa Rosa that Miri remembered Cefalù's reassurances. She herself was the beneficiary of her husband's modest holdings, and her mother-in-law's as well, Cefalù had told her; Serafina, Pina and Leandro were assured of a living and a home at the Casa Rosa as long as they and the house stood; the town would in any case have found them inexpensive housing had it not been so, he added. But the image of Serafina away from her kitchen and Leandro from his vineyard was not one Miri had wanted to contemplate, and she had shrugged off the town's modest generosity along with the memory of what Cefalù had been telling her.

The biggest change since Miri had been away lay elsewhere, and it was Serafina who revealed it. Some of the invitations Miri had received to lunches and cruises were from people Miri had never heard of, and some were from names she distantly knew, Piero's friends and acquaintances, perhaps, who she could only imagine to be visiting on their yachts. They weren't locals. Oh but they are, *signora*, Serafina said when Miri mentioned some of their names over the kitchen table, they were recent, they were *forestieri*, blow-ins, but they were firmly entrenched, with great big houses on the track up to the Vessinaro. The *cancello* had been opened. Hadn't the *signora Contessa* heard?

The *cancello,* opened? – the *cancello* which had been closed for centuries, the *cancello* whose war had provoked a final, terrible rupture between Piero and Cipriano, over Piero's lordly behaviour? Miri didn't know the full extent of that rupture and the way that it had stoked the lifelong fires of resentment in Cipriano's heart; but she had some sense of how much Piero's triumph over Cipriano, unsought and therefore all the more to be resented, had led, in time, to their family tragedy. Cipriano's defeat had sealed Vittorio's fate. All over a gate, for God's sake, a gate!

And now it was open. *Montagna aperta.* Just like that, the mountain was an open house.

It was the final insult, the final testimony to the town's blithe ability to ignore its own murders.

Cosa vuole, signora? Serafina had said, wheezing and nodding, as she saw the effect of the news on Miri. What can one do?

Well, she would do something, whether or not people preferred to forget.

But the *cancello*! Open just like that! So it was with wars, Miri reflected, little wars no less than big ones. All those tempestuous emotions, speeches, insults, vendettas sworn, feuds to the death, and a few years later someone signed a little piece of paper and it was all consigned to the past. Never mind that your son lay in an unmarked grave outside Stalingrad; that he drifted in ash across a Polish countryside. You signed a form and moved on.

It was bizarre to stand beside the great *cancello* now, locked wide open on the very chain and padlock that had previously kept it shut (had the key been handed from *sindaco* to *sindaco* for a thousand years?), the symbol of everything that had formerly declared the inviolability of the mountain, its dignity (its *continence,* Piero had called it!), its rights and privileges, its history. Now the gateway yawned, twenty feet wide. Snarling Vespas, along with kindred vehicles, tiny Vespa-drawn buggy-like carts, poured down through the gate as though the mountain were disgorging mechanical beetles and earwigs in flight from the marauding rich, whose cars now lumbered uphill, hooting and pooting like the *beee-bah* buses on the coast road below, towards their new *palazzi.*

(And was Cipriano grimly happy now, to see his old campaign justified now – the crusade to open the *cancello* that had ended in his bitter defeat at Piero's hands? Was he smiling to think that history had been on his side after all? And was his own property now accruing value, up on a more accessible Vessinaro? The thought of Cipriano in smug comfort enraged her. Miri made herself a vow: despite Andrea's cynicism, Cèfalu's prevarications and Massone's political opportunism, despite all their negativity, she would write to every lawyer in Genoa, seeking someone to help her mount a prosecution. She would write to her father – might Avram not have powerful contacts here? Through the Berlins, perhaps? She would *not* abandon hope.)

The palazzi and the busy antheaps of construction on either side of the re-paved goat track were shocking, as if the town had abruptly squirted itself all across the hillsides, where once only Dario's reproachful cries, as his mules battled with the giant, slippery stones of the track, had disturbed the peace. Miri couldn't bring herself to march through the immense open gateway, along with everyone else. The gatehouse beside it was no longer a hovel but an enormous pink stucco'd building – had the hovel really been as big as this? – seething with inhabitants. The little gap, now unused, remained between the gatehouse and the pillar at the gate's jamb, the gap everyone had used for centuries; it still beckoned, though already neglected and unloved. Weeds were growing in its three small steps, a purchase they had not achieved in the preceding centuries. In memory of the old days, Miri stepped between the weeds, up the steps and through the gap. It was unnecessary and absurd, but it was a final gesture to honour the vanished monastery and the old ways whose last trace was now gone. Some superstitious spell lodged itself in Miri's heart as she stepped through. Thereafter, she always took that route, and never, I believe, took the easy route through the wide open gateway, on its refurbished, newly paved slope.

It was also, of course, a way to refuse the event itself, the opening of the *cancello* that revealed the town's effortless overcoming of its own vendetta-ridden past, regardless of the innocent lives those vendettas had taken. No, the *cancello* was not open as far as Miri was concerned, would never be open until the town paid its debts. She would go around it, through the gap, as people always had. It was a way of keeping Vittorio alive.

VITTORIO. DID SHE have to ask Vittorio's permission, to do what she was doing? Surely he would not withhold it. He would want her to confront the man who had sealed his fate.

And beyond that?

There were nights, now, when fury woke her, shaking as if she had a fever, and she wondered if this was entirely sane. If Andrea handed her a gun, as he did in her imagination, if she killed this man – and it was no good going on pretending, as she had at first, that the thought didn't enter her mind – if she killed him (she had no idea how it would happen, since the event in her mind was a single moment, an eruption of her rage, and a body, the man's body, falling, far below her, to the cliffs and the sea) – would she be sanctioned by Vittorio or only by herself?

Just the man's body, falling, black-coated, tiny, tumbling towards the sea-splashed rocks of Punta Vessinaro. She had no face to put to him, although she knew she had seen Cipriano once or twice. She had tried to recall some part of him, eyes, mouth, but without success, nor would any invented features stick. His anonymity had been a part of it, all along. He was a figure in the dock, blurred, bulky (hadn't he been stuffing himself with food, all alone in Prospero Velo's restaurant?), and still faceless, in her mind. This had granted a judicial form and a judicial conclusion to her emotions. But now – now what form would they take, and towards what conclusion?

Miri didn't dwell on it, during the day. The very question belonged to the craziness of the nighttime fever when the Casa Rosa seemed like a tomb and to wake in it alone cried out for violence. Was it Vittorio's presence in the walls, calling her to violence? What *was* the fever in her? Revenge, undimmed by the passing of time? She wondered if it was madness pure and simple; whether somewhere in the past four years she had slipped the bounds of sanity and that now she had put on this unlikely habit of the brisk, imperious

Miri in order to fool people that she was normal. The new Miri *felt* normal to her. A person inside her, unanticipated, and slightly surprising, but completely at home in her, had taken the helm. This Miri spoke through her with calm authority. Perhaps it was just too much of a surprise for others, after the diffident *Contessa Miri* they had known. Her schoolmarm impersonation, as she some-times felt it to be, drew attention and seemed to make people look at her strangely. Old acquaintances like Andrea and Cefalù studied her – how could they think she didn't notice? – in a way that made her want to shout at them. But this would only have confirmed their suspicions. Were they thinking, Poor woman, no wonder she's a bit dotty – or was she always a little neurotic? No doubt they had always found her shy and tense, and thought her highly strung. Now their penetrating stares sat oddly with their condolences, and surely meant they'd heard, as Miri feared, that the *Contessa* had been in hospital. Everyone in the town knew that, perhaps. Yet how would they know? Who could have told them?

Serafina too, with her wheezing, asthmatic, exoph-thalmic *gravitas*, with the shortness of breath that made her speech so curt and forced her attention inwards, eyed Miri strangely from time to time, it seemed to her. Were they wondering, she and Leandro? Is the *signora Contessa* all right now, or not? Her determination to eat with them probably seemed like a symptom, a clear sign that she wasn't quite right in the head. Was the whole town discussing it? Were reports circulating of her brusqueries, her raging ascents up the steps to the Casa Rosa, her refusal of invitations and her failure to call in on old friends like the bookseller?

When she tried the matter in the court of her mind, Miri judged herself to be perfectly sane. Excessive grief and rage, these were surely sane, in the circumstances; and that was her only way to understand Miss Brisk, the person who had taken control of her, beginning right back in Hemel Hempstead on the day of the taxi, and continuing in the way she had treated her mother (there had been no choice but to top her mother's own abrasiveness). Miss Brisk was there to keep Miri's tears at bay. There was no other way. The accused is acquitted of all charges.

Yet shouldn't she, Miri sometimes allowed herself to ask, have passed this stage? Not 'be over it,' since it was unimaginable that one could ever be over such things, but should she still be waking in the night, in the grip of the Furies?

Again, there was an explanation. She had dodged them, the Furies, for years. For most of her time in England she had pretended they weren't waiting for her, at the gate. They were fresh and unappeased, now that she allowed them full rein. They were in her bedroom, camped around the mosquito net that covered her bed and clouded her view of the rest of the room.

When she woke, they were strangling her – in a manner of speaking, because she felt no hands at her throat. But she felt the claustrophobic press of their anger, and their discontent with her. The little world of the bed inside its mosquito net had always seemed so cosy when she and Piero shared it. Miri had assumed it would be distressingly empty now, but instead it felt crowded, as if the night had thickened around her, and as if the Furies themselves were like Serafina's asthma, agents of unbreathable air.

She had been sleeping for so long in a ward full of tormented sleepers, some who cried out, moaned or spoke in the darkness. The ward had never been silent, not for a minute of the night, and Miri wasn't used to waking to the utter silence of the Casa Rosa – she knew this was part of her night terrors – with its distant cricket chatter like accelerated hearts, silvery hearts, unappeasable as the sea. They were like faint metallic *beee-bahs* patrolling the night.

And Miri knew that of course it was Vittorio's absence, not his presence in the walls, that commanded her to wake. She could feel Rosanna's absence too, no less than Piero's. Indeed Piero's absence – it was shaming to admit it – was the least disturbing. Miri had expected to be most alert to it, above all to his absence from their bed. She reminded herself that she had slept alone for four years, and was used to it. Yet that wasn't the unsettling part. Piero's ghost lay quiet on her soul and on the house, and she wasn't sure why. His beauty had withdrawn into the realms of death as if (and why did she think this? – it was absurd!) his physical perfection had made it easier for death to take him back entire, like a natural experiment successfully completed, leaving no unquiet portions behind. It was as if he was telling her that he was happy to have died in battle, to have died when his beauty was still on him; even, that he was happy to be lying in the *cimetiero* back at the inland end of the town, where the hills came together to complete the inlet. Was that possible? Or did it make no sense at all? She had visited the grave, the headstone still oppressively new, so new it seemed like a fake, a gravestone erected for a movie, with no body beneath it. He wasn't there, it seemed to her. Where was he? And why was he so utterly at peace? Why wasn't his spirit, too, raging beside hers, in the night, demanding vengeance for Vittorio?

There had been some cut flowers, withering fast, and several small wreaths, on Piero's grave. From when? And from whom? Miri couldn't think whom to ask. Dutifully, feeling as if the eyes of the whole town were on her, she had brought flowers of her own, the second time, and tended and tidied the grave, although few weeds had sprouted to disturb the pebbles. This time, too, the headstone seemed to have nothing to do with her or with Piero himself, and she felt as if she were coming to an empty grave, or to a simulacrum put up to deceive her. His spirit wasn't here. But where was it?

In the night, when she woke to the Furies, she needed to know that there were other lungs reaching for air along with hers – besides those of the harsh, relentless, tintinnabulating crickets – in the silence of the Casa Rosa. Sometimes Miri pushed back the mosquito net and went out to the stairwell and stopped there, listening, hoping to hear Serafina's hissing breath. If she couldn't, Miri would tiptoe down the stairs, getting closer to Serafina's bedroom with each step, stopping to listen until she could hear Serafina, like the thrumming heart of a ship, snoring, and pausing, and sometimes sighing an *oh Lord* aloud in her suffering, *ossignor!*

Ashamed to be eavesdropping on Serafina's night agonies, Miri would slip back to her room. She was always afraid that Serafina had heard her nonetheless, Serafina for whom the Casa Rosa was a body whose faintest twitches she could detect.

But Miri found it easier to sleep now, on returning to her room and imagining that she could feel the faint vibration of Serafina's snores, through walls and floor. The Furies had relented and withdrawn, having extracted their price. Heavens, how unnatural they were, the early hours of the morning, still night and prey to night-terrors; no wonder we were supposed to sleep through them, these graveyard watches when spirits walk! As she drifted into sleep, Miri could feel the sadness in her chest that was the real, inescapable sadness, for Vittorio. There was nothing wrong with her. She was still grieving.

AS SOON AS she passed through the gap between the old *cancello* pillar and the new, repainted gatehouse, as soon as she climbed its three ancient steps and set foot on the new paving above the gateway, Miri felt she was on Cipriano's territory.

Serafina had been able to tell her only that the demon lived on the Vessinaro, somewhere in the promontory's warren of cliff-face dwellings, many of them invisible from the sandy orange track above, on the ridge. *Il demonio*, the demon: it was Serafina's word for him. *Si vede poco, poco. Pare che sia malato.* Cipriano was rarely seen in the town, according to Serafina, and was said to be ill. Miri couldn't tell whether Serafina's sceptical tone was meant to cast doubt on the matter of Cipriano's ailing health, or expressed undisguised *Schadenfreude* at his condition. The loathing with which Serafina spoke of the former mayor, and Leandro and Pina's expressions when Miri brought up his name, made Miri half expect Serafina to cross herself at the mention of Cipriano. *Il demonio.* It was if Miri had asked about the devil himself.

The paved, level roadway that had replaced the old Homeric goat track felt strange to Miri's feet. By force of habit her soles and toes were still reaching tentatively for purchase, only to come down on a puzzlingly flat surface. For the first time she was able to proceed uphill without looking down for footholds, on the long climb up to the Vessinaro. It was disturbing and, at first, faintly nauseating to be able to ascend a mountain while gazing out at the view, without studying where your feet should go. The only thing that every climb in the *paese* had always had in common, as richly various as they were in landscape, was that each one was uneven, treacherous, and required continuous attention. If your mind wandered for a moment, even on a track you had navigated all your life, you'd find yourself sprawled on the hard ground of the barren terrace or the vineyard beside the path. Until now, the hills had always been considered too steep for a paved road. Climbing this one gave Miri the curious sensation, the first time, of having been turned into a wheeled vehicle herself.

If nothing else, it allowed her to study the transformation of the mountain without having to stop each time, as had always been the practice for everyone ascending to the Vessinaro: first set your feet, then look around. Almost every former peasant dwelling, every farm and every cottage, it seemed, had been acquired by a newcomer – here and there she saw one whose owner had obstinately held out – and was in the process of being turned into the Milanese idea of a villa by the sea. In many instances the new owners' idea was preposterously wrong. Miri had to remind herself that these invaders really were Italians; the Milanese idea of gracious living appeared to belong entirely to northern, not to southern Europe. Was there a class distinction at work here, bringing the news that north meant sophistication, and south lacked class? Behind the tall wrought-iron gates that each new mansion sported, the old vineyard had gone and in its place a lawn, as odd on a volcanic hillside as turf in the desert, battled for its life, attended by a dozen sprinklers working day and night like intravenous hospital feeds. Olive and fig trees had disappeared, replaced by swimming pools, over which cypresses, imported fully grown, now stood like a Pretorian guard, to keep out prying eyes. The houses themselves were barely visible, but pink, ochre and yellow, the wall colours that echoed oleander bushes and bougainvillea, had been supplanted as the dominant colours, to judge by what Miri could glimpse, by white and gold. To hide the villa even better, there were stands of bamboo (why on earth bamboo?) in exotic shades – some were bright blue. No more dusty ground; well-kept pebbled paths led between box hedges and around scrubbed-looking statuary.

So be it, Miri thought. It was no good feeling nostalgic for the picturesque discomfort that had preceded this new world of the *montagna aperta*, the open mountain. Progress would always look like this. She was glad, all the same, that the hundred steps up to her Casa Rosa would discourage similar developments, pending a hardier race of invaders, or one determined to tunnel into the mountain at sea-level, beside the little beach, and install a lift, as the Berlins had.

The Berlins themselves were not in residence yet this year, Serafina had told her. But they would come. Miri felt a measure of dread at the prospect. They would be gentle with her, grieving with her and no doubt aware that she had been recuperating for a time – was it 'a breakdown' that people would have reported? You couldn't disappear from circulation for almost two years, once the war was over, without some word being attached to it. The Berlins would be kind. They were civilized people. In fact they were the very essence of 20th century civilisation, almost its poster family – look up the word 'civilized' in Larousse, Miri thought, remembering her school dictionary with its little black-and-white illustrations beside the entries, and you'd probably find a tiny photograph of Isaiah Berlin. But that was just the problem. The Berlins would hardly approve of whatever she was doing with Cipriano. Miri had no idea yet what that would be, but she was fairly certain it wouldn't be civilized.

As she climbed, studying the mountain's facelift, Miri couldn't help pausing to gaze into the few remaining farmhouses, hoping to spy familiar faces. She didn't really want to be called in for a glass of sour wine and respectful conversation, as she feared she would, with all the family called in to stare at her in fascinated awe, and the chickens driven out and the dog hushed. But these old, grey shacks were her own past now, as they were the mountain's, and she couldn't just walk by, indifferent. They belonged to the years before her return to London, the years before the hospital, as vivid and as strange as another life. They beckoned, the old hovels, bearing clues to the Miri she had been. The *Contessa* Miri; it had been four years, and an age of pain and confusion, since she had imagined herself in the role.

Could the old farmhouses help her recapture it? Or was the role itself outdated? *Montagna aperta; mondo aperto,* perhaps, a world free of rank, or at any rate ruled by wealth, not title. The farmhouses seemed almost comical, now that their dilapidated frames, which once had fitted the mountain and its goat track so comfortably, looked almost wilfully ramshackle beside the new paved road. The improvised little structures with their tiny windows, stained old walls and collapsing roofs, mended so often with whatever came to hand, had come to resemble a museum exhibition of life in poverty, thanks to the contrast with the manicured lawns and soaring gates of the new *palazzi*. Amid the general facelift, the old dwellings stood out like their owners' balefully rotten teeth, still grinning, still defiant, the dogs barking as if only the more delighted to have cars and trucks and builders on whom to vent their perpetual anger, and the washing draped from tree to tree like the flags of the undefeated. No doubt they too would be gone, one day, Miri reflected, but for the time being the *contadini* enjoyed the pickings that construction work brought right to their door. Now, barely a stone's throw away, there were jobs for even the least educated and least handy members of the family. They were living in a different century from the Milanese, but they stepped happily through a time-warp portal onto the new road and into the new houses to put on livery, tend the lawn and the pebbled paths, the hedges and the pool, and then return to the reassuring squalor of home, just across the way. It was as if, Miri thought, a doorman at an American skyscraper could slip off his uniform and cross the street, each evening, to enter the cabin where his grandsire had been born.

During her later climbs up the mountain, Miri did indeed find herself invited into the crumbling old houses; it was as if, on the day of her first climb, their inhabitants hadn't been expecting to see her, and were too startled to call to her, or simply too unprepared. On all subsequent occasions they seemed to be waiting for her (had Serafina put the word out, and sent Leandro and Pina scurrying across the hilltops to inform the backwoods farmers?). The hillbilly house had been scrubbed and the entire family summoned and dressed in their Sunday best, in anticipation of her visit. If this wasn't Serafina's work, then certainly it seemed as if each family alerted the farmhouse farther up on the mountain, as soon as Miri reached the first one, telling them the *Contessa* Miri was on the way, because there was no escaping a sip of wine and a ritualized conversation (*la salute, il stagione, la uva* – health, weather and the state of the grape) in every one of the farmhouses between the *cancello* and the Vessinaro. Happily, the mountain was still a tracery of secret paths and tiny steps cut almost invisibly into the terraces, and Miri knew most of them, enabling her to reach the Vessinaro with the minimum of lady-of-the-manor visits, when she chose to. It touched her, nonetheless. Some things hadn't changed. She was the *Contessa* Miri; it was still Piero's *paese*. Vittorio's *paese*.

Miri didn't stop, on that first climb, until she reached Olimpio's hillside bar, where everyone paused, regardless of their destination. Here the road forked, taking you west towards Camogli, and ultimately Genoa, along the ridge over the sea, or south to the Vessinaro promontory. You had been climbing for the better part of an hour, unless you'd stopped at the tiny chapel of San Sebastiano, which was, perhaps, the last surviving relic of the vanished monastery; the chapel's doors were always open – or so it seemed to Miri – and usually disclosed a farmer or more often a farmer's wife in prayer. It was only when she passed San Sebastiano, this time, and reached Olimpio's bar, that it occurred to Miri how remiss it was of her not to have stopped at the chapel. She had never lit a candle in her life. Now she would learn.

Miri knew that she must also stop at Olimpio's so as not to give offence, and that if she took a place or a little table on her own, no one would dream of coming to sit beside her or disturbing her after their initial greeting. But the little outdoor bar was crowded; Miri could picture it falling silent at her presence, bubbling with surmises and speculations that no one would yet sound, while she was there, but which were so much more interesting than their current conversation that they could barely keep these going. She dreaded that silence, and wished with all her heart that they could pursue their gossip about her, unhampered. She sat down a little distance from the bar, on a bench – more exactly a mossy seat cut into the rock, opposite the Madonna whose effigy sat on a little altar, at head height, in the little low volcanic reef which came to a point at the place where the two paths, south and west, diverged. From where she was, she could see everyone who came and went, to the Vessinaro or instead on up towards the Vetta, a place of decaying buildings and radio towers which had once sported a glamorous hotel where the national poet Gabriele d'Annunzio had held sway, overlooking Golfo Paradiso, Liguria's Paradise Bay. This fork in the road had been her goal, on this first venture. If Cipriano passed, she would recognize him, she believed. And he would see her.

She was also visible, sitting there, to Olimpio's customers; close enough to acknowledge greetings, and far enough away to permit the farmers – yet no, they were in fact mostly workmen from the construction sites, she thought, since she recognized only a few faces – to discuss her to their heart's content.

Olimpio came out with a tray and descended to her bench. *Un bicchiere di vino, signora Contessa?*

The wine, she knew, was on the house. Olimpio, grey-haired, a man of unfailingly distinguished bearing, bowed as she thanked him and took the glass. He stepped back two paces, and waited, in case the *signora Contessa* had any further requests.

Miri made conversation. Had the roadway greatly increased Olimpio's trade? It had, of course, along with the presence of the construction workers. Was he now able to visit the town more easily, by Vespa perhaps? Olimpio had a leg full of shrapnel from the first World War, an injury which confined him to his house and his beloved bar above San Sebastiano, where he was the reigning *boccia* king. His unerring aim with the heavy metal bowling balls required no agility from his legs, and drew competitors from all over Liguria to challenge Olimpio on his own *boccia* court.

But Miri's tongue was heavy. Suddenly the sense that Cipriano might arrive, might pass at any moment was upon her, and she could barely speak. She wanted to ask Olimpio if he had seen Dr. Cipriano today. *Il demonio*. Had he gone down to the town? Was Dr. Cipriano often a passer-by at this hour? Hearing the hearty chatter at the outdoor bar, where the noise had revived after what she took to be a few minutes of *Contessa Miri*-murmuring, she wondered whether the former mayor didn't avoid this route with its gossiping voices, if he was as unpopular as everyone had indicated to her, taking instead the long, narrow flights of steps, chipped from the rock and finished in cement, that led directly from the Vessinaro to the coast road. It was an uncomfortable descent of a thousand feet and more, and an even more arduous return, but a private one since it was so little used.

She wanted to ask Olimpio, but couldn't bring herself to speak.

Instead, she downed her wine, returned the *bicchiere* to Olimpio's tray, stood up and nodded to the assembled workmen at the bar, and walked back along the path a few paces to the chapel of San Sebastiano, wondering for the first time whether her skirt was long enough. The proper *Contessa*-length was something that had concerned both Piero and Rosanna, her mother-in-law, but it was so long since Miri had thought about it.

In the tiny chapel she lit three candles, and sat in the pews, unable to pray.

How could she pray when all she could think about was whether, while she sat in the pew and her back was turned to the door, the murderer was walking by, escaping her?

IT WAS THE strangest experience. For the first time she had to keep Vittorio at bay.

He could be no part of her hunting of Cipriano. She had to shut the door on the boy. Was it that he mustn't see her do this? – that it was all right for him to share the misery and the rage in her heart, but not to be with her when she took action? Or did this feeling come from *him*? Was it the Vittorio in her mind, the true Vittorio, who drew back, who looked away or even disapproved? Miri puzzled over it, but she couldn't tell. They were too much a part of each other, herself and the boy in her head, for her to be able to sort his initiatives from hers. But she had to tell him that this was her business only, hers alone. This would not be his hand in Miri's, but only hers.

She thought more and more often of their last moments together on the quay, at Genoa. She had placed her hand on Vittorio's chest as if to brand it on him, to show him where she would always be, at all times, forever. Yet it was as though that gesture separated them, establishing a him and her, distinct from each other. Miri had seen an echo of this in Vittorio's eyes. The gesture had not reassured him.

They were in each other's heart in a way that could only be lessened, or even contradicted, when rendered physical, when it was dramatized. Such closeness needed neither to be shown or spoken, and when either of them tried, the meaning turned into its opposite, into two people reaching towards each other, two people seeking to be intertwined, when in fact they were interchangeable, that was the whole point, there were not two people at all.

It was nothing like the love she had felt for Piero, or for her father, or the intense puppy-loves she had known at school. In love, she had pined for the loved one's presence, his embrace, his gaze; to be apart from him was an insufficiency that only he could end. With Vittorio it was completely different, and she could never have brought herself to say this to anyone for fear of being thought mawkish or crazy or neurotically possessive, or all three. There was no insufficiency; she was never apart from Vittorio. She never had to pine for him, only to look forward, when school hours or other unavoidable separations parted them, to the moment of reading in his eyes, his face, the content of their hours apart. It left surprisingly little to say, when they were reunited, and Piero, who would demand a report of the day's news and activities, would watch her silent reunions with their son in bewilderment. Aren't you interested? he would sometimes ask. Why do *I* have to do all the questioning?

All Miri wanted to know was how it had been, not what had happened, which Vittorio would tell her in his own good time. She could tell at once *how* it had been, from his face.

When they walked in the hills he would tell her about his teachers and his schoolmates, conjuring the teachers vividly. He was a mimic, although shyness kept him from showing this side of himself to others, and brought her back little playlets from school. As with all true mimics, he himself never figured in these sketches. Miri knew the schoolboy that he was, invisible, head down, a perfectionist in all things, who suffered the slightest error or reproach as if burned by it, and who dreaded being called on to speak in class. His reports praised him extravagantly in all things except in this, his *manca di confidenza*, lack of confidence. Lack of assertiveness, they meant. He didn't lack confidence; he knew his worth. It was precisely this that made him vulnerable to the slightest failure, and that made him ashamed, when he was called on to speak in public, that he could not already be a d'Annunzio, a glorious rhetorician and warrior poet. In his mind, he *was*. Then when he heard his voice, he knew himself to be, as yet, a boy searching for words. It was hard, Miri felt, to have inside you the spirit of a thinker and a teacher, as Vittorio surely would be, like Avram, his grandfather, to have that spirit fully matured in you from so early on, and still to have to wait, trapped in a child's body, until the rest of you caught up.

He was one of those children, it seemed to Miri, who is born an adult, with his direction fully mapped out, within. It affected his friendships, inevitably; one or two were bound to him by ties of intense admiration, adoration almost. Most were made uneasy by his gravity. As gentle a soul as he was, he could so easily have become the victim of bullying, but here Piero's heritage came to the boy's rescue. He was tall, agile, and surprisingly strong, as anyone who tried to pin Vittorio to the schoolyard swiftly discovered. He was fast, too, and chosen early for a pick-up team at any sport. He revelled in this and, though Miri knew that among his peers he would have been modest to a fault, he couldn't wait to reach the Vessinaro on their daily walk, where the broad sandy path allowed him to demonstrate some of the moves he had brought off that day, at school.

What seemed to Miri so remarkable – it could hardly seem as strange to Vittorio as it did to her – was the boy's seeming inheritance of the smallest of her traits and mannerisms, including his vices. Although thin as a rake, as Miri was, and quite unable to acquire puppy-fat, he snatched food whenever and wherever he could, often to Serafina's exasperation, and guarded his platefuls, at meals, with a watchful fury that reminded Miri of herself at home, a child whose plate was raided by her sisters as soon as her back was turned. It evoked a quite different Vittorio, as wrathful as a dog over his food bowl when another dog is present. Miri knew that expression on the boy's face; it had been hers once, and she knew she had been a Tartar to Hannah and Rifkie when they were young. These days Tartar Miri was back again, she knew from glimpsing her pinched mouth and in-gathered brows in the mirrors of the Casa Rosa. The snapping dog in her was back.

She and Vittorio, both obsessive about animals, had often joked that they themselves were part canine. Rosanna had owned a lapdog which has predeceased her, Ciampa had been its name, a nasty yapping spaniel of some miniature variety, unyielding and liable to sink its tiny teeth into any stroking hand but Rosanna's. All the same, Miri and Vittorio had been unable to prevent themselves cooing ceaselessly over this ratty and ungrateful creature, despite Rosanna's warnings and Ciampa's own growls. Ciampa by name, chomper by nature, had been Miri's rueful word for the spaniel, as she bandaged another bite on Vittorio's fingers. Piero wouldn't allow the house a bigger dog, a proper guard dog, for all Vittorio's pleas. It was a matter of pride: dogs, all the way up and down the mountainsides, raged and howled to protect their owners' property and sound the alarm. *Il Conte* could not have such a beast, for who would dare to rob *Il Conte*? To own a guard dog would show unseemly suspicion, and even more unseemly fear. To own, instead, a placid beast that didn't bark would seem unworthy of a *Conte*. The solution was: no dog. The *Contessa madre's* lapdog was another matter, it was hardly a dog at all, more of an accessory, like a handbag with legs (and teeth). So the Casa Rosa had cats, plenty of them, fed by Serafina at the kitchen door, and adored by Miri and Vittorio.

Most of all it was Vittorio's trustingness she remembered, his sense of awe. She had seen that unguarded look in other boys of his age. At twelve he was still a child, playing alone in a garden. The girls his age had already guessed something; they had glimpsed the larger picture. Or maybe it was the smaller picture they had seen. The world was not a garden. The shadow had not yet fallen over Vittorio's eyes when she left him. Pain, but no resentment yet.

Cipriano's men had pulled him from his bed, while others held Leandro at bay outside the room. There was screaming in the corridor as Vittorio pulled on his clothes at gunpoint – Serafina had described it to Miri in her usual terse sentences, but there was only so much of it Miri could bear to review.

Later, she made herself face it, against every impulse that cried out not to indulge in the futile details. It was too late to be with him.

Yet no: it *wasn't* too late, time and courage taught her. Step by step she retraced the journey with him, restoring herself to the Vittorio who had held her in his heart all the way, Vittorio to whom she had said with her hand on his chest that she would be there at every instant. She followed him to Fossoli di Carpi, where he was still waiting for her. She followed him onto the train, through the days and nights in the cattle truck, without water, crammed upright like the damned she had seen on the front elevation of Orvieto Cathedral.

And beyond; she followed him all the way into the gas chamber, where he was waiting for her too, waiting in line, shuffling forwards towards the promises of a cleansing shower and a mug of hot coffee to follow, at last disrobing, folding clothes – make sure, the guards called, that you know where they are, make a mental note of the number on the hanger, so you can find it swiftly and without confusion, afterwards – entering naked and shivering and unshriven into the last room he would know and waiting in the dark, still trusting, still hoping, until breath wouldn't come and the screams began.

Some, she read, a few, instead of scratching and fighting their way towards the top of the seething, screeching pile in search of the last gasps of air, and rather than join the mass tearing their fingers raw against the doors, withdrew, and sat, breathing their last, against a wall. She was quite certain that Vittorio had been one of these. Too proud, even in death, to claw a few more instants, when clawing meant ripping into fellow-human flesh. That was where he was waiting for her, at the wall. He had known she was watching, and at last she was.

ON THEIR WAY up to the Vessinaro to collect *pinoli*, to squat or sit on the sandy, orange path and gaze out at the horizon that hid Africa, they had often paused above San Sebastiano. At Olimpio's

Miri would take a glass of water and Vittorio an *aranciata*, a gassy
San Pellegrino orange juice out of a small bottle. They would sit on
the bench opposite the little altar in the rock with its effigy of the
Madonna, where Miri now sat awaiting Cipriano.

He would come in time, and of time she had an endless supply.

She recalled Vittorio's curiosity about the effigy in its blue dress.
Now, as then, there were flowers, some dried, some fresh, around
the statue, which was no more than a foot tall, in its glass case. Why
does no one steal it? Vittorio, raised without religion – without ritual,
at any rate – and curious about humanity, had wanted to know.

When they passed the chapel of San Sebastiano with its door
forever ajar, Vittorio had always turned his glance away, in a kind
of shyness or piety, it seemed to Miri, not wishing to penetrate the
interior with a gaze he himself felt to be too raw. No matter how
curious he was about others (and even sceptical – *Why does no one
steal it?*), he had never doubted, she thought, the sense of reverence
that was intrinsic to him.

They had never visited the chapel. Piero himself had been no
churchgoer (Rosanna had been more faithful, attending Mass on
Sunday), except on ceremonial occasions when the town expected
their *Conte* to be present. Miri had explained to Vittorio the little
she knew of the religion of her own forefathers, and told him about
Christian ritual and belief, to the best of her understanding, assuring
the boy that he would find his way and make his own choice, both
as *Conte* and as an individual. And, as yet, it had not occurred to
her to regret having failed to bring Vittorio into the religious fold as
a child. Her first thought had been: how much would prayer have
helped him, at the last?

Yet now she was drawn to San Sebastiano every time she came to
the crossroads beneath the Vessinaro, and it was Vittorio, not just
herself, that she felt she was introducing to the interior of the chapel
at last, to the idea of sanctity, and sanctuary.

She showed him how to light a candle, where to put the money.
And she would explain to him how it was not the lighting of your
own candle but the blaze of other candles – a very little blaze at
San Sebastiano but a blaze nonetheless – that told you why you

were performing this act: you were attaching yourself to others' prayers, to all men's prayers, to prayfulness itself. It was not your prayer that counted, but humanity itself as a flame to be re-kindled over and over. The candle flames, straight and still until the chapel door opened or closed and made them all flicker briefly, in concert, bespoke trust in a greater meaning than your own – this you could embrace without needing to be a Catholic.

You stepped back into the pews, you took a seat and sat down to pray (it would feel quite wrong to pay and hurry out, Miri thought), or at least to meditate.

No form of prayer came to her, no words. This surely didn't matter. It was quiet here, serene, comfortable even, where so much pious emotion inhabited the walls.

Miri ceased to instruct Vittorio in her mind and considered the chapel in solitude. She was perfectly willing to pray. She felt no allegiance to the agonized eyes that watched her from the luridly painted baroque altarpiece – at second glance they didn't seem to be looking at her at all, but out above and past her at the open chapel doorway, as if drawn by the sunlight, or rather, Miri thought, as if watching for Cipriano for her, keeping guard – but if there was a deity she felt free to address Him here, regardless of her Jewish origins. To be in a church was of itself in no way strange to her. As a student of culture she had visited a great many churches, and had entered this one with the same sense of polite interest and respect for the hushed atmosphere. She would not feel out of place, she thought, praying here. If the Lord of hosts was here – how did *that* phrase arrive in her head, and where did it come from? – and was listening at all, he would surely listen to her.

Cricket-chatter (was it *inside* the chapel? – no, the wristwatch-steady sound was coming from behind her, flooding in at the door) and then, soaring over the cricket recitative like a soloist above a drone bass, birdsong penetrated the tiny space, humanizing it, Miri thought. Before she could even parse that thought it occurred to her that at any moment a *contadina* might come in at the open door to pray or light a candle. Miri had so often glimpsed hunched, praying figures in the pews, from outside, as she walked by. And what would such people think, to find the Jewish *Contessa* here at prayer? Perhaps they'd be delighted. But she would feel self-conscious.

Yet she *should* be here, shouldn't she? It was her parish church.

Birdsong came again, scratchily, from the open door. A halting sound, yet with a purity of – of what? Of *authority*, yes, a voice of authority that this chapel could only mimic. Well, she could pray to the voice of the bird, the guiltless bird, couldn't she, here in this chapel that, unlike the great churches of towns and cities, allowed the birdsong in?

And so what if the *contadini* caught her in their chapel? Not on her knees, perhaps – couldn't she pray, here, sitting at the back in a corner, without going to her knees? Did the Lord of hosts require the act of submission?

And of what hosts was he Lord? Was he the Lord of *armies*? Abruptly it struck Miri as absurd that she, anyone, should be here, in a chapel, or in a church, bowing to a Lord whose armies had stayed peculiarly clear of battlefields during the past ten years. Churchgoers were strange folk, she thought. Churches and chapels were their refuge against the horrors of the world, and yet the good, dear, all-forgiving Lord they prayed to – that Miri herself had been about to pray to – failed or refused to forestall these horrors. And their Pope, their God-inspired leader, where did he stand? Where had he stood, while millions were slaughtered? Now she felt ashamed of herself at being here at all. The God of Auschwitz, and surely if there was a God, he had to be the God of Auschwitz too, was here. The thought dizzied and nauseated her. The saint – or was it Christ himself? – on his altarpiece stared out through the doorway like an anguished avatar of the death camps, it seemed to her now. His suffering eyes beneath the crown of thorns seeming to beg passers-by to come and join the throng – come on in! *More* sufferers, please. More, more!

Standing up unsteadily, sickened, she felt shocked at herself for coming here for comfort. Wasn't this the headquarters of voluntary suffering? If life was one long crucifixion, as the agonized martyr-face seemed to be saying, then let's all greet Hell on earth without a protest! Let's walk obediently into the gas chamber. Thy Will be done, o Lord! Let's forgive ourselves for suffering as we forgive ourselves and each other for torturing. She wanted to run out of the door and lock it behind her, before the place could give comfort to the Ciprianos and the Cipriano-forgivers of the world.

THE DAY SHE came upon him, it was as if *il demonio* had been waiting for her, not the other way around.

Miri had walked up to the Vessinaro itself, up to the promontory where she feared that not only he, the demon, would be waiting for her there, under the umbrella pines, but that Vittorio would be there. It had been their favourite place of all. Nowhere in the *paese* resounded so much with his presence.

This was precisely what had held her back. It was one thing to carry Vittorio with her, another to come upon a remembered Vittorio unawares, especially now when she needed to be focused and alone. This spot, high above the waves crashing onto the Punta Vessinaro, had held a curious fascination for them both, unconnected with the treasure of the *pinoli* lying waiting on the ground, and the *prigionniera* perhaps lurking behind the laurel hedge. The promontory held the terror and finality of the sea. For any eyes and soul already gentled by the bay – the bay that the promontory so successfully protected from the sea – it was a shock. Sea without end. There was no view, nothing to be seen from the Vessinaro except the waves. It was *all* view. The Vessinaro drew Miri and Vittorio to look, always with a thrill of fear, but not to stay. High up as they were, above the mangy scrub and sheer volcanic slabs that plunged a thousand feet and more towards the waves, there was a comfortlessness to it. Gazing out at emptiness, at absence, you couldn't help thinking, Why would anyone want to live here, gazing at murderous emptiness and the single mood of sea and sky, when you could turn and face the other way, towards men, towards the multifarious pleasures of the bay? Vittorio had once asked her this very question. Miri could only nod. But they were both aware, Miri felt sure, of an unspoken rider to their thought. This, the seaward view, the absolute, was the sight that drew them to the Vessinaro, day after day.

At the Casa Rosa or in the town, on the esplanade, or on the little beach, the bay held you cradled in its looping arm, with the *tricorne* of the peninsula at one edge, like a dragon guardian half-immersed and sinking slowly into the waves. At the opposing edge the bay unfurled a coastline without end, land without end, Italy stretching into blue beneath the long ridge of the Appenines, its peaks overlooking one fishing port after another, inlet after inlet, straight on south as far as the eye could see. Within the curve of the bay and its calm, lake-like waters, colour itself promised safety. The hillsides dotted with pink or yellow where a wall peeped through its bougainvillea mask, the flicker of sails, even the *beee-bah* of the buses, spoke of home and harbour. Up on the Vessinaro, peeping over the edge of the world to where the pitiless horizon held nothing but water, you were at the mercy of a unanimous sea. It filled your sight and senses. Below the sandy path, glimpses of rooftops told you that the cliff held houses, alive with Chinese wistaria and a tempest of attendant bees that came and went, soaring over the promontory. But to live there! – to gaze out all day at the comfortless waves, a view so stark and unforgiving: it seemed a kind of voluntary imprisonment.

Four or five times, over the years, Miri and Vittorio had dragged themselves out of bed on a baleful March morning following a storm, and marched to the Vessinaro armed with a pair of binoculars. On such mornings, and such mornings alone, Africa could be seen. This altered everything. Once, when they rose in darkness and reached the promontory at first light, they saw the distant coast, the other side, without the binoculars. It was only a little blue rind of land, but it closed the ghastly circle, the infinity of the sea, like a glimpse of the afterlife. They had been permitted to see that there was something beyond, that the fearsomely empty vista beyond the Punta Vessinaro was bounded. Before them was a giant lake, a giant bay, with its own encircling arm. It too, then, was a mothering sea, not the void it seemed.

The old man was sitting on a bench overlooking the Punta, on the side of the orange path closest to the cliffs, looking out over the Mediterranean. He wore an overcoat, and even though the day was mild, cool even, the long coat looked out of place. He sat hunched, the back of his neck hidden by the overcoat collar, but his profile clearly visible.

Miri recognized his pouchy face by the bags of darkening skin under the eyes and the soft, curved nose. It was the man Piero had pointed out to her, not only in passing, in the town (with a warning hiss of "Cipriano!"), but at Prospero Velo's, eating alone, without looking at anyone, his doggy features at once sagging and severe.

On the path, Miri stopped and stood, studying him. If he had heard her approaching, as he surely must have done, she thought, and heard her footsteps halt, he showed no interest but sat gazing out to sea.

What was to be made of a demon's face, now that you had it in your view?

It was the face of an ailing, vegetating old man, reviewing the past. Or simply gazing at the sea? The demon was inside, unappeased, the demon at whose orders life had been extinguished, slowly, amid barely imaginable horror.

Since returning to Italy that horror had become familiar to Miri in a wholly new way; it lived in the Casa Rosa, and every time Serafina gasped and cried out in an attack of asthma, Miri had to fight not to run into the garden where she could escape the soughing, desperate sound of lungs fighting for breath.

And now here he was, the instigator of the horror, Cipriano, ailing but unharmed, freely breathing the sea air over Punta Vessinaro.

She had formed no plans for him, other than perhaps for him to see her, day after day.

And if he locked himself in his house? Then he would still know she was outside, waiting, tireless. Waiting to follow him when he went to the town to do his shopping; to sit at an adjacent table as he drank his coffee; to tail him steadily – she was younger, stronger – as he climbed the thousand steps up to the Vessinaro, stopping when he stopped, continuing when he continued.

This much she could picture. And then?

Would he move away, move to a city somewhere? She would follow.

But sometimes, at night in the Casa Rosa, this *via dolorosa* of shadowing Cipriano to his death, although it slaked her heart (as entering a convent, Miri reflected, must have slaked the heart, for some), held one troublesome glimpse that disabled her sense of purpose. It hid, this glimpse, like an assassin in a side-street doorway. It was the vision of a future Cipriano calmly going about his business, barely glancing to see if Miri was, as always, there behind him; the vision of a Cipriano to whom, over the years, this stalking had become routine, uninteresting, unthreatening.

What then?

There were nights when she saw herself setting fire to the Vessinaro houses one by one, torching the little ghost village to flush Cipriano out. And then what? On such nights, lying in bed, Miri returned in imagination to the police station, to Andrea's shuttered office.

Did you mean it? She would ask Andrea. *Then lend me your gun.*

But that was in imagination. Here was the sick old man before her, in the flesh.

Miri had known all along that it could only be a disappointment to come face to face with him, to see the tired ordinary features of a fellow human being. She knew his would be no more than another pitiable human face, whether she pictured it defiant, frightened, or indifferent. It was the demon inside that waited its hour, gloating, hiding from punishment, ready to rise again unless it was dragged before the people, spitted, and destroyed.

That was why she had wanted a public hearing so much, to put the crime on trial. To put the demon on the rack, not merely its human vehicle. All men needed to know that such things did not go unpunished.

The crime, yes; the crime needed to be punished, not the man. Because – *was* there even a demon? It would be hard to see it, even in the dock, where so many murderers had shown only their bewildered, craven face. It was hard to see it now when it was right in front of her, hard to be sure that it was there in the hunched figure on the bench before her, no more than thirty feet away. Perhaps there was no *demonio* as Serafina seemed to picture it, no spirit of purest evil, only weak men thirsting for the raw, heady wine of revenge, the wine of the hillsides that Miri knew well, harsh and immature but still addictive. No demons; just men believing that power would permit them to act out their vilest fantasies. They knew the consequences, if they fell from grace. Nonethless: the world had to be reminded. The world knew, too, what those consequences should be, but surely it had to be reminded.

Didn't it? Miri could feel her certainty faltering. Faltering already? – was it possible? – Vittorio, come to my aid!

Close to Miri, on the other side of the path from Cipriano's bench, a rocky seat offered relief, scoured from the volcanic schist like the seat opposite the Madonna, at Olimpio's. Miri took it, and sat in silence, gazing at Cipriano. Instead of the Madonna, now she had the devil in view. She wanted him to turn and see her, but he didn't, and something inside her prevented her from calling out to get his attention.

He knew she was there, waiting, and watching him. For the time being, that was all that mattered.

AMONG THE GRIMMER tasks awaiting Miri at the Casa Rosa had been the matter of deciding not only what to do with Vittorio's things, but with both Piero's and Rosanna's; their clothes and books and papers awaited her in perfect order, dusted and expectant, still awaiting their owner. Miri's too had been kept impeccable by Pina. It was like entering a museum. There had been days, at first, when Miri had found the upper story of the Casa Rosa so spooky that she knew she had to act on this sensation quickly while it lasted, before she became used to the house the way it was and woke one day to find that years had passed and she was living in a mausoleum. This determination had taken her downstairs to Vittorio's room, adjacent to Serafina and Leandro's quarters, to start there on the worst and hardest task. Miri knew that if she left Vittorio's room till last, she'd leave it untouched. Even now every impulse had cried out to leave it alone, but she repeated over and over to herself that by cleaning out his room she was taking its every portion of Vittorio into her heart instead, where he resided.

Nonetheless, the experience had been so dreadful that it had stopped her from proceeding to the upper floors. Clearing out Vittorio's room had taken every ounce of strength from her. Let books and papers rest where they were. Why did she need to sort them out, let alone throw them away? What harm were they doing? Clothes too, mothballed, harmless. Leave them be.

But did she want them hanging there in their closets, and heaped in chests of drawers, into all eternity? She had returned to a house three-quarters frozen in time, in which – this was the truth of it – she could only bear to be in the kitchen, even when food wasn't being prepared and no one was there but herself. It was hard for Serafina and her family to accept her behaviour, she knew. They wanted Miri to be upstairs, where the Contessa should be. But couldn't they see for themselves? The kitchen was the part of the house that was still alive.

No, there had to be a clearing out before the body of the house could live again. Time – time was at the heart of it. The house had to stop looking back. She was tempted to ask Leandro to strip the bougainvillea away from the outside walls. They hadn't seen direct sunlight in at least a generation.

Instead Miri began with Rosanna's desk, a surface she had never touched, let alone explored the drawers. All she wanted to do, Miri realized, was to address the contents. Nothing had to be removed. Why should it be, unless the desk was to be sold, or someone else took up residence in Rosanna's "apartments," as Piero had liked to call the two interconnected rooms. "She is in her apartments," Piero liked to say in English, with sumptuous precision.

A leatherbound journal lay before her, carefully centred on the inlaid red rectangle, also leather and trimmed in gold, that occupied the greater portion of the surface of the desk. Had Rosanna kept it like this, centred and perfectly ready, albeit closed, and surrounded by fountain pens, blotter, and ink? Miri had no memory of the configuration while Rosanna had been alive. To one side, sheets of writing paper. To the other, a small pile of letters received, held down by a marble paperweight. All very symmetrical and neat. Or had Pina arranged it this way? Miri knew that Rosanna had been particular about her letter-writing paper, which was made specially for her in Genoa. It was grey and deliberately rough in texture, with an artificially ragged edge, top and bottom and on both sides, as if mimicking some antique document – even though Miri could think of no antique document (unless you went back to the Dead Sea Scrolls) that had been so negligently prepared. On the whole the past had prided itself on cutting paper along a straight line. Not a very demanding art. But letters from the *Contessa Madre* Rosanna, on their pebbly grey paper, emerged from their matching pebbly grey envelope folded at strange angles, as if to stress their ragged edges, like some hastily penned and clumsily folded medieval *billet-doux*. Presumably that was the intention, that each one should look as if a Sforza or a Medici had torn off a corner of Leonardo's sketchpad and written a quick note on it. The pile of letters to Rosanna, under the marble paperweight, included several penned in sepia ink on similarly eccentric and proprietary writing paper. For the first time, seeing them all together, Miri saw it less as pretentiousness than as an endearing schoolgirl game.

Dare she open the leatherbound journal? Should whatever thoughts they contained be consigned to a future generation who could not be hurt, but at best only amused, by their references? But *what* future generation? Not in this family.

What then, for the diaries of the dead who lacked descendants? The bonfire? Or the bric-a-brac shop? Even without opening the journal, Miri knew it would be written in Rosanna's beautiful italic script, and how could one possibly throw out a life annotated in such a wonderful, old-fashioned hand? Even Rosanna's letters, as trivial as their content might be, made you want to frame them. And no local bookseller or antique dealer should be granted possession of the *Contessa madre's* secret thoughts. They'd be all over the town within a week.

Let it lie, then. Let time and history decide.

But what harm could a quick look do?

To Miri's astonishment, the front cover, when lifted, revealed a loose piece of Rosanna's letter paper, and under it, page after page of the same pebbly grey paper with its ragged edges, covered in writing, and on the top sheet, in Rosanna's sweeping hand, hugely written, just one word, one name: hers.

Miri, it said.

Turning it over, Miri read, on the page beneath:

Dear child. In English. Then, in Italian, *Cara figlia.* Dear daughter.

Miri found herself in tears, unable, for the moment, to read on. Had Rosanna ever addressed her as *Cara figlia*? Perhaps – yes, perhaps, but to see it written, in that sumptuous antique hand –

And what was it doing *inside* Rosanna's diary, if it was penned for her, meant for her? Had Rosanna wagered that Miri would be unable to resist prying? Or was the letter precisely aimed at a Miri who did pry, and at that Miri only?

More likely, Miri thought, the grey letter paper had been left protruding invitingly from the journal, and Pina had tidied its pages into place.

Or was the letter still only a draft, interrupted by Rosanna's death?

No, it was dated, Miri saw as she wiped her eyes clear, May 20th, 1944. More than three years before Rosanna's death. Miri sat at the desk and read on, lifting page after page of the strange, heavy grey paper.

DEAR CHILD. CARA figlia –

Yesterday I received the news that our beloved Piero has died in the retreat from Monte Cassino to Rome. Rome, German Rome, will surely fall now and the war will be over and it will be poor consolation to those who lost a loved one. For some who survive, our life is over whether the war goes on or not. And it is especially cruel when someone dies in the final days.

I know I must sound calm, unnaturally calm, to you who read this. There are many reasons for this, some of which I mention below. I was prepared. Also, I know from Piero himself how to understand his death. As I write this, my dear daughter, I have not yet begun properly to mourn for Piero. There will be time enough, and I want to write with my mind clear. Yesterday in any case, when the news came, I knew that I would have to act at once. I knew it would not help if I gave in to emotion. I had the plan already in my mind, and a day has not passed since Piero went to the war (as I say, I was prepared) when I did not expect to hear the worst. Even as a medical orderly, he would go where it was most dangerous. That was Piero.

So when the news came I put on mourning, I had it ready, and I went to see the Comandante di Polizia.

This is a man, I'm sure you know, called Cipriano, who was once the mayor. I knew him many years ago. His sister Paola, may she rest in peace, was my closest friend when I was a girl. I went to beg him not to take Vittorio now that Piero was dead and the boy was without protection. But Cipriano would not see me. I sat all day in the police station although out of embarrassment they begged me to leave. And still he would not see me. I was going to return, today, and every day until he saw me, but this morning they came and took Vittorio from his bed.

I cannot write this with a steady hand, forgive me. All I can think of now is to permit you to know the truth. Many years ago I behaved like a foolish, fickle young girl. I was 20 years old and everyone was saying that a new spirit was born with the new century. The fireworks that year, to celebrate the new year, were the finest and the most expensive the town has ever seen. I have reason to remember this, as I will explain. I hope you will think that the girl I was could never have foreseen what would happen. But what use is it to try and escape the responsibility? Now you and Vittorio are paying for my foolishness, and I must live with it the best that I can.

At least I will not hide it any more.

I have instructed Pina that when I die this letter is to be left in my diary, on my desk, which I trust is where you have found it. The diary is old, as you will see. I stopped writing it in 1928, the same year that you and Piero met. When you read it, as I hope you will, you will see why I stopped. It has nothing to do with you and Piero, needless to say. In fact you will find one happy and prophetic reference to you, my dear. Only one, but it came true. I was wiser than I knew. I wrote that if my Piero had a sensible head on his shoulders he would fall in love with a girl like you instead of the pampered principessine *he had always yearned for. And if he was lucky, I thought, although I didn't write this, you would love him too. And you did, my dear, as well and as long as you could. Please don't think that by this I make reference to your return to England to escape death, a journey every one of us at the Casa Rosa wanted you to make and begged you to* make and were only afraid that you would not make out of love for us. To have died for this, for your love of us, would not have been a loving choice. No, when I say you loved Piero as well and as long as you could, what I mean is – and I beg you to forgive my candour, because at this time when I'm writing now I have little patience with anything else – that by forty a man like Piero has outlived himself. It is hard to love a man who knows this. (I can tell you so, because his father was the same.) Perhaps it is in the biology. Not so very long ago, 40 was the age when a vigorous man, if he had lived fully, might die without being ahead of himself. 40 was no longer young. Today it's different, but not for everybody. When my Vittorio died in his car, it was recklessness. Everyone knew he was a reckless driver. Only I knew it was a little more than recklessness. Don't misunderstand me. It was more than recklessness and a little less than suicide. But when you make the gambles bigger and bigger, one day you must lose everything, because that is your intention.

I write this only to explain to you that I know how things stood between you and Piero. To him it seemed that you were occupied with the boy, as a mother should be. Does the father need attention as if he too were still a boy? Of course not. But to need and to want are not the same thing. In any case what you did was right. And Piero too was occupied. He was busy, like his father, with his own disappearance. Having seen it in two generations, my dear Miri, I am now an expert in this. He was busy, I say, with his disappearance. Watching it, and fighting it. His father took risks he would not have taken at 20, at the height of his courage. I was afraid Piero would go to war, to make himself appear again. I believe he did this successfully, I know it from a letter he wrote in which he speaks of recapturing himself (I will leave you this letter), and I know that he died happier than he had been for many years. I hope you understand this and are happy, as I am. Other people perhaps will not be able to understand, but to me it is simple. For some people a few minutes of living at the height of their passion is better than years of only surviving. Speaking for myself, I can't pretend that I don't know what this means.

But I was also afraid for Vittorio, for our young Vittorio. And so I went to see Dr. Cipriano, to talk to him.

When you read the diary, you will get some small idea of what this meant, to go and see him. Not the difficulty of doing it, for me. It was not difficult at all. I would have spoken to him at any time. For him, for Cipriano, I could anticipate how difficult it would be. We had not met for almost forty years. Forty years, Miri. Can you imagine? In the life of a small town, this is nothing, but in our hearts it is an eternity. It felt like two hundred years since I had seen him. He was 23 then, the year I married Vittorio. I had known Cipriano all my life, we had been as close as sister and brother, because his sister Paola was born in the same month as I was and she was my best friend, inseparable. Renzo (I wonder if you know his first name, Miri, since our dear Piero never used it and so few people call him by any other name than by Dottore Cipriano) – *Renzo was three years older. It seemed a lot when we were young, Paola and I. When we were twelve and Renzo was fifteen, the difference was enormous, and we looked up to him and were a little afraid of him. He was always very quiet and private, and serious, and often it was important not to disturb him at his books. Once he took us fishing, not on the sea but up in the mountains, and also showed us how to use a rifle. After some years, suddenly the difference in age was not so much, and when I was 18 (the same as you were when you met Piero, and so I know that you can imagine it clearly), Renzo kissed me during the fireworks on the esplanade, at New Year, and I thought I would faint from the shock.*

He had been planning it, he later told me, for two years. Perhaps more, because after all we are not entirely innocent when we are young, but he said two years, and I did not want to think that he had been dreaming of kissing me for longer than that.

Did I let him think that I liked it? I did, of course, but a girl does not have to show how much. How much did I encourage him, during the next years? It's the question I have had to ask myself all my life. Of course I did not give him very much encouragement. I was 18 and even if it was a new century and a new spirit, I was still a girl of the 1800s, and I was not a wild girl, by nature. So I gave Renzo very little encouragement. But in those days even a smile was almost an engagement to be married, so the little encouragement I gave him was also a great deal.

*Did I want to marry him? Here I must not lie. I did dream of it,
because he and Paola and the Cipriano family were like my second
family and to be part of them forever seemed to me like a perfect life.
But I can say honestly that a part of me resisted. A foolish romantic
part, perhaps, that wanted a fascinating stranger and not to marry
into a family that was mine already, with people I could always
be with whenever I liked. So that when Vittorio noticed me, who
was a friend of Renzo's but someone so exalted that I think I had
never once looked him directly in the face, in his eyes, I was terribly
distracted and excited.*

*We had no understanding, Renzo and I, that we would be married.
But can I even say that much without lying? Because perhaps
everybody else understood that one day when Renzo finished his
medical studies we would be married, and no doubt Renzo thought
so too and even I thought so, and went on thinking so even when
I made secret meetings with Vittorio. These meetings were a life of
fantasy. Renzo was the life of reality. You understand? But I had
never said anything to Renzo, or Renzo to me. We never even kissed
again after the first time, the night of the fireworks. But was that
enough, perhaps, to settle everything? Was it as good, for Renzo, as
if I had written my name to say, yes, I will marry you? The kiss was
something I could not avoid, even if I wanted to, because he was
kissing me before I knew it, and then another firework went off and
everyone was jumping up and down and screaming, and I remember
I was quickly trying to forget that it had happened, the kiss, in case it
was a mistake, or simply the excitement of the fireworks. And even,
did it happen at all? But I knew it happened, and so did Renzo.*

*And we went on seeing each other, every day almost until he went
to Genoa to study, but it was the three of us together, Renzo and
Paola and I, it was not just Renzo and I. At the same time I knew
that this was a kind of a way that we could be together, he and I,
that was not improper. So in another way it was just Renzo and I.
And I liked him. I'd known him all my life. He was more serious
than Paola, and it annoyed Renzo sometimes when we laughed
together, Paola and I, over jokes that we had been making since we
were young. But it was good for a husband to be serious, and be*

studious, as Renzo was, with plans not just to be a doctor, but to play a part in the new Italy. He was always talking of the new Italy and then later, when Mussolini spoke about it too, I understood that there had been many people like Renzo, dreaming of Rome and the old Imperial Italy, which to me was chiefly statues and a dead language. But to Renzo it was the future.

In any case, as a doctor he was a good 'catch', I think, Miri. And I'm sure everyone thought that this was my future. And even when I went behind Renzo's back, when I was kissing Vittorio, and more than kissing, because I didn't want to lose him, I thought it was my future too, to be Mrs Doctor Renzo Cipriano.

Well, my daughter, I must tell you that history repeats itself. If you don't know it yet, you will know it, it will happen to you in time. The birth of your little Vittorio was of course a little early to me who knew the date of your marriage in London, as the town did not. Although I could not be sure (and would never have asked you to tell me) whether you knew that you were pregnant when you married Piero, I couldn't help smiling to myself at the way life repeats. You probably knew, didn't you? And Piero too? Knowing Piero, I'm sure he was delighted. They had this in common, the father and the son, and it was a delightful quality. They loved to see new life come into the world, and they were loyal to their love, above everything. Do you know, I have thought it was for a curious reason, this. Not for a moral reason, although of course they were both very moral men, even more moral than most men, with their belief in democracy and equality and the rest. (Pardon me if I speak like this of their politics, but from reading about history all my life I have very little confidence in the great plans that people make for the world.) No, do you know what I think? I think that Vittorio (my Vittorio) and Piero were loyal above all to one thing, and that thing was their body. They lived so much in their body, and understood it so well, it was so obedient for them and so strong and acrobatic. Of course later when it betrayed them, this was much worse than for other men. To others, looking at Vittorio and Piero as they approached 40, all the others can see is their astonishing, youthful beauty, their vigour the same as always. But for Piero as for Vittorio the story from the inside is not the same. Enough of this. I speak of them in their pride and their beauty. Be truthful, Miri. Wasn't it Piero's body that you fell in love with? I don't mean you fell in love with his legs and not with his face. He was a beautiful boy. But what made you look at him, and his father was the same, was not just the face but the perfect expression of the body. In every movement it did exactly what he wanted it to do, and often this was something extraordinary, a jump or a turn that no one else would have dared make. But also just when he was sitting and reached out his hand to pick up his drink, it was (isn't it so?) like no one else. It was like water, how it flowed. Or like an animal, so easy and graceful that it made you almost gasp and ask him to do it again. He lived in his body, my Vittorio, and I saw at once that my son was the same. Whether he had it from Vittorio in the biology or from watching, I don't know. Perhaps both. In any case he adored his father, and to see the two of them swimming together like two fish, or playing tennis, or just walking down the street, or sitting, perfectly calm, like two leopards, watching each other's cigarette smoke, it was like seeing another tribe of men. I'm sure when you read this you are nodding.

So I think, and I am afraid to return to my subject, for reasons you will soon understand, that I know how Piero reacted when he knew you were pregnant. It was a thing from his body, and he loved it, regardless of whether it was improper to be married to a girl with a big belly. And you see, I already gave away the game, didn't I, when I said that history repeated itself? Yes, I was pregnant too, Miri, when I married Piero's father. But it was not so simple as it was for you, to go to London and after a time get married, and then to go on honeymoon, and finally to come back months later to the town, pregnant.

From the very beginning it was dangerous, and for me it could have been a disaster. If Vittorio had been anyone but Vittorio, I think, he would have said, She's pregnant? Accipicchia! Che sfortuna! *What bad luck! And he would have turned the other way and left me with my life destroyed. Renzo Cipriano would not have married me. No one would have married me. I was not, as I told you, a wild girl, and so I was not the kind who would run off to Rome, or even to Genoa and make a bohemian life for myself and my child, and never come back except once or twice to laugh at everyone for their sad provincial life. I would have stayed, the child would be adopted, I would be famous in the town (not the only one, but famous all the same), and that would be the end of it, I could become a spinster shopgirl, or I could become a nun. Instead, to my amazement, Vittorio was delighted. Delighted! He was* il Contessino, *he would be Count any day because his father was in poor health ever since the Great War, but he was delighted, and it was hardly possible for me to believe this, he was delighted that little Rosanna who was not a* principessa *but whose parents ran a* biancheria, *a cleaning business, was pregnant with his child. (You didn't know this, did you? Yes, my parents ran a* biancheria.) *I could hardly stop him from telling everybody he met. He wanted to marry me that day. That he wanted to marry me at all I thought at first was just a cruel joke. But then I understand that he meant it, and that I wasn't going to be Mrs Dottore Renzo Cipriano at all but the Contessa Rosanna. I could barely whisper the sound of it in my own mind, it was so incredible. If someone had made me Queen of all Italy it could not have been more strange. And of course once I did dare to say it, Contessa Rosanna, Contessa Rosanna, I couldn't stop saying it in my mind like someone who was drunk.*

And what chance did poor Renzo with his medical studies have against this? I was blinded with excitement and love and disbelief that this beautiful panther, this leopard with a title to give would give it to me. *I had thought I was just one of many fortunate girls (and there were many) in the town who had enjoyed some visits from the panther, and now when I discovered I was pregnant I would pay for those visits with the rest of my life. Instead I would receive a fortune, I would get as a husband the man of whom the entire* paese *dreamed and I would get a title, I would be the Contessa Rosanna for ever and ever and ever.*

And Vittorio loved me. This I could not entirely grasp. Not in fact for many years. I thought he was a saint, a miracle, a man who loved me for having his baby, which I knew was the easiest thing in the world, to become pregnant by him, and if this was all that was needed to win his love then any of a hundred girls could have done it. So there was nothing special about me, only that il Conte was going to marry me, out of all the other girls, because my belly was full and theirs was not. And perhaps it's true that this was why Vittorio loved me. I think he liked me well enough until the day he learned that I was pregnant, and then he could see nobody in the world but me. And when he looked at us together in the hospital, little Piero and I lying together, I saw in his eyes that this was a kind of love that he had never felt before, and I believed it would never die.

And if I was replaced, in time, in his heart, it was not by another woman, but by time itself, which wounded him in ways he had never expected. He was like a man who wakes up to find he has been put in chains during the night, and the love of his wife, his child, and his friends are no use since none of them can undo the chains. Nobody can. Suddenly there is a price for being a leopard, and it is a heavy price. All this you know, Miri, I think.

But Renzo Cipriano, of course, was also in chains, and worse than chains, already at the age of 23, when I married Vittorio and took away Renzo's life.

It is shameful to admit it, but I prayed that all Renzo's dreams would come true, and that they would take him away from our paese. He should not only become a Dottore but a grandee of the new Italy, he should go to Rome and have a glorious future and find a glorious wife and we should read about him in the newspapers.

Instead, of course. he stayed here. Here, where he would be tortured all his life by his disappointment, because now it was more real to him than anything, more real than dreams of Rome and glory, and he was afraid, perhaps, to put it behind him, because then he would not know who he was. It's strange what we become: he discovered that he was his disappointment. (Perhaps it was this he had been looking for, and waiting for all his life, when he dreamed of glory or when he went hunting or fishing, it was disappointment he was really hunting for, and when he found it, he knew it belonged to him. Yet perhaps when I think this I am only trying once more to escape responsibility. Perhaps, and if there is anyone who can tell me this for sure I would like to meet that person, Renzo Cipriano would have been a happy and *prosperous man who never knew the name of disappointment, if I had not betrayed him to become Contessa Rosanna.) So whether it was because of cruel fate or because of his character, or both, he stayed here and he stayed single, and Paola did the same, giving up her life to cook for him and sew for him, and be the housekeeper to disappointment, because it was all she could offer him. She could give up her friendship with me and she could give him her life, up on the Vessinaro, where they lived like two secret people who inhabit the attic of a great house and climb up by the back stairs, those one thousand stairs of penitence that lead from the bus stop to the Vessinaro, if you choose that straight but cruel path. In truth, Paola never entirely gave up her friendship with me, and we met once or twice a year in secret, and I don't believe Renzo ever found out.*

What happened then, not then but many years later, you will now read when you open my diary of 1928 (you will also understand why it ends there, in that year and on that particular day). I say many years later, and we were all twenty years older, more than that, twenty-five years older, but Renzo and Paola's life had changed as little as the pini *on the Vessinaro in that time. Twenty-five years the wind blew on them in their secret house, whether it was the good wind off the hills, the* tramontana, *or the* sirocco *from Africa which affects the mind, but they were as indifferent as the pine trees which are built to survive all winds. And at once everything changed again, as if time had stood still for twenty-five years, and then, as if a clock suddenly came back to life, it jumps forward like an old car starting.*

That's how it is with life, my dear. It sticks, often for years, and you think it will never move again. And suddenly in an instant a door blows opens and nothing is the same anymore. You will find this out as we all do.

Enough. Read, Miri dear, and forgive me if you can.

FINDING WHERE EXACTLY it was that Cipriano lived, on the Vessinaro promontory, proved to be harder than Miri could ever have imagined.

She reproached herself for not having followed Cipriano at the end of their first encounter (although as she discovered in time, this would not necessarily have resolved the problem of finding him again). That afternoon they had remained sitting on their respective benches for what seemed to Miri like an interminable period of time. Perhaps it was no more than an hour. At last the old man got to his feet, without looking round at Miri. Sometimes she still found herself calling him the old man in her head, both out of habit – Cipriano had already seemed old to her when she watched him eating alone at Prospero Velo's, before the war – and because this was confirmed by the way that in the past Serafina had always preferred to call him *il vecchio*, the old man, rather than use his name, long before he became *il demonio*. From Rosanna's journal Miri had calculated that Cipriano was 68, old enough and yet a few years younger than she had imagined. Now she watched him walk stiffly away along the level orange path towards the umbrella pines. He hadn't glanced back at her once, but she was sure he was aware of her presence. To follow him, it seemed to her at that instant, would not give the message she intended. She had not come to track him to his lair, but to wait him out. She wanted him to understand that she was in no hurry. She would always be there.

But on Miri's subsequent visits, Cipriano never reappeared. She haunted the Vessinaro for longer periods, without success. Where was he, *il vecchio*? There wasn't a living soul, amid the ghostly rental properties of the promontory, whom she could ask. Not one. No dark eyes were visible behind the laurel hedge. Not even a *prigionniera*, a prisoner, to ask.

A letter came, the second one (or was it the third?) from her father, begging for news and announcing his arrival to lend succour and, if she refused, simply to see her. To find out how she was. Miri read the letter in bewilderment. Hadn't she already written to Muswell Hill, making it plain that they could visit her only in her own good time, not now? Hadn't she written? Or only in her mind? She wrote again, trying to keep her tone gentle yet firm. No visits. Not yet.

For a week, Miri waited instead on the thousand steps down to the coast road. No one came. She had all the time in the world, it was true, but there was a mystery here. How did Cipriano get his supplies, his food and water?

One day, up on the Vessinaro, Miri discovered the answer. *Il demonio*'s deliveries came by sea. Instead of descending to the road and catching the bus, Cipriano clambered down to the rocks of Punta Vessinaro – Miri saw him from way above, on the clifftop path – and met a boatman who unloaded supplies and helped the old man carry them up to the promontory.

But where to? Which house? Miri hadn't been able to see where Cipriano and the boatman went. Serafina didn't know where exactly the demon lived. Leandro, who played *boccia* at Olimpio's every weekend, and supplied Serafina with her gossip, didn't know. Olimpio himself, when Miri asked him directly, admitted he didn't know either. How was it possible, Miri wondered aloud, that no one knew? It was strange, Olimpio's carefully-set baffled face seemed to agree. In a tight-knit, garrulous community where everybody knew their neighbours' business to the point of noticing a new pair of underclothes on the washing line, no one could tell her where the town's former mayor lived?

Couldn't – or wouldn't? Were they afraid of identifying the house in question to a Contessa with heaven knows what mayhem on her mind? Did each of them shrink from being the one who told her where to find Cipriano? They hated him; she believed that; yet at the same time they didn't want to finger him, it seemed. She didn't look like an avenger, surely, a reckless person, did she? Miri thought not. She kept her voice calm, her dress sober. Of course, she reminded herself, if they'd all heard that she had been in hospital, it was possible that for all their cordiality, the entire mountain regarded her as mad or, at best, as barely recovered. Why else, after all, had she kept away from the *paese* for so long?

Besides, what could Olimpio think Miri was up to when she asked him where to find Dr. Cipriano? It would hardly be a pleasant social call that the *Contessa* had in mind.

Olimpio's face, as impassive as any politician's, and his ponderous formality, his *sì signora Contessa* and *no signora Contessa, mi dispiace davvero*, I'm truly sorry, remained impenetrable. Was it even possible – this was her most disturbing suspicion – that Olimpio knew everything and that Andrea, the police chief, was as indiscreet as everyone else?

What if Andrea had not only let it get out that Miri had come to him demanding justice but that he, Andrea, had told the *Contessa* that she could take it herself, with his permission? For all Miri knew, that kind of thing swiftly became common knowledge in a community like this. It might be the very stuff of life in the hills – watching and waiting for the day of revenge. Or was she simply falling for a Wild West idea of Italy and its vendettas, peddled by pulp fiction and the movies?

When Miri questioned Serafina, or asked Leandro directly – Leandro who in his shyness had never spoken more than ten consecutive words to her – she received no hint of what they knew or suspected. Was there talk about herself and *il vecchio?* Miri demanded to know. No, there was no talk. What talk could there be? Serafina replied. But Miri found it impossible to tell, as with Olimpio, whether their shrugs revealed genuine ignorance or whether they were trying to protect her from the fact that they knew her every move and her every purpose, that they knew she had gone around the town seeking a prosecution of Cipriano, in vain, and that now she was planning to take the law into her own hands. Was their silence tacit approval of this, or not? Serafina and her family didn't disguise their loathing for *il vecchio*, and Olimpio's distaste was evident even through his dignified restraint.

That didn't mean they would approve of the *Contessa* Miri stooping to stalk the old boy. Or worse.

But if it did, if all their cordiality was real, and they didn't regard her as mad, if they hated *il vecchio* and were behind her all the way in whatever she did, why were they trying to hide Cipriano from her? Why wouldn't they tell her where he lived?

Non si sa. This was all Olimpio would say, shaking his head in sad puzzlement. It isn't known.

How could it not be known? Yet as Miri patrolled the deserted Vessinaro, she began to see that this might very well be the truth. The houses – there were perhaps eight or ten, all tiny, hanging on to the cliff and clustered around the knob of the promontory like snails – were shuttered, all of them apparently summer rentals. At any rate, the landward windows were shuttered. There was no way to see the windows that looked out across the Mediterranean.

And suddenly it came to her.

What if Cipriano had gradually acquired them all? What if he owned every one? He would be able to move between them – could *il vecchio* really be so paranoid? – like some wary dictator shuttling between one residence and another, pulling out a crowded key ring and deciding which soulless semi-furnished rental property to stay in tonight? Was it from her, was it only from Miri the old man was hiding, or from others too? She pictured him hatching his plans, preparing for the day if it should come (and long before the end of the war he must have known it would come) when he needed a bolthole. She saw him acquiring houses and at last retreating from the turncoat town and its rejection; the heavy-footed old man climbing up towards his promontory fortress, thinking *try and find me now*.

Yet some part of him wanted to be found. Wasn't that true of all who hid out of resentment rather than love of solitude? They couldn't resist the temptation to come out and sit on a park bench, sooner or later. Like Miri, Cipriano had climbed up to the ridge and walked along the path, the day she had found him sitting on the bench. Why? To get a different view? Why else other than to risk showing himself? To let some passer-by see him and spread the report: *il vecchio*'s still there, still alive.

It was the prey who would give the game away.

One day there came the old, familiar rustle in the laurel hedge, as Miri sat underneath the umbrella pines, opening and savouring the *pinoli* as she had done with Vittorio in the unimaginably distant days before the war. They had sat on the same spot, perching on a low concrete wall with their back against a chain-link fence. The same cypresses bulged against the fence now, planted too close, growing too large, but serving better than ever to hide one of the little rental villas from view. Directly opposite was the house with the laurel hedge. Now, at last, the eyes were visible again, between the green and yellow leaves, and the same incomplete glimpse of a face.

Except that now Miri knew who she was, *la prigionniera*. Rosanna's journal had told her.

UNTIL THE FINAL entries, the journal seemed to have been a vehicle for her mother-in-law's development of an italic hand, a skill the young Rosanna would hardly have troubled with, let alone had time for, while working in her family *biancheria*. The diary recorded social events at length, along with reports of her friends' children and their progress in the world. It chronicled the books Rosanna was reading and passed sweeping judgements on them for posterity.

Then abruptly the tone changed, and with it the quality of the script. The lordly syntax gave way to shorthand. Abbreviations and coded words could have made some of the entries hard to follow, but thanks to Rosanna's letter, Miri could see that *R* stood not for Rosanna but for Renzo Cipriano. *Vo* was the Vessinaro. *P* stood for Cipriano's sister Paola, whose death, Miri discovered, brought the journal to a close in a rush of appalled shorthand.

Al Vo ove orrore P deced.

A message from *R*, from Renzo, had begged Rosanna to come at once. At the Vessinaro she had found, to her horror, Paola *deceduta*, dead, in childbirth, it seemed, from the subsequent, final entry. So far as Miri could tell, there had been no one present other than Renzo Cipriano, when his sister died. To all appearances, Cipriano had been trying to deliver the baby himself.

Per miracolo, read the final words of the journal, seemingly written some while later, to judge by the restoration of syntax and the firmer, finer hand, *la piccola vive.*

Miraculously, the child, a girl, is alive.

THEY HAD BEEN, all three of them – Rosanna, Paola, and Cipriano himself – in their forties when this happened. Up in the hills, Miri knew, childbirth often occurred before a doctor could be fetched, and usually without a doctor being sent for at all. There would be at least one midwife, locally, and plenty of healthy babies born with or without the midwife's help; there would also be plenty of *sfortune,* unhappy accidents, in which the hand of the Almighty would have to be read. But it would be read, more often than not, without the aid of a priest or of any intruder from outside the family. Officialdom was not welcome in the hills. Cries in the night were a family matter, whether they derived from joy or pain, or even murder. If they were heard at all.

On the depopulated world of the Vessinaro, life went on. Renzo Cipriano had a child to raise.

BUT WHAT COULD Miri do with the information Rosanna had bequeathed her? Shout it through the laurel hedge?

What could she do with it in her heart? It was shocking to be confronted with a separate tragedy belonging to Cipriano's life, one that had little bearing on the role the old man had played in Miri's life. Shocking, and confusing, too. What should she feel? Disgust? Pity? Rosanna's story seemed to offer something to Miri's understanding of *il demonio*'s warped life and nature. Yet it had to be put aside, out of her mind, if she was to concentrate on her quest to bring the former police chief to justice.

At the same time it resonated, this horrible tale, with her sense that she was out of her depths here, in this barbaric *paese*, trying to trap some ancient savage beast that had gored others, and been gored, in its time. And she couldn't even find its lair! The seeming futility of her waiting game was beginning to colour everything.

There were terrible nights at the Casa Rosa when Vittorio seemed dead to her, and all her searching for a way forwards 'in his name' appeared hollow and pointless. To maintain her resolve she returned over and over, in imagination, to the victims, as they stood in line in the place called Auschwitz. To Vittorio among them. They were on no account to be forgotten, she told herself over and over. But this abstraction was failing her.

I'm dead, Vittorio said. Let me go. What are you doing? *Mamma*, let me go, and let me dwell in our happy memories, as I was. As we were together. The only thing worse than my death is having to re-live it. You keep bringing me back to the camp, to the queue, to the ante-chamber, to suffer again. Let me go.

(How was it she could she hear his voice so clearly in her head? Was this normal? Or was she close to another mental collapse?)

And there worse nights, too, when Miri woke in a rage, a fury directed at Jews, all Jews, at Jewishness itself, which had risen up and led them by the millions, two by two, into a basement to die – at such moments all she could think was that but for Jewishness he would still be here with her and the world would have, for her, a reason for being in it. All she could think as she woke to remember yet again that he was dead, and wanted to scream against the suffocating knowledge, was that Jewishness had come down on them like the gas that took away his breath, and was still, slowly, killing them both.

It was even a relief to surrender to this rage in place of the chills of regret that attended her days, the fear that she had not given him Jewishness enough for him to be able to give that word, at least, the word *Jew* and his place in it, to his role in the nightmare.

It was an aspect of the tragedy from which Miri knew she was still shying away, as she was still shying away from visiting Baldini the bookseller. As guilty as she felt about this, some part of her continued to refuse the thought that it was as a Jew, and not just as the *Contessa* Miri, or even as Miri Gottlieb, that she needed to confront Cipriano. How could she confront him on behalf of millions? Or even on behalf of the handful of victims from her own town? If there was a sense in which she could or should be speaking for *them*, Miri couldn't locate it at all. Of course they deserved a voice. And in Vittorio they had an emblem. But it was as Vittorio's mother that Miri was hunting Cipriano, not as the avenger of the Jewish people.

To do otherwise would be to pretend that she didn't know about Cipriano's vendetta; it would be to ignore the fact that Cipriano had an added reason for having persecuted her son, a personal reason that had everything to do with his life and the life of Vittorio's grandparents, and nothing to do with Jews and Jewishness. (It had also often occurred to Miri to wonder whether it wasn't purely and simply to get his revenge on a member of her family that Cipriano had embraced anti-semitism and even fascism, which allowed Cipriano to commit risk-free, bureaucratically sanctioned murder. To whatever extent this was true, it argued that the others who had been deported with and died with Vittorio, the Schmitzes and the

Baldini clan, were stage dressing to camouflage Cipriano's real and sole target, Vittorio. This was too gruesome a thought to rest on for long, but it played on Miri's conscience whenever she thought about visiting the Baldini parents, sole survivors of Cipriano's pogrom. How could she face the Baldinis if their children had been sacrificed to lend an official disguise to the police chief's vendetta against Piero's kin? It was possible to imagine that if there had been no Vittorio – no Miri, that is, and no Vittorio – Cipriano might not have bothered to deport a handful local Jews against whom he had no special grudge. Like other police chiefs, he might have looked the other way. Cipriano's nemesis was incarnate in Vittorio, not in Jews. What if the young Baldinis had in that sense been sacrificed *to* Vittorio?)

It was only as herself that she could avenge him.

But this defiant thought failed to banish a host of questions from Miri's mind, as it failed to banish the Baldinis. *Was* it as a Jew, as his mother's son, that Vittorio had been sent to his death, or as his father's son, the scion of a hated line? Only Cipriano could answer that. And the other, separate yet dimly connected question tormented her: had she sufficiently connected Vittorio to his heritage to allow him to understand – futile understanding! (or was it precious nonetheless?) – what the fatal virus of Jewishness was, that he carried in him? She and Vittorio had been a tribe of two. It had seemed more than enough, far more than most human beings were permitted. And was it now found wanting, that extraordinary, all-consuming bond?

One of the glimpses that had haunted Miri's imagination ever since the news reached her about Vittorio's deportation was of Vittorio alone among pious, observant Jews, a breed he had never even met. She had no doubt they would have treated him well; he was a fellow-deportee, towards whom kindness would surely be the order of the day. (And he looked so Jewish, so Sephardic even! – though Miri could have wished him a little less so, for once. What Jewish family would not have adopted him on sight?) But what would he have made of *them?* Would he have felt even more alien, even more alone, to be one of the doomed and yet not *of* them?

A dam was breaking, inside Miri. She couldn't help wishing, now, that she had flouted everyone and everything, even the resistance to religious observance that her father had instilled in her, and opened the door, for Vittorio, to his ancestral religion. What would it have cost her, to give him the opportunity to decide for himself whether to join the 'modern', despiritualized Jews of Vittorio's immediate Gottlieb forebears, or to rejoin the ancient tradition to which he was heir? To which she was heir too – and might she too have found an unanticipated resonance in it, even an unanticipated home?

Yet in asking herself this question it was hard for Miri to avoid a sense of disloyalty to her father. Avram hardly deserved the epithet 'despiritualized'. He was an intensely spiritual person, she believed, in whose vocabulary the words 'spirit' and 'soul' were in continuous use, and who constantly invoked God. May God strike me dead! he even said, sometimes, when claiming a surprising truth. An involuntary oath, perhaps. Yet it reached his lips, uncensored. Was it somewhat absurd – and Miri realised she had never previously ventured this critique – that Avram had rejected his religion (or rather continued in a rejection initiated by his own mother and father) while continuing to pay his respects to religion's underlying concepts?

The way Miri had always regarded it, only a fanatical materialist – surely a dreadfully incomplete kind of person – would be able to do entirely without words that acknowledged the immanent and the invisible, both in man and outside man. Such terms were surely necessary, and what they referred to was just as real and as decisive in everyday life as anything you could identify under a microscope. So of course you used the words 'soul' and 'spirit'. 'God,' too, even if like Miri's father you only used it as a gesture of humility before the totality of all things inaccessible to men, was a hard word to replace. Observant Jews wrote 'G–d', not 'God'; Miri had always known this and found it both faintly silly, as if the omission of a letter ensured true piety, and rather beautiful in its abstention from fully naming the thing that stood for what can never be fully encompassed. But Miri (and Avram would say much the same, Miri believed) still felt that the same gesture of abstention and humility could be made as truly in the heart as on the page. *More* truly in the heart, indeed, where it had to be renewed in order to be truthful, and not merely transcribed. Like Avram, she had always clung to this idea of freedom from formal, automatic worshipfulness, a freedom obliging her to summon more authentic piety, not less. And what Avram's parents had fled, Avram had told her, was not God but the archaic, anti-democratic spirit that ruled Judaic custom as it ruled so many other religions, relegating women to ancient roles from which secular life had long since emancipated them. This had driven enlightened, socially progressive Jews into the arms of atheism. (Well, she knew it wasn't as simple as that, but she had always assumed that among social progressives her immediate forebears had found a common recognition of the reactionary aspects of church and temple, and that this recognition had led inexorably to an idea of religious belief itself, particularly monotheism with its trust in an all-wise heavenly father, as a brake on social revolution.) Yet the very virulence towards religion that Miri had encountered in some of her parents' friends – didn't it bespeak the deep roots of spiritual devotion among her people and the need for something no less consuming to replace it?

Her people. Could she call them that? Her co-religionists hardly fitted, and 'my former co-religionists' was a ludicrous mouthful. Her fellow-Jews, yes. But her people?

The question, *how Jewish are you?* had simply never come up for Miri. It had never been implied, let alone asked, inside or outside her family, where the question could not have arisen. How *observant* are you? *That* was a question. Not very, was the answer, or more candidly, not at all. But neither answer addressed your Jewishness, in the non-observant world in which Miri lived. In that world, Jewishness was a blood tie, and could no more be denied than your blood type. In answer to *how Jewish are you?* you couldn't answer, "Moderately" or "Not very" any more than you could be "moderately" or "not very" blood type A positive.

So why was the issue now a pressing one, drumming in Miri's head. *How Jewish are you?*

She knew the answer. It was, "That's not a question."

But it was.

It would have been a question, Miri knew, to an observant Jew, one who might have looked at her and thought, precisely, *not very Jewish.* Or that's what Miri imagined an observant Jew thinking of her and her family. With reason, too, in her mind. She could see the force of the argument that Jews who abandoned their religion were abandoning not only the faith of their forefathers but the very thing – their faith, far more than their blood – that had enabled them to survive as a community. If theirs was simply a community of blood, *Jewish by descent*, what did it mean? We were all Africans by descent; *homo sapiens* and *erectus* by descent; tree-shrews (or arboreal creatures resembling tree-shrews) by descent. So what?

This was where, from time to time, Miri had imagined an observant Jew to stand, in relation to herself. The few observant Jews she had met had not picked an argument with her, nor she with them. It was easy, in twentieth century England, to be a Jew raised in and belonging to intellectual, left-wing metropolitan circles and never even meet an observant Jew. Miri had an idea, though, of what her father would say in answer. We, the no longer observant Jews, he would say, are proud of our heritage, proud of you, our observant brothers and sisters, and proud of our own free-thinking intellectual kin, who have taken the rebarbative, combative element in Jewish tradition to its logical extreme and accepted what so many non-Jews have also, no less independently, and departing no less radically from their own forebears, accepted, namely that there is no God.

(Fine, said the observant Jew in Miri's head. But don't call yourselves Jews, please.)

God. There was a concept to be conjured with, after the death camps. Or rather G–d: that was the problematic concept. It was G–d who was the all-knowing Father on whom ultimate responsibility fell. The 'God' to whom Avram referred was simply a deficit in human knowledge, an insufficiency in our understanding of the world. God, that symbol of our ignorance, was still there, as gnomic, as apparently cruel, as ever. But G–d? What happened to *him*?

It wasn't so hard, Miri imagined, for non-observant Jews, stoical students of history, to accept the reality of the death camps. The camps were simply the latest, and debatably the most shocking, in the long tradition of human savagery. But for believers in G–d? If there was such a thing as divine justice, never mind divine love, what had the Jews, His chosen people, done to deserve this? Was it a mark of exceptional favour, turning half the Jews on earth into a crucified sacrifice? No – no, that was completely impossible, as a way of understanding it. Each murdered Jew a Jesus? Hardly, since Christ's claim to be the Messiah, fraudulent in Jewish eyes, had contributed to his crucifixion in the first place. Only fanatical anti-semites could see the death camps as the site of the ultimate Christian revenge, putting every available Jew on the cross for which, in the most extreme Christian view, every Jew remained reponsible. But *where*, *where* was G–d if he was witnessing this incomparably systematic carnage?

And would observant and non-observant Jews now be divided by this question, as never before? Ironically, they were bound together as a people, as never before, regardless of religious preference. They had been singled out and murdered for their ties of blood, not belief.

That was the fact of it. And that fact meant one thing: they were her people. To think otherwise would be to remove the last vestiges of meaning from Vittorio's suffering and death.

Yet even as she thought this a shudder went through Miri. Under what compulsion did that thought lie? Was she not allowing the Nazis to re-define her relationship to her ancestral past, to a heritage which she should be free to embrace – if freedom meant anything – as fully or as little as she chose, as *she* chose, not as a pack of insane butchers directed, driving her back into the fold.

But *did* freedom mean anything now, after such atrocities? To imagine that you could still be 'free', free to embrace or reject your heritage, free to determine your own affiliations as if mass murder had never occurred – was that a vicious, selfish cynicism, or was the price of freedom, now as ever, the risk of being seen as insufficiently recognisant of the past?

Avram was a scientist. Life, for him, was about throwing off unthinking shackles and looking at the world around you with your own eyes, not those of the past. But what was Miri? Who was she? She was a Gottlieb – but since that couldn't mean she had to love

God, or even G–d, simply to live up to the meaning of the syllables, it meant nothing. So what was she? She had been, before anything else in the world, a mother. (And then a nurse; yet somehow those two brief busy years had become inseparable in her mind from the two that followed, as a patient. Throughout, she had been a mother in exile, in abeyance, waiting for news, at first, and then pretending that it hadn't arrived.) As a mother, she was not 'free' in any sense that she could presently imagine. The death camps were something she would never be free of, nor even desire to be free of. How could she even imagine such a condition?

What did that mean, then, for her Jewishness? It made it harder to banish regret that she had failed to give Vittorio a faith to carry into his final days and hours, and to share with those who were his kin in one inescapable sense: they were doomed alongside him. She too, at one remove, was stricken by the same doom, and wasn't it possible that faith would even now be giving her some comfort and enable her to feel more united to her people in their suffering than she currently did? – she who couldn't even face the Baldinis, her fellow-sufferers, for fear of being recruited to a tribal grief? Wouldn't it make life more bearable? Should she seek out a synagogue, now, now even though it was too late to do it with Vittorio, and too late to do it for him, since every visit would only remind her how very much too late it was?

But something else, resisting this as a counsel of despair, stirred inside Miri. She hardly dared call it hope; yet it was the obstinate belief that she could find peace in something other than a choice between forms of mourning, more and less pious; that she could do something in Vittorio's name that would look forwards, not back. To suppose that the road to this led through the Vessinaro seemed perilous in the extreme. Wasn't vengeance the very essence of looking back? Wasn't that precisely what had brought Cipriano to his private hell, and killed Vittorio? Yet that obstinate strand of hope told her that it was precisely here, at the Vessinaro, that she had to begin.

THESE DAYS DOTTORE Cipriano was in the habit of spending the daylight hours in his dressing-gown.

His father, Giuseppe, would have been shocked, Cipriano reflected with sour amusement, to think that a son of his might spend the entire day in a dressing-gown. No matter how old or ill a man was, one did not do such a thing voluntarily. Cipriano had even, on occasion, descended in his robe to meet Ataulfo the boatman, on Punta Vessinaro, in order to bring up a month's supplies of groceries and other living necessities. A long tedious climb, heavily weighed down. But it was worth it, to render futile the crazy *Contessa's* siege. Would she try to keep it up forever? Surely not. Everyone knew she was crazy, and would one day be put away again, in a hospital. All the same, why couldn't they have kept her in England?

Poor stupid woman – avoiding her, he had even, on occasion, slipped out (there were many back ways, known to one who had spent childhood years up on the promontory) and paid a discreet visit to the town in search of a missing item – sometimes it was simply a newspaper – which he purchased in his usual manner, without looking right or left, and without seeking or exchanging greetings, indeed without acknowledging any salutations that came his way, and making himself as unobtrusive as he could.

It would not do as a long-term strategy, however. He could foresee how much attention it would draw if the mad *Contessa* were to discover his secret routes and follow him around in the town, undoing all the work he had done to achieve invisibility. The prospect alone made him Miri's prisoner, and could not be tolerated.

One morning around eleven o'clock, he went to his bathroom, shaved meticulously, put on a white shirt and a tie and the suit he had often worn as the town's mayor, and examined himself in the mirror with the mechanical, resigned attentiveness of a man going to the gallows.

Did he toy for a moment with the thought of putting on his medals, one or two stupid, boastful civic medals that he had always secretly despised, and his smaller, dustier medals from the Great War that also reminded him of sadness and loss rather than vanished glory? Ah, why bother, Cipriano must have thought. For whom?

To impress whom? Hadn't the country already gone to the dogs?

But I fancy that another possibility will have entered his mind – I who intrude here once more, if I may, because although I scarcely knew Renzo Cipriano himself (who, indeed, could put their hand on their heart and say they knew him?), I knew his father, Giuseppe, that stern old warrior who wore his medals every day of his life. Geography brought me together with old Giuseppe, who had sailed with Garibaldi in '62 for Palermo, in my native land of Sicily, where I was born beneath Mount Etna in the city of Catania, and where Giuseppe marched with Garibaldi's famous red-shirted Thousand and claimed the kingdom of Sicily. I knew the places where Giuseppe had walked and fought, and it made us fast friends. And I can picture Renzo, his son, on the morning I'm describing, setting aside his own badges of office and the medals he had won in the Austrian campaign in 1915, and thinking for a moment about putting on a more ancient set, the medals his father had won in the war of liberation. They represented, after all, everything he had tried to stand for in his life, everything Italian, everything that had been betrayed.

Old Giuseppe had been the son of a family of *contadini* from the hills beyond the Vessinaro. Tall and strong, he had marched off to join Garibaldi, and returned to our *paese* a hero, honoured wherever he went, but alas no longer tall and strong. A permanently damaged leg and the loss of his right arm had made him the town's icon, a living emblem of the blood spilt in the name of freedom. For the rest of his life he wore his medals and was unfailingly saluted by the townspeople, more and more lazily, of course, fondly, humorously even, as the years went by, and in the end even ironically. After all, wasn't it time, forty years later, to get up one day and put those medals and their weather-worn ribbons aside instead of wearing them at the street corner and in the café and on the esplanade, where old Giuseppe sat and dozed, sometimes indistinguishable from the rogues and beggars who used the esplanade as an ambush?

After all, Giuseppe had a living legacy, his son, *il dottore*, who had so splendidly made good. From dirt-poor Vessinaro farmer to doctor and mayor in two generations – wasn't Dr. Renzo Cipriano himself the old man's true medal and testimony to what paternal heroism had inspired in the boy? (And no wonder it was property up on the Vessinaro promontory that Cipriano gradually, secretly bought up! – land from which he could look up the coast and see the poor, rocky, terraced hillside acres his grandfather had farmed – he who now *owned* the Vessinaro – all of it.)

Yes, Renzo had done his father honour. In turn, he had been fortunate to be raised, Renzo had long believed, in an atmosphere of pride – of fully justified pride – and self-discipline, and a faith in national destiny which had been forged in sacrificial deeds, not just in the empty rhetoric of politicians and local time-servers who followed the game by naming their piazzas and streets after Cavour, Mazzini, and Garibaldi. As a young man Cipriano had often wanted to tear down these beloved names, parroted so obediently on every street corner, and replace them with more ancient revolutionary names, simply to call a halt to the empty piety. Did they think it evoked the true spirit of liberation, to turn every town in Italy into a saluting echo of every other town? It evoked enslavement, not freedom. No town dared keep whatever old names their streets and squares had once proclaimed, names not in themselves worth keeping – unless they were local. Yet surely, in place of Cavour and Mazzini, which were deserving names but ones now more than sufficiently memorialized, a town should celebrate its local heroes, real people rather than history-book effigies? People like his father, indeed.

But by the time Cipriano himself was in a position to act on his youthful impulses and, as mayor, commemorate men and women from the *paese* in place of national heroes, Renzo Cipriano – as so often happens – had different aims in life. He was no longer the Renzo who had wanted to see a Via Giuseppe Cipriano celebrating his father's sacrifice. When had he changed? He wasn't sure himself. His sense of a personal mission, of a destiny that would fuse his life with his country's glory, had been bred into him by his father, and it survived the first, deepest blow, that of the loss of Rosanna. It was true that his image of domestic happiness had never overcome this loss; ten years later, on the Trentino front in the Great War, and during the terrible, humiliating retreat after Caporetto, he had only been able to think of her. But his will to thrive – to thrive and show her the poor choice she had made – had survived her defection and his unceasing grief. When was it, then, that he had turned into a different man? His service as a doctor on the Austrian front had hardened and darkened his already martial spirit, and robbed him of some of his confidence in national endeavour. But it had been after the war, living at home and witnessing, as his mother and sister had, the crumbling of his father's will as the old man grew bitter and resentful of his wasted life – it was then that Cipriano had begun to change. His father lashed out unceasingly at his family, in the way that angry and frightened old people will, especially if they have been pampered and revered and given space in which to become a tyrant. And how they had revered Giuseppe! Giuseppe the hero, the Garibaldino! Yet what undid Renzo Cipriano, suffering his father's tantrums, was not that Giuseppe was now angry and afraid of dying – young Renzo had seen plenty of fear in the Alps, and at Caporetto – or that his father now looked back with indifference and even resentment at the very history, his personal history, that had sustained the family and inspired them, or even that he now proved to lack the courage to face old age and death without taking it out on those around him. No, what undermined the very person that Renzo had thought he himself was, beneath the stern, imposing *dottore* Cipriano exterior, or more exactly what undermined the strength that fed this persona, was the growing realisation that it had *not* been in pride and self-discipline that he was raised. That had been an illusion created by his father and maintained by Renzo's mother and sister, and carried into the world like a banner by Renzo himself. The truth was that he had been raised in bitterness. What lay beneath his father's unyielding exterior, as he refused all help, despite his disabilities, in managing his daily life, was not the fierce substance Renzo had believed it to be, a sense of ineffable worth tested in the fire of the struggle for his country's freedom. No, despair lay behind the ferocious military bearing. Was *that* all it came to, the legacy of suffering that Renzo and Paola had bowed to and believed in and carried proudly into the schoolyard, setting them apart from their peers, those who chanted and sang the empty slogans but had given nothing to liberty? Was it all simply dust, inside the painted effigy? Rage and resentment fermenting away behind the mask of proud severity? In his mother's eyes, Renzo now believed he saw the truth. The great Giuseppe Cipriano was a hollow person. They had lived for a puppet-show.

It had never galled Renzo, the thought that the town had elected him mayor as a tribute to his father, the *paese's* Garibaldino hero. Renzo had been proud of it, for as long as he had been able to feel proud of his father. Yet in the end the truth poisoned everything.

No one knew what that was like, to find you had been nourished and sustained by a lie. Only Paola, his sister, knew, Paola who had shared his dedication to the myth of his father (in his fury, Renzo had even allowed himself to wonder whether Giuseppe had really been wounded while storming the barricades at Messina, as he claimed, or was it perhaps in some inglorious explosion behind the lines, a munitions dump erupting, set alight by a stray spark?). Like their mother, Paola had given her life to tending the lifelong invalid – a man who now railed at his family as lazy ingrates who knew nothing of sacrifice. Was this the fruit of true heroism? Only Paola had understood the shame Cipriano felt. The disgrace didn't lie in his father's failings; it lay in Renzo Cipriano himself, for having fallen so completely for the illusion his father had fostered, that they, the Ciprianos, were better than the rest. They were no better. He had known that for a long time.

So no, no medals today. Just a clean shirt and a little dignity of bearing – there was enough of his father in him (at any rate of the Giuseppe of Renzo's youth) to insist on this. That would suffice.

Tie straight, shoulders straight.

A last glance in the mirror. Then he went to his front door, opened it and, seeing Miri seated dispiritedly on the low wall beside the orange path, called to her.

"*Venga, signora.*"

Come. Cipriano turned and went in, leaving his front door open.

WHEN THE SOUND came of bolts being drawn back, and the heavy door opened, and Cipriano appeared, Miri didn't react. Her eyes saw him, her mind registered the fact that he was there, incredibly, at last, but her body refused the message altogether. It was only after the old man had turned and walked back into the house, leaving the door open behind him, that Miri realized she had simply remained sitting crouched on the little wall beside the sandy path, shoulders bowed, eyes dull. She hadn't even drawn herself up at the sight of him.

And all she felt, as her legs carried her mechanically down the steep path towards the doorway, was that she wasn't ready, that she wasn't even present, that this was happening at the wrong time.

Praying to come to her senses and somehow master the moment – at least be equal to it, after all the waiting – she followed a short, dark, corridor and emerged, dazzled, into a wide sitting room. Sea and sky filled the windows and the room with light. Bare walls, and furnishings almost military in their simplicity. She was reminded for a moment of Andrea's office. A desk and chair; a smallish rough-hewn table with two chairs; a small wicker settee. That was all. Was that because he lived elsewhere some of the time, in the other houses? Or did he relish these spartan surroundings?

With a balcony behind him, Cipriano stood against French windows, where he could study her in the blaze of light off the sea. Miri, squinting against it, could hardly make out Cipriano's features. But she could hear his heavy, asthmatic breathing. Even the short walk to his front door and back, Miri noted, troubled his lungs. Perhaps his heart too.

The air itself seemed to be humming.

Si siede. Cipriano was pointing to the settee.

Miri moved to the settee and sat down, pulling herself erect. She was afraid she might be about to faint.

Che cosa vuole di me? What do you want from me?

Miri was staring at him so hard she barely heard the words. This was the moment, in imagination, where speech always failed her. You are a criminal – could she say that? – a murderer! Even in daydreams the words had always sounded melodramatic and absurd. And then what? Could she demand that he surrender to justice, to a justice that didn't even want him?

What she wanted, what she had wanted all along, was to *see* him. To look into his eyes and see him, and have him see into her soul, to understand what he had done. He would see Vittorio there.

But now she couldn't see his eyes. Even as she grew slowly more accustomed to the flooding light, she could barely make out his features. It made her feel, as no doubt the demon intended, as if she were the one under interrogation. As if she were the criminal. In the bluish shadow, the old man's skin itself looked bluish, and the heavy bags under his eyes had a purplish hue.

She realized that he was waiting for an answer. *What do you want from me?*

Just this, she wanted to say. This, here, now. But the words wouldn't come.

She saw movement in his arm, his shoulder, and then he was fumbling at his jacket pocket with a trembling hand. He brought out a pack of cigarettes, extracted one with difficulty, and put it in his mouth.

Miri felt her head give a faint shake of disbelief, and was shocked to find herself about to say, *You shouldn't smoke.*

She watched him light the cigarette, his hand shaking almost too much to do it, and his fingertips almost white, swollen-looking in the light.

"I do what I like," Cipriano said softly.

Had she said aloud that he shouldn't smoke? Miri felt so faint and so estranged from herself that it was possible she'd spoken aloud. Or had he seen it in her face?

Abruptly a wave of emotion swept over her, reassuring in its clarity and intensity. But it was the wrong emotion altogether, a belated response to his question, *What do you want from me?*

She wanted comfort. It was shocking, absurd, a feeling that should disgust her. But she could only sit there, enduring it, recognizing its awful power. She wanted comfort from the demon. An embrace, even. With all her soul she wanted him to console her, because he was the only one who could.

Cipriano had said something, in the silence. What was it? *E allora?* Well, then?

Trying to distract herself, Miri returned to her old script, the one that belonged to this encounter. Instead of answering, she introduced herself.

He shook off her words in a pall of smoke. "I know who you are, signora. If you don't leave me alone I will call the police."

"Please call them," she heard herself say. This she could manage, it was like playing tennis with Vittorio when he was little. It only needed a part of her mind. Was Cipriano, too, simply going through the motions? Was his mind elsewhere? She still couldn't see his eyes. The voice was rasping, low. She saw him suppress a cough, before continuing.

"You can't harass a person like this. It's against the law.'

"I'm doing nothing to you, signor Cipriano. I've been coming to the Vessinaro for 20 years. I shall go on coming here."

"No, you can't do it. I shall take out a complaint against you."

"I can do what I like in my *paese*, signor Cipriano. But if you wish to talk about it to Andrea, please do so. He is a friend of mine."

The words failed to convince her. They were the right words, the words she'd planned to say, bouncing the ball back to him, returning serve. But she seemed to be sitting next to herself, watching herself speak, and she was afraid that this sensation might turn into panic unless she could control it.

She focused on Cipriano's shaking, swollen fingers. She should be counting symptoms, perhaps, while she had him in her sights. But wasn't there anything better she could do? (Why didn't I attack him? She thought afterwards. Why didn't I simply rush him, force him back out of the French doors, out onto the balcony and over the edge? Why did it never even enter my mind to seize the opportunity while I had it?)

Abruptly she realized where the humming sound came from. Outside the French windows, behind Cipriano, there were wistaria vines, full of blossom – she hadn't even noticed them, so intently had her gaze been directed at the demon's face – and the vines were swarming with bees, the ones she'd seen soaring up, on blowy days, over the promontory.

"Andrea is a child," the old man was saying, more firmly now. "A boy. I hired him. I put him there, in that office."

When would this sparring stop? Would it go on all day? But what was the real business, here, between them? What was she supposed to say? Perhaps nothing, Miri thought. Perhaps my role is simply to be here, as it was outside his house, to sit here like a statue, so that he will always see me here, in his mind, as I am now; so that every time he comes into this room he will avoid glancing at the settee, in case I am on it. And slowly, as he lets me into his life because he is afraid of the ghost of me outside his house, and now inside, in his sitting room, he will let me in closer and closer until my spirit finds him in his bed, all night and all day, asphyxiating him.

He was still speaking. "You think *I* don't have friends, more powerful than Andrea?"

The panic was beginning to recede. There was nothing she had to do or say. She was here, inside. How would he ever get her out? Was he even strong enough to force her to the door?

"And you speak of 'your' *paese*, signora. You seem to forget that your husband formally surrendered his title. This surrender extends to you, whether or not you want it. And whether or not the *contadini* want it. It's too late to ask for it back. Those days have gone."

She would leave in her own time. Perhaps she would ask to see the balcony first, and admire the wistaria.

"I ask you again. What do you want of me?"

"I want my son," Miri heard herself say, without thinking.

Studying her, Cipriano shook his head.

Yes, Miri thought. He pities me. The mad *Contessa* wants her son. This is the madwoman speaking.

At last, Cipriano seemed to realize he was spilling ash on the tiled floor. The cigarette was almost burned out. For the first time, he moved away from the windows, and walked stiffly to the desk to grind the remainder of the cigarette into an ashtray.

When he turned, Miri was shocked to see how blue his skin was. It had not been an effect of shadow, then, but of disease.

"What is it you want?" he said again, impatient now. "What do you hope to get?"

"I wanted to meet you."

How long has he got? Miri wondered. The nurse in her wanted to check his pulse, and she had to restrain a smile at the thought. Yes, perhaps she should start laughing – that would really scare him.

"Now you have met me. Now go, please, and don't come back."

"I've met you, signor Cipriano, but I don't know you yet. That's what I want. I want to know you."

No, this was the wrong tack. Now she was playing his game, making it easy for him. She could almost hear, before he spoke, the ponderous contempt that would fill his voice.

"You will never know me. That I can tell you. You could be here every day and you would never know me."

"What's your niece called?"

She too had barbs. Why should she endure his contempt? In her mind, she summoned Rosanna to her aid.

"I have no niece."

"Your daughter, then. Is she your daughter, signor Cipriano?"

"You will leave now, please."

Now she allowed herself a smile, right in his face. Yes – why had she allowed herself to be bullied by his patronizing words, by his sarcastic tone? *She* was not the prey here.

She watched him walk around his desk, and sit in the chair, carefully. Looking across the desk at her as though she were a petitioner. Miri held his gaze.

"I ask you to leave," he repeated.

"Why did you invite me in?"

"To explain to you clearly that I will not tolerate what you are doing. I have given you your warning. Now I ask you to leave."

"You will have to tolerate it, Signor Cipriano, for the rest of your life."

"No."

"Yes. You'll see."

"No, signora. This will not happen."

Now she understood why he had sat behind the desk. It was all choreographed. In his daydreams as in hers. He was fumbling audibly, his hands letting him down, at a drawer. How smoothly it must have gone in imagination. Now he had the drawer open and his hand came up, holding a service revolver.

"You see. I have this."

"If you want to kill yourself, please go ahead."

"It's not myself I will kill."

"If you want to kill me, you can."

Instead of finding the gun alarming, she felt as if it enabled her to catch up with the present. A large, heavy old gun. Pointed at her now. Would it really fire? Could it put an end to everything? Exhilaration was running through her, and Miri was afraid of what it might do. She told herself to stay quiet, but the words were tumbling from her now, directing her.

"You can try," Miri said. "Why don't you shoot me now, signor Cipriano? Then you can put an end to the suffering you began four years ago."

He was staring at her. The madwoman, said his gaze. The madwoman *wants* me to kill her. So that then I will be punished at last. It's what she wants.

"You don't understand, do you?" Miri said. "You *can't* kill me. You can put a bullet in me, but you can't kill me, because you already did that four years ago, when you sent my son to Auschwitz."

"Not to Auschwitz. That was not my doing."

"Of course it was, signor Cipriano. You sent him to Fossoli di Carpi. You knew where they went next."

"No."

There was a part of her that, through all this, calmly studied Cipriano. His skin. His hands. It was the nurse in her. Surely it was the nurse in her – and yet as they duelled, she and Cipriano, it was sometimes as if it was her father she was gazing at, as if she couldn't avoid looking at the elderly, ailing man in front of her through the eyes of a daughter.

And wasn't there a daughter in the house, somewhere, listening, watching even, from the balcony, between the wistaria vines, or behind Miri, perhaps, in the archway, in the dark corridor?

"Tell me about the girl, signor Cipriano. What's her name?"

In the silence – was it her imagination? – Miri thought she could hear someone breathing, behind her. Cipriano's gaze was still on her, unflinching. The gun was pointed at her.

"Did you raise her on your own?"

Now the silence lasted it seemed forever, until Cipriano laid the revolver down on the desk.

"What do you want from me?" he said again, and this time the anger was gone from his voice.

Miri had not meant to say it; the thought had never occurred to her until she spoke it.

"I want you to come with me to Auschwitz," she said.

A sound came from Cipriano, and for a moment Miri thought it was laughter. Then his face buckled, and she saw that it was another cough withheld, a stronger one. She watched him reach into his pocket, still fighting the cough, for a handkerchief.

Before he could bring it to his lips, there was pinkish liquid running down his chin. Cipriano dabbed quickly at it, but she had seen the colour. Blood in the sputum. The handkerchief was there, in his hand, but the coughing fit was upon him, and Miri saw him fall forward onto his desk with the violence of it.

As she rose to hurry over to him, to the desk, she felt someone fly at her – before the sound or sight of the girl, she was thrown to the floor and blows were raining on her head.

"Giacomina!" came a hoarse cry from the desk, between gasps for breath. "Giacomina! No!"

EVERY TIME MIRI replayed the scene it was the immense, astonishing emptiness outside the windows that came back to her, the way the house, perched on the cliff face, showed nothing to the southward gazing eye, nothing aside from sea and sky, framed by wistaria vines. From the balcony itself, you'd look down at live green scrub and straw-coloured dead scrub and grey volcanic cliff and, in the waves below, the Punta Vessinaro, outstretched fingers of volcanic rock. They would be dotted black with sea urchins, vicious little migrants, sheltering in the pitted surface of the stone where bubbles in the molten flow of magma had popped and left them bowl-shaped homes.

But inside Cipriano's sitting room, so vivid now to Miri, there was only the surging light, the distant sound of the waves far below and the nearer sound of the bees. Only a blank blue view, as if she and Cipriano were meeting at the farthest fortress at the edge of the world.

She had bearded the demon. She had met Cipriano at last. But the chief impression Miri carried away of their meeting was its unreality. He had brandished a gun. But that was all theatre. Their words had all been theatre. The only reality she was left with was of his illness. It wasn't hard to diagnose – the stertorous breathing, the swollen fingertips, the cyanosis – the blueness of the skin – all bespoke advanced emphysema.

Miri had known an emphysema sufferer in London, an outpatient at the Middlesex, but he'd been at least ten years older than Cipriano. It was a story with a grim ending: the man had jumped under a train at Colchester railway station, out of dread, Miri had assumed, of a terminal asthmatic attack. But Ward Sister had seemed dubious about this. One thing you know about your disease if you have emphysema, she told Miri, is that it has a saving grace. People who suffer from it usually die in their sleep.

At night in the Casa Rosa, Miri saw Cipriano's baggy face staring at her across the desk. There was no cure for emphysema, as he doubtless knew. It was irreversible. How long did he have? She had wanted to take Cipriano's pulse – and then when he had his coughing fit, she couldn't help jumping forwards, only to be intercepted by a small, ferocious, dark-eyed person seizing her legs and bundling her to the ground. *Giacomina!* Between racking coughs, Cipriano had still somehow managed to call out to her. The child – the girl – had rained punches on Miri until Miri had begun to protect herself, and had finally thrown Giacomina off her and risen to her feet. Giacomina had run to Cipriano, who was still coughing and gasping, and hugged him, cradling his head. The child: small and stocky, with a child's wide-eyed, stupefied face. But she wasn't a child at all, if she was the one whose birth Rosanna had chronicled. *Per miracolo*, the child is alive. By a miracle. She looked like a young teenager, fourteen perhaps at most. Defending Cipriano…

The bruises the girl had left on Miri's face were enough to warrant her slipping upstairs in the Casa Rosa, avoiding Pina and Serafina and calling out that she would forgo supper, that she wasn't well and would go straight to bed.

Miri had opened the door to Rosanna's rooms with infinite care, so as to make no sound that would reach Serafina's quarters, and left it open while she reread the passage in Rosanna's diary.

Paola Cipriano's child would be 20 now.

Miri slept little that night, her altercations with the demon more vivid now in retrospect, more real than they had been at the time. She hadn't planned to suggest to Cipriano that they visit Auschwitz – what had possessed her? – it was a grotesque idea. Even to imagine travelling with Cipriano was impossible, never mind violating with his presence a journey she had supposed she might make, one day, with Vittorio, and for Vittorio. And yet it resonated with her, the moment she said it. Cipriano should make the journey. He should see the fruits of his work. Miri had no idea whether this was feasible, or even where Auschwitz was exactly. She had found the place on an old map that said Upper Silesia. But where was Upper Silesia now? Was it Poland, and did Poland still exist? Whose armies controlled it? Miri had no idea. As for the camp, how would one get there? And would there be a stick or a stone still standing, or had it already been obliterated from the earth, in shame, torn down and ploughed under and planted and ploughed over? Surely it could not have been allowed to endure, as a place? No geography could contain or tolerate it – the name would blacken all maps. Auschwitz: the word belonged only to the acts committed there. How could they have a local habitation? Auschwitz was the North Pole, a place you might reach without knowing you were standing on it, a place that was only a name, where all compasses went haywire. But one could always set out for it – that much was clear in Miri's mind.

She slipped out of the Casa Rosa early, climbing in the first, thrilling light, uphill through terraced vineyards and orchards, feeling intensely, inescapably alive in the keen smells of the hillside. Tiredness found her soon enough, after her sleepless night, and she dozed on the little wall beside the Vessinaro path, her back against the chain-link fence, her face in the sprigs of cypress that poked through the fence.

Now, though she knocked at Cipriano's door, and called out to him and to Giacomina, no answer came, no sign of life.

Sometimes, as the hours went by on the silent, soughing promontory where the wind would come and shake the umbrella pines, shake them hard before discovering their indifference and going away again, Miri thought about the fire. It had come to her aid, this memory, on many an occasion, during an arduous shift at the Middlesex, or at Hemel Hempstead when one of the nurses was pestering her for a response.

The wall of fire was already eating its way down the hillside opposite the Casa Rosa when Pina's cries had alerted Miri, in the middle of the day. Afraid of communicating to him her own alarm, Miri gave Vittorio, who was less than a year old, to Serafina, and went up to the roof to look out over the neighbouring hills. The sight was astonishing, lurid and quite unforgettable. Beautiful, too, though utterly terrifying. Vittorio had often asked her to describe it – it formed part of one of his favourite stories. What looked like a twenty-foot high band of flame, half a mile wide, was munching its way steadily down the mountainside directly facing the Casa Rosa, with a sound like herd upon herd of elephant stampeding through a jungle and sending trees and bushes crashing to the ground. Behind the flame, where the smoke allowed glimpses of it, a purple and grey moonscape was also descending the mountain in the wake of the fire. This is what you'll look like shortly, it said. I am death and this is my colour. Watch me eat the colours of day and vent them into the air as smoke. I am the destroyer, and I only halt for my watery cousin, the sea. "Shall we pack? *Signora! Signora Contessa!* Shall we pack?" Pina's cries came from below, from the garden.

Miri gazed across at the fire. She would not let it come. It could see her, and she was sending it back.

And then, as breathless inhabitants watched in neighbouring houses, that was exactly what had happened. The fire trembled and paused, all along its half-mile front, while disappointed, hissing, thinning plumes of smoke hesitated like cavalry awaiting further orders. Then it growled – the fire growled audibly, like a beast, and afterwards it was what everyone on the mountain remembered: that growl, like a creature cowed before the *Contessa* Miri's will. Leandro had described, in the following weeks and years, to a perfectly serious and respectful audience at Olimpio's, how he and Serafina and Pina and even the little *Contessino* too, gazing up, had seen the Contessa Miri standing on the roof, glaring at the fire as if it were a disobedient dog. She hadn't spoken. She didn't have to. The power – *il potere* – had been in her eyes, Leandro declared. The fire had growled and started back up the hillside, amid grudging, furious sparks as it devoured the poor, burned seconds left by its initial *Blitzkrieg*.

Miri had willed it not to consume the Casa Rosa, that much was true, and it had not done so. Perhaps, Miri had thought at the time, she did have supernatural powers. It turned back. The wind had shifted, of course; that was why. But shifted at her command. Keep away from my child, she had said in her mind, to the shouting all-devouring wall of flame. Get back.

Rain now swept the Vessinaro, forcing Miri to shelter under the umbrella pines. A chilly breeze accompanied the rain, threading its way between the little shuttered houses. Would Cipriano ever emerge for her again? He would have to, Miri knew. Hour after hour of waiting in the melancholy grey light of the promontory was beginning to numb her spirits. But this was the test, Miri knew. If it was only the beginning, she would endure it. He knew she was there, that was what mattered.

One day the fog had come down, and as she climbed the narrow steps that hugged the walls above San Sebastiano, she found herself ascending into the mists. On the Vessinaro, she could see nothing, no glimpse of the sea. She could barely see the houses, only the path at her feet, and the laurel or cypress hedge that identified each property. The silence of the Vessinaro was eerie now. Could Cipriano and Giacomina have slipped past her in the fog? What if they'd left altogether, one night, and she was now stalking an empty cluster of houses? In the mornings, at the Casa Rosa, glimpsing the wet trees and the grey light at the window, she could feel a despairing torpor overcome her. Did she have the strength for another day on the dark, discouraging promontory?

And then the letter came.

At first sight, when Leandro deposited it on the kitchen table, the missive had such an official air, with the glistening dark letterpress on its cream-coloured envelope, that Miri's heart missed a beat, thinking it must be from some government source, or from the *guardia civile*, roused by Cipriano's protests. It would tell her to cease and desist, to keep away from a retired civil servant full of years and dignity and long service to his country, an invalid who was living in quiet seclusion and doing nobody any harm. To her alarm, she realized that what she was feeling, as she opened the envelope, was relief. She could stop going to the Vessinaro now – Vittorio was nowhere in her head, he was asleep and she would tell him later – because she would have no choice. This was a formal warning, the letter would say. *Contessa* or no *Contessa*, she had no right to –

But the letter was from a Milanese law firm. They had been contacted by Avram Gottlieb, the lawyer wrote, in connection with the matter of Dr. Lorenzo Cipriano, a former police chief whose prosecution the *famiglia* Gottlieb were now seeking, on the grounds of the unlawful deportation of Dr. Gottlieb's grandson, Vittorio…

Miri read on, through tears, and over Serafina's anxious questioning. *Every reason to believe…successful prosecution…*

Reading aloud now over Miri's shoulder, Serafina was crying too, and Pina and Leandro joined her at the table, embracing Miri, which made her cry all the harder as she struggled to read the rest of the letter.

It was Vittorio's status as a *mezzo-ebreo*, a half-Jew, a fact of which the former *commandante di polizia*, Dr. Cipriano, had undoubtedly been aware, that would form the basis for a charge of wilfully and inhumanely exceeding orders, and would pave the way for a wider test of the legality of the orders themselves and of obedience to orders as a defence against a murder charge. Miri read this section over and over again. It seemed too good to be true. It was time, the lawyer said, to find out what the law was made of in Italy. No civilized person should tolerate the proposition that criminality can be sanctioned by law, or that tyranny imposes a higher duty than morality.

It was a long letter, written as though the author, one Maestro Signorelli, hoped that one day it would find its way into print, or at least into a court record. But who was Signorelli? Was he one man, out of step, a Quixote tilting at universal indifference, or did his view carry some weight? Could a prosecution really be mounted? Clearly, he was going to try – and this changed everything.

Up on the Vessinaro that day, Miri read and reread the letter, wanting to speak it aloud like a town crier, to hire someone with a bullhorn to declare it over and over, all around the Vessinaro until the crier lost his voice, anything to make sure Cipriano heard it and understood that his stonewalling days were over. She almost wanted to ball up the letter and fling it over the laurel hedge, except that it might only rot there in the dripping vegetation, and she wanted to read it again until she had its words off by heart.

Much of it was not as high-flown and rhetorical as the opening salvoes about criminality and the law. Reassuringly, the second page got down to what her father would have called brass tacks and addressed various legal considerations, not all of which Miri could follow. It was a question, Signorelli wrote, of whether those who executed deportation orders while Italy was under German rule could apply to them the racial categories laid down in the Nuremberg Laws, whereby a Jew was deemed to be someone who had three out of four grandparents who observed the Jewish religion, while a half-Jew was someone with two observant grandparents, and a *meticcio, 'Mischling'* in German, was someone with only one observant grandparent. Italian law had no such provisions; the deportation of all Jews, regardless of category, was clearly illegal under Italian law – but what was the status of Italian law under German rule? This, Signorelli pointed out, would be one of the legal morasses they would have to cross.

More to the point, Miri thought, drafting her answer in her mind, if the Nuremberg Laws were the final authority and they defined Jews in terms of religious observance rather than blood, Vittorio would not even be a *meticcio*, since he had no observant grandparents or even great-grandparents.

(For the moment, Miri didn't even want to think about the sense in which her prosecution might then rest on the fact that Vittorio wasn't 'technically' a Jew at all, as if it had been quite all right to murder anyone who was inescapably a Jew by Hitler's definition.

No, better to bear in mind Signorelli's argument that in puncturing obedience to orders as a sufficient defence they would breach this legal wall and blast a hole in it for others to follow.)

The main problem, Miri suspected, and Signorelli's closing sentences confirmed it, lay less with prosecutorial strategy than with whether the courts would accept to try such a case at all. Signorelli didn't say as much, but Miri knew that they – she and Signorelli, or perhaps the *famiglia* Gottlieb if that was how the plaintiffs were going to be designated – would be attempting to set a fearsome precedent. It would be no good pointing to the Nuremberg Trials and the judges' rejection of a just-obeying-orders defence. Signorelli reminded Miri that in many people's opinion the very function of the Nuremberg Trials had been to draw a line beyond which there would be no further legal reckonings. Its purpose had been to close a door, not open one. Otherwise, where would such *retribuzione* stop, as Andrea had asked her? Where indeed, Miri thought bitterly? There would be no hiding place for uniformed murderers any more.

So was her prosecution feasible? Or was Signorelli's letter, with its philosophical grandstanding about the law, largely an attempt to placate her and Avram, and to establish Signorelli's bona fides in case it all came to nothing? Miri didn't want to think so. All she wanted to concentrate on was that at last there was someone on her side, someone with a legal lance who was prepared to point it at the enemy, as she would point this letter at anyone who questioned her behaviour.

There *would* be a prosecution. *Ogni ragione… – every reason to believe in a successful prosecution.* She would take it to court if she had to forget the Vessinaro and Cipriano himself, and sit outside the High Court with a sandwich board telling the world what she was about, for as long as she lived.

Or rather for as long as Cipriano lived.

EXPLAINING THAT SHE was getting them for Serafina's asthma, Miri obtained prescription medication and an inhaler, penned a note explaining their use and dosage, and left them at Cipriano's door.

Then she withdrew, abandoning her post and returning to the Casa Rosa. The medicine she had left was potent enough, if used in excess, to kill a man with a weak heart; but if Cipriano were so inclined, he had the revolver, the cliff below the balcony and any other means at a suicide's disposal.

Recurringly, in her mind's eye, Miri saw Giacomina soothing and stroking Cipriano, cradling the old man's head. The image stood between Miri and any thoughts of violence on her own part, just as the existence of Giacomina surely stood, Miri speculated, between Cipriano and any desire to end his life prematurely.

Rosanna had known when she wrote her letter to her daughter-in-law, Miri reflected, how much was changed by Giacomina's existence.

The following day, Miri was glad to see that the bundle she had left on the doorstep was no longer there. This disappearance guaranteed nothing, of course. How could the besieged pair imagine that she now suddenly meant well? They could hardly be expected to exchange their image of the *Contessa* as a deranged persecutor for one of her as a kindly saviour, merely on the basis of a parcel of medicine. Miri had written in her accompanying note that she was a trained nurse, that she had recognized and was familiar with the *dottore*'s illness, and could help. The message was intended for Giacomina rather than Cipriano, but even if it had reached the girl, there was no knowing whether she could read. Illiteracy was common in the hills, and something about the childish, broad face with its wide-spaced eyes – fixed in shock and anger, perhaps that was all it had been – put Miri in mind of some of her fellow inmates at Hemel Hempstead. They too had looked strangely untouched by time.

Per miracolo, Giacomina had survived the ordeal of an inexpertly assisted birth that had killed her mother. Paola had been born the same year as Rosanna, according to Rosanna's letter, and although in life she had been coy about her age, the letter Rosanna left to Miri acknowledged that she was 20 in the year of the turn-of-the-century fireworks, when she and Cipriano had kissed on the esplanade. That made both women, Paola and Rosanna, all of 48 in the year that Paola gave birth to Giacomina.

Miri was aware of the statistics, the factors that increased the likelihood of a retarded child. Everything had been against Giacomina; but whatever ill-starred oppositions had attended Giacomina's birth, the fierce tenderness with which she had protected Cipriano, and held him, stroking his cheek, had survived all adversity. Perhaps such love, Miri thought, had been fostered by adversity itself.

A few days later, with no sound or movement in the laurel hedge to alert Miri, she saw that Giacomina had returned to stare at her once more, the dark eyes as unblinking and as severe as they had been ten years earlier when they watched Miri and Vittorio gathering *pinoli* from the path, on their afternoon walk.

There were *pinoli* on the path now too – Miri had ceased to eat them with any relish – and for a moment she considered collecting some to hand to Giacomina, passing them through the leaves. As a small child, Giacomina had always resisted the gesture, backing away as soon as Miri had approached, then running back around the house and out of sight. And today Miri had come prepared to perform a different drama, if and when, as she'd prayed, the girl returned to the back garden. Perhaps an idiotic charade, she thought, was what it truly was; but Miri forced herself to go ahead nonetheless, now that she had an audience. From her bag Miri extracted a packet of cigarettes that she had bought in the town. They were Nazionale, Cipriano's brand, as Miri knew from watching his trembling fingers extract the single cigarette he'd smoked in front of her. Now Miri took them all out of the pack, tearing off the top and pulling out the cigarettes in twos and threes until she had them all assembled and clenched together between thumb and forefinger, in her right hand. With her left she screwed up the empty packet, letting it fall to the ground, and then used both hands to snap and shred the twenty cigarettes until they too lay in the path, a broken heap.

What now? Miri felt almost ashamed to look up at the laurel hedge, seeking out Giacomina's eyes, as if to say: so – d'you see? Did you get it?

But what if Giacomina didn't connect her demonstration to the medicine she had supplied? Might it seem, Miri wondered, as if the evil, crazy *Contessa* were merely gloating over her unlimited possession of Nazionale cigarettes – rather as if an encircling army were to torture the besieged by deliberately parading delicacies and then disposing of them uneaten? What if she were now to grind the cigarettes beneath her shoe with a deliberate flourish – but no, that risked giving the same impression of conspicuous waste. And to mime the dangers of smoking by lighting up and coughing would probably come across as mockery pure and simple. *Male*, Miri called out, lifting the mangled cigarettes to show Giacomina. *Molto male.* Bad, very bad. Surely the girl would get the message, if she didn't know it perfectly well already. How much intelligence did it take to make the connection between smoking and coughing?

Smoking would kill Cipriano – Giacomina had probably guessed that already. Had she tried to stop him herself? There wasn't much else, other than belatedly to discourage emphysema sufferers from smoking, that you could do for them, short of providing oxygen and a respirator to alleviate or forestall attack – and Miri had fought off a vision of herself heaving an oxygen cylinder over the laurel hedge, hoping Giacomina's head wasn't in the way. It was too absurd, this business of trying to keep the demon alive simply so as to be able to put him in the dock (put his *crime* in the dock, Miri kept reminding herself) and make him suffer even more, by doing so, than he was already suffering. Worse than that, it was loathsome to pretend to be genuinely solicitous. As Miri was writing the note she had left with the inhaler, she'd had to repress her nurse's impulse to add to it a helpful regimen: *limit salt intake, no coffee, smaller but more frequent meals.* Writing it would make her feel like Cipriano's mother.

And wasn't her very change of tack from tormentor to nurse not only loathsome and absurd but cruel too? To be arrested and brought to court would probably kill Cipriano faster than three packs of Nazionale a day.

She had not felt she could inhabit the role of the Jewish avenger; could she nonetheless be the avenger for justice, putting a sick old man on the rack simply to find, as Signorelli had put it in his letter, what the law was made of in Italy? *No civilized person should tolerate the proposition that criminality can be sanctioned by law, or that tyranny imposes a higher duty than morality.*

Fine phrases. Important truths. But did Miri have to be the one who enforced them, if it meant dragging a gasping, choking, moribund victim to grovel at the bar of justice? Would Vittorio have demanded this? – Vittorio whom Miri now summoned, as she sat on the little low wall in the pawky sunshine (after the week of rain and mist, the sun seemed unsure whether it was yet permitted to return), with the crumbled cigarettes at her feet, and Giacomina's unyielding gaze boring into her through the laurel hedge.

She saw Vittorio in the crowded transport that carried its death camp victims across the Alps, days and nights without food and water as the trains took them to their distant killing ground; she saw his calm, courageous, frightened face in the press of bodies, and asked him: should she let the demon die in peace?

No, came the answer. There was no hesitation in it. *No*. Look around you, came Vittorio's instruction, as his dark eyes held hers, look around you at the people in this freezing cattle truck, parched, famished, utterly humiliated, on their way to die. In their name – and in the name of those in this truck, within a few feet of me, who have already died, standing up, of heart failure, of asphyxiation, of terror – you cannot set free a man responsible for this, to live his final breaths in peace. Did *we?* – did we live *our* last breaths in peace, or were they drawn in a terror beyond imagining?

And you're tempted to let the demon off? Because an arrest, a cell, a courtroom would be too much for his heart and lungs to bear?

Have you forgotten what our heart and our lungs had to bear?

FORGOTTEN, YES. BECAUSE she hadn't been there. How could she remember where she hadn't been? And wasn't that really why she was hounding Cipriano to his death? Because she couldn't forgive herself for having left, having run off home, and failed to be there with Vittorio, in that cattle truck, holding his hand into all eternity. Beyond gas, beyond terror, beyond asphyxiation. That had been the death for which she had been intended, the test of courage and love and motherhood, and she had flunked it. Never mind excuses. She had flunked it, and damn all the talk, inside the cotton swaddling of her head, prating about a preternatural bond with her son. None of it could efface the truth.

Cotton swaddling. Sometimes it was unnerving, at night in the Casa Rosa, lying there in the strange white wadding of the mosquito net around and above her bed, the chrysalis that had been so cosy when she shared it with Piero. Now it was like a bag around her head. She had a fake body – she could see her limbs, but they weren't real, they were a Miri doll that lived inside her head, inside the mind whose limits were the cotton weave of the mosquito net. It was like her life: in it she moved and walked and spoke, but it all happened inside her head. There she pretended to be a mother still in love with her son, and he with her, and she acted accordingly. But it was all shadow-play, like the silhouettes that lamplight threw onto the netting, when you came into a room and saw that there were bodies under the net. In reality she was simply a liar and a coward, and she had run home and left Vittorio to die.

And now was she going to punish a sick old man for it? Yes, Vittorio, you're right, caro, of course he deserves to die in pain, not only once but once for every life he doomed. No single suffering death could ever be enough, let alone too much. Yes. Yes. But if I'm doing it to ease my soul or to distract it from the lie I've been telling myself, is it for me to sentence him – to sentence anyone?

It was a way of not thinking about the truth.

Why did she never think about Piero when she lay here in the bed they had shared? Folded into Rosanna's journal, she had found his letter, the one from the front at Monte Cassino, that Rosanna had saved for her. Piero had sent Miri a similar one, in the days before his death, full of excited, breathless sentences. Shells bursting around him, he said proudly, as he wrote. It had infuriated her. I'm of use now, he had written to Rosanna. It's all I ever wanted, Mamma. Miri refused to take it as his epitaph. You could get drunk on war. Drunk on danger. (All, Piero? All you ever wanted?) She would put it all in perspective another time. Not now. She had her own war to keep her busy at night, she was up on the Vessinaro in her mind, on sentry-duty, waiting and scheming.

Saying, Can you see me, God, in my penitence? In my dutiful atonement?

(Whom did she mean by God? Whom did Avram, her father, mean by God, when he said, May God strike me dead!? God the all-seeing, all-watching? God the final judge?)

Why did she never think, even in her body, about Piero?

ALL THIS TIME, unbeknownst to Miri, I had been keeping an eye on her, at a distance. Or rather, the eye was Leandro's, who brought me information. I, in turn, kept in touch with Miri's family, a connection opened almost three years earlier, in October of '45, when I phoned London to tell the Gottliebs that Vittorio had not survived the death camps.

Leandro was one of the quietest men I have ever known, and one of the best (I would not say that the two are connected – are there no quiet villains in this world? – but to a babbler like myself the idea is appealing). I knew him by sight, as we all did, and from chance encounters when our shopping rounds happened to coincide, or on the bus. I am not an early riser, and so I was never among those who, like Leandro, met the newly returned fishing fleet at the dock, at dawn. But once or twice you might meet Leandro on the esplanade, sitting and taking the sun, smoking a cigarette, if he had 20 minutes to spare before catching the bus. He would probably be on his own, not for lack of friends – as I've mentioned, Leandro was a weekend *boccia* regular at Olimpio's, up in the hills – but because his friends knew and were loath to violate his evident serenity. Even at *boccia*, when Leandro ran up to fling his steel ball, a brief respectful silence would fall instead of the usual catcalls or cries of support; until his eyes began to fail, in his seventies, Leandro was a formidable player, and cries of admiration would erupt as soon as his boccia ball landed. But by then, Leandro had already quietly turned his back, having judged its trajectory by the ball's flight, and returned without comment to the back of the *boccia* court, impassively certain of the outcome, good or bad. Somehow Leandro created a zone of silence around himself – more exactly a zone of peace, since silence can be threatening, and the aura Leandro brought with him was anything but saturnine. Rather it was gentle, patient, all-accepting. It was said that to be married to

Serafina would break a man if he was anything less, and no doubt this was true; equally, I've no doubt that Leandro already had these qualities as a young man – his daughter Pina shares them, though with a flash of Serafina's temper visible behind her eyes – and that it was a case of Serafina's wise choice and not of her bringing a man to heel.

He always stood a little crookedly, one knee bent as if to say, Don't put me in a uniform, I belong to the hills, where we keep low, like cats. "Angelo, bend the knees," Leandro would sometimes tell me in a sweet, soft undertone, when I walked back after a particularly bad *boccia* shot, delivered on tiptoe – I am a bookseller, a bibliophile, not an athlete – as if trying to deliver the ball to its intended spot by sheer willpower. "*Ginocchie*, Angelo," *knees*, Leandro would whisper, or even mouth in silence, when I looked at him despairingly after another bad shot.

His face, too, was crooked, one eye higher and smaller than the other. Beneath the tortuously broken nose (and how I would have loved to have known what duel of honour had exacted this payment), a ragged moustache disfigured his mouth, and his thin cheeks were corded with muscle as though from years of binding his jaws to stop himself speaking. How was it possible (there are many such faces, of course) to look so noble without a trace of handsomeness? – that was the meditation Leandro's face inspired. In a different face, regular features made one wonder at the compelling effect of the whole; Leandro's features made you traverse them again and again, as familiar as they were, looking for their secret. It lay within, needless to say, but that doesn't stop us from hunting for the outward and visible signs.

And one day, Leandro was there on the sunlit esplanade, sitting on a bench, alone, legs spread wide, his shopping set on the ground between his shins, staring out to sea with such blind benevolence that I hesitated to seize the opportunity and interrupt his trance. He could have been an old shepherd on Ithaca, watching for a sail, awaiting the return of Ulysses in tranquil confidence. On rare occasions I had seen him here, on a bench, with a pair of gossiping pals at either shoulder, Leandro obediently smiling and nodding, wordless, wedged between his two friends like the book they were trying to decipher, or like a necessary punctuation in their ceaseless talk. Seeing him alone now, it seemed a shame, a violation, to approach him; but I knew his good heart, and I had wanted a conduit to the *Contessa* Miri for a host of reasons, all of them personal, though some more secret than others. Happily married as I had been for over twenty years, I had adored Miri from afar – as my wife was amply aware, since according to her my gaze hides nothing – for almost as long; I badly missed, as my wife did, the consolation of her presence, that's to say of the presence of someone who had suffered a loss like ours (and not just 'like' ours! The same shipment had carried Vittorio and our own boys to their death!); having already written to and spoken to Miri's family in London, I felt some obligation to maintain the role of go-between in which both the *Conte* Piero and Miri herself had installed me, providing me with addresses and phone numbers to the purpose; and finally, I read in the fact that Miri had not contacted us since returning to the town a reticence which permitted me to fear for her state of soul. I could say it was unlike her not to call on us, but that would be to refer both parties, Miri and ourselves, to an early time and an earlier incarnation. We could never be what we were, Miri and Angelo, fellow-townspeople. Auschwitz had not only separated us from the rest of the *paese* but even more cruelly from each other, precisely when we were each other's only available source of comfort. There are griefs that need to heal in private; I understood that well. But my wife and I had each other, by whom to measure the slow return of vitality to the shattered spirit – of a measure of vitality at any rate, since severed limbs, after all, remain severed. Who did Miri have? Not hearing from her, I worried about her.

And the question mark that Miri now was, in her failure, or refusal, or inability to contact us – perhaps simply her understandable fear of the very connection that now bound us – also magnified a question in our own minds. What were we doing here, my wife and I? Back here in the place that would forever resonate with the life of our vanished boys, in every street; here beneath the hills we shrank from climbing (I should add that unlike Miri we are neither of us devoted to exercise), because beyond the Vessinaro lay the abandoned farm that my cousin and his family had tended so lovingly. Now, as I knew from my few timid, appalled visits, the terraces were overgrown, the peach trees and the vines ragged and steadily throttled by weeds. The house – ah, the house; I had only once been able to make myself enter it and bring out a cartload of personal possessions that had been sitting there mouldering from the morning the inhabitants had been taken from their beds at gunpoint, to the day fourteen months later, when I re-entered it. We had stayed in Tortona, my wife and I, with her family, the Rietis, until the Germans were gone. And when we came back and made our way up into the hills and found the farmhouse still with washing on the line, now stiff and contorted by wind and weather, and dishes in the sink all but fossilized with grime, we asked ourselves how we could possibly return to live in the vicinity of this place, this museum of horrors. The beds from which my cousin's family had been dragged were still in exactly the disarray from which Cipriano's thugs had pulled their sleepy, terrified occupants, a year earlier. Somebody had liberated Rufo, their dog, it seemed, or he had finally chewed through the rope that had secured him to a tree outside the kitchen door. (My secret suspicion was that Cipriano's men would have silenced Rufo with a bullet, just for convenience's sake, and that later, some visiting neighbour or scavenger with a vestigial sense of decency had cut the rope and disposed of poor Rufo's body, probably over the edge of the cliff. Better, from a purely practical point of view, than have the sirocco waft the stink of a decaying Rufo to neighbouring farms.)

No one had gone in and made the beds, or washed up, and perhaps that made crude sense, practical peasant sense: make the beds for whom?

Yet seeing them with the sheets and blankets askew, evoking the bodies they'd contained as vividly as if they'd just risen from them, tore the last of our self-possession to shreds. We took everything perishable, without lingering, towed our hugely loaded cart laboriously down the mountain as if we were hauling corpses stricken by the plague, and never went back.

If the farm hadn't been the last and farthest, on the cliff path that leads across the hills toward Genoa, someone would surely have bought it. But these days, even with the paved road that takes you up as far as San Sebastiano, no one wants to farm the barren, rocky terraces another hour's climb beyond that. We want our comforts on the doorstep. Perhaps one day I shall receive a phone call from Tristana, the real estate broker who keeps the property on her roster, to say that some recluse wants to live up there. Or perhaps not. This is a country of abandoned villages, simply because it was once a land of hardy mountain men, and they're a vanished breed.

Meanwhile our town has prospered; our bookstore has prospered, though neither event has brought us any great gladness, here where everything was taken from us that motivated our existence.

And yes, you might wonder: why, in God's name, did we stay?

The Rietis begged us to return to Tortona, where we had begun to make a new home, over the fourteen months of our hiding with them, in a house depleted and made empty by their own loss of a son to the death camps. Yes, we said, thanking them profusely, yes, of course we would. We simply had to go back to our old paese to redeem possessions, our own and our cousins'.

Yet that day of bringing back the keepsakes and the perishables from the hills, as we sat exhausted at our old kitchen table in the town, and answered knock after knock at the door, bringing us neighbourly food and love and comfort, I think we both knew we would never go back to live in Tortona. It wasn't the townspeople's love and kindness that compelled us, as touching as this was. It was simply that there was nowhere to run to, no way to get away from a storm of suffering that spread from horizon to horizon, in our heart; it made more sense to sit here in the eye of it, where at least we were not undermined by the sense of trying to escape, and by the constant, guilty return in our minds to the fountainhead – this town, this house, these rooms and these beds from which our own boys had been torn, on the same morning as their cousins – of our grief. Better to be here with it. It would in any case always be with us, no matter where we were.

And there was something uncomfortable – as shameful as it was to admit this to ourselves – about our life with the Rietis, whose loss matched ours. (If nothing else, this discomfort helped me to understand Miri's reluctance to revive our old acquaintance.) It was

like living in a house of mirrors. Simply seeing each other re-installed
the pain we were trying to keep under control. And wasn't that pain,
then, only worse, in our *paese*, when we returned to it? Worse, yes,
but we had embraced it deliberately, and (if you can understand the
distinction) the reminders were continuous, rather than an ambush
attending would-be escapees. The town, our own town, was a ghost
town to us, crowded with memories, but we had the consolation
– this may sound curious, and perhaps it has had a certain morbid
element to it – of having chosen to inhabit this graveyard, cheek by
jowl with loss. The best way I can explain it is this: in later years, I
learned that certain death camp survivors had banded together and,
unable to find a place they could call home, anywhere on the face
of the earth, had returned to the concentration camp itself, their old
prison, and, with the state's reluctant permission, set up house in
the empty barracks (do you doubt me? – this is a true story), where
they, their family and their descendants live to this day. Discovering
this, I felt a surge of kinship, and more than that, a tremendous sense
of gratefulness and release. Someone had showed the world what
lay inside our hearts. These pioneers of retrenchment painted and
decorated the old bunkhouses and put flowerpots (and glass) in the
bleak, dreadful windows, which are now bright with geraniums. I've
seen photographs. The very sight of it is grotesque, alarming, comical
even – as if Disney had spread its soulless theme park culture so
successfully that even a concentration camp could be redeemed and
sprayed and varnished, to become Auschwitzworld or Belsenworld.
But for those who grasp its meaning, there isn't a trace of mockery
in it. I understand completely this need to reinhabit hell, when
everywhere else simply feels like hell deferred.

So we stayed. We turned and faced it, and set up house in the past,
as perhaps everyone does (I have to remind myself of this) in time.

In those days, though, when Miri was newly returned, and hunting
il vecchio on the Vessinaro, as I discovered from Leandro, we were
still struggling to adjust. It had never entered our minds to wreak
vengeance on Cipriano, that instrument of the devil. This was not out
of forgiveness. We had heard he was ailing, and we wished him pain
with all our hearts. But the very thought of pursuing justice (which

to us seemed a mere wraith, another death camp victim) was fraught with temporary distraction and ultimate disappointment. Our need was too large, and the vessel, a vicious animal like Cipriano, too mean. To me it seemed like this: if I could roast him on a spit in public every day, would it drive away the ghosts and fill the hollow places in my heart with satisfaction? A mirage, surely.

So what was I to judge of Miri's state of mind, from Leandro's patient account of her one-woman posse? (It was Olimpio who noted the *Contessa's* comings and goings on the path to the Vessinaro, and kept Leandro and Serafina informed.) Did it betoken purpose, determination? – was that what I should report to the Gottliebs? Or would her purpose abruptly founder like one of the abandoned terraces below the Vessinaro path, to crumble into the sea? So I feared. Should I be warning the Gottliebs of my fear?

It wasn't my place to simply turn up at the Casa Rosa; and I knew I would feel like a spy if I did. But if I was to give the Gottliebs fair warning that Miri was losing her way, alone in the hills every day from morning to night, I would have to base this on a first-hand impression, not second or third-hand gossip. When I asked Leandro how he thought the *Contessa* was, in herself, a stillness came over Leandro's twisted old face, an extraordinary absence of expression. Had I been a visitor to an ancient Ithaca still awaiting the return of their king from Troy, and asked the shepherd how Penelope was, in herself, I imagine that exactly the same impermeably loyal face would have gazed back at me, divulging nothing.

Non saprei, I couldn't tell you (literally, "I would not know"), Leandro said at last, and I believed it was the literal truth. I should have to see for myself.

I CHOSE A fine day, and timed my arrival for an hour or so before *pranzo*, having learned from Leandro that Miri returned from the hills for supper.

The *Contessa* wasn't yet home, Pina told me. She showed me to the terrace – I knew my way, but it had been a good few years since my last visit, and Leandro's work, along with time itself, had created a denser, darker garden than I remembered – and brought me a glass of Leandro's wine, made from the Casa Rosa's small vineyard. It was tart enough to be mistaken for medicine at first, but the aftertaste was rich and raw and true, the wine of the hillsides, utterly unlike any other. To this day, when I visit the Casa Rosa, knowing that there will be no more wine now that Leandro is gone from us (and the little vineyard itself replaced with pebbles and a formal Milanese garden), I can still taste Leandro's wine, warm and harsh as the aroma of the terraces, as I climb the cliff-cut steps up to the house.

At last I heard footsteps on the paved road, footsteps regular as they could never have been in the days of the goat track and its monumental, perilous stones that forced even my old friend Dario the muleteer to curse his surefooted animals for hesitating as they felt for footholds on the path. I glimpsed a disshevelled-looking Miri, through the orange and the fig trees, and then she was gone again. Pina returned to tell me that the *signora Contessa* would be with me shortly. When Miri emerged at last, ten minutes later, it was with her hair carefully coiled and a polite, contrite smile on her face which was utterly contradicted by her blazing eyes and distracted hands.

Then the smile collapsed utterly. Shame seemed to be spreading from her eyes to her trembling mouth, and I couldn't think, at once mortified and horribly moved as I was to see her features in such disarray, whether to let her speak or forestall her.

"*Per carità.*" For mercy's sake. "Please. No apologies, *Contessa*. We have been leaving each other in peace, that's all. That's all."

I made to stop her, as she tried to speak and tears only came instead. She raised a hand.

"I should have come to see you long ago," I said, unable to control my own tears.

"No. Let me say it, please. You were the only one who thought of me, and now look, this is how I've repaid you, to make you come here at last – "

"To *make* me come here! I would have come the first day."

"And I should have gone to you the first day. But with every day that passed I became more ashamed –

"*Please, signora Contessa,* let's have no more of this."

She asked me if I'd always addressed her so formally. I was flattered, but in truth I always had, and always would.

"How is your wife?" she asked "How did she... I hope she managed better than I did. You know I was in hospital for a time?"

I nodded, and I could see the anxiety in her face, at the very fact that I knew.

"I knew from speaking to your family, *signora*, and I can assure you that I have told no one any private matters concerning yourself."

"I know that," she said. "But rumours fly on the wind. The whole town knows that I am *la pazza,* the madwoman."

"You're quite wrong," I said. "No one thinks any such thing. You are loved above everyone and above everything in this town."

She shook her head, crying again, and we sat in silence for a time.

"If it was so," she said, "They would not have let Cipriano go free. Tell me," she said quickly, before I could reply – and what, indeed could I have said, other than ineffectually to remind her that Cipriano was an outcast and a pariah? – "about your wife. How did she cope with your loss?"

"Poorly. But we had each other, *signora Contessa,*" I said. "You had nobody."

Suddenly – I could see from her expression that her own change of subject had quite failed to remove Cipriano from her mind – she astonished me with a smile and a small, mocking heave of forced laughter, more troubling than the tears that had preceded them.

"Do you know what I'm doing, Angelo?

The hectic flush was back, darkening her eyes, and her fingers were flicking so badly that she had to put them in her lap.

At that moment, footsteps came, on the paving stones leading to the terrace, and we were silent as Pina brought Miri a glass of water, and refilled my glass with Leandro's savage nectar.

"I'm nursing Cipriano," she whispered as Pina retreated. Her tone was almost childishly defiant, but she could hardly get the syllables out. "I'm nursing him. What do you think of that? Will you ever speak to me again?"

My heart was too full. I was trying to find the words to tell her

I would follow her to hell and back, ministering to Cipriano all the way if needs be, but the words stuck in my mouth, and I could see that although she was staring at me, she wasn't seeing me at all. Today, when I have heard her story a dozen times, I know where she was and what she was seeing, in that shuttered bedroom filled with a dying man's gasps for breath.

"Can you even believe it's true?" she asked. "He's sick. Emphysema. There's no cure. Only waiting. I had a patient – did you know I was a nurse in London?"

I nodded.

"Of course you knew," she muttered. "Can you believe me that I'm nursing Cipriano? Last week he let me into the house, then again he wouldn't come to the door, he or his – his – "

She stared, as if seeing me once more.

"His daughter?" I said. "Paola's child?"

She shook her head at me in puzzled surprise.

"*Signora*, that *is* something the whole town knows. The story's been going around for many years. Some of Cipriano's supporters still deny it, of course. But old Ataulfo the boatman is a dreadful gossip when he's drunk. I don't suppose *il vecchio* knows that, or he wouldn't use him to deliver his groceries."

Still flustered, she told me about Rosanna's letter and her journal. (Indeed, many years later, Miri showed me the letter itself, and permitted me to copy it. But the journal she kept private, telling me only fragments of its coded and abbreviated tale.)

"And today," she said, and then stopped, as if amazed at the memories the word brought. She looked at me as I might be reading her mind, and be shocked at what I saw there.

"What happened today?" I asked.

She shook her head. I waited in vain.

"You say he let you in, last week?" I said eventually.

After a time, when my question caught up with her, she nodded. "Yes. And again, four days ago, after I left some medicine. And then again nothing."

"And today?"

She gazed at me.

"Forgive me, *signora Contessa*," I said, about to add something that would change the subject, but she was already speaking.

"He had a fit. It was bad. Giacomina came to the door and tried to call me, but only a kind of cawing sound came out. I haven't heard her speak, and I'm not sure…"

She gazed at me. *Giacomina*. Named, as Miri could not have known unless *il vecchio* told her, for Cipriano's grandfather, Giuseppe's father, Giacomo the old hill farmer that my cousins had known in his extreme old age. *Giacomina*. For me a synoptic vision came with the name, a montage that began with young Giuseppe Cipriano the future Garibaldino marching down from Giacomo's farm to join the forces of revolution; returning crippled to the town and raising Renzo and Paola in an angry pride that made of them an exclusive clan – just as Miri and her son had proved to be in Piero's life – of suffering brother and sister; then Renzo and Paola, after *il Conte* Vittorio's intervention, taking their broken lives back up to the hills where Giuseppe had come from, where Giacomo had farmed and Giacomina, his namesake, now hid.

"She let me in today." Miri's hands were flapping on the table again, clasping and unclasping until I took my courage in both my own hands and clasped hers and held them still. Perhaps it was Leandro's wine that led me to do it.

"Angelo – I'm nursing him, the man who took our children from us, I tell myself I'm trying to keep him alive for a trial but all I know is that I went up there to kill him and now I'm giving him every last bit of comfort I can. What I did… you can't imagine…"

I squeezed her hands, trying to calm her. I was really afraid that in this condition she might easily fling herself off the Vessinaro onto the rocks below. "Vittorio would be the first to approve. Think of Vittorio not in the terrible hours at the end of his life but as he was as a person, as Vittorio, kind, forgiving, loving and trusting you in all things."

She was doing her best, gazing back at me and nodding faintly as I spoke, to convince me that she was hearing what I was saying, and that she was seeing me in front of her, but I knew she wasn't.

AS SOON AS Miri had got through the web of wistaria and into the house, she could hear the ghastly sounds of the old man fighting for breath.

Following Giacomina down a darkened corridor towards the sounds, she came to a shuttered, spartan bedroom, where Giacomina ran to Cipriano's side.

For an instant – there were fewer such moments, and this was one of the last – there were two Miris present in the room, the nurse and the mother, and while the nurse noted the absence of the inhaler from Cipriano's hands or bedclothes or the bedside table, the mother considered calmly the sublime appropriateness of the demon's calvary. Gasping for breath, not just once and for all in an underground 'bathhouse' where breath-annihilating gas, not water, spewed from the vents, but daily, hourly, he was condemned to strive over and over again, like some doomed Titan in Greek mythology, to fight for the very breath of air that he had in effect denied to those he had deported, until one day he breathed his last, or at any rate until he had the courage to end it. But it was the mother, too, in Miri, who knew it was not simply a lack of courage that kept Cipriano from putting an end to his living hell. It was the presence of Giacomina. And that, in turn, was a bitter irony to savour, if Miri had it in her to savour Cipriano's pain: it was parental love that was keeping him on the rack.

"Where's the inhaler?" Miri heard herself say, and, seeing Giacomina's expression, realized she'd spoken in English. "*Inhalatore!*" Was there such a word? "*Ventilatore.*"

Together they crawled around the floor, under the bed and behind the bedside table, as Cipriano's breath howled in his chest like a banshee, until they found it, behind the bedhead, and applied it to Cipriano's lips.

As he calmed, slowly, Miri avoided looking at Giacomina. In the shadowy room she wasn't even sure whether the girl was still there.

But when she turned to look, Giacomina's baleful stare told her clearly: your job is done, now clear out and leave him with me.

Miri ignored her and took Cipriano's pulse. Then, without compunction, while the old man watched in amazement, Miri searched the drawers of the bedside table, and when Giacomina rushed forwards to stop her, this time Miri was prepared. She took the child by one arm, spun her round, and sent her reeling across the room. Then she turned back to the drawers, brought out pack after pack of cigarettes, and placed them on the bed.

She picked up one of the packs, ripped it open, and looked at Giacomina, who was still nursing her arm.

"*Fai tu?*" Miri enquired. D'you want to do it?

Giacomina made no sign.

Systematically, Miri stripped the packs of their cigarettes, as she had done on the path while Giacomina watched, and reached for a small raffia-work waste-basket on the floor beside the bed, filled with pink-stained tissues. Into it she crumbled pack after pack.

Cipriano's eyes, over the crude rubber inhaler-mask, studied her, calmly, it seemed.

"You can always get more. I know," Miri said. "But each time I come here, I shall destroy them. You'll have to find somewhere better to hide them, *dottore* Cipriano. I shall look everywhere. It could become an interesting game."

Eventually he pulled away the inhaler, and let out a long slow breath, before speaking.

"You're even crazier" – *ancora più pazza* – "than I thought."

Miri couldn't help smiling, as she continued to destroy the cigarettes, making sure no smokable butts remained. She knew smokers.

Cipriano wasn't smiling back, but there was something in his eyes, something other than dull hatred.

Ancora più pazza che avessi creduto. A joke. Again the Miri-double who sat beside her, wondering at her every action, made her presence felt. A joke – she was sharing a joke with the demon.

When she finished the shredding and glanced up at him, the light was still there in Cipriano's eyes. But perhaps it was only the desire to speak, and the contest of wills between that desire and the fear that if he spoke it would once more require a deeper breath than he could manage. Now that he'd put aside the inhaler at last, he would want to lie still, Miri thought. But she could see the battle raging inside him, and at last the need to speak won out.

"Aren't you here to kill me?"

Miri shook her head.

"Don't you want to kill me?"

She made no answer, but watched him struggle for breath. Her presence, she knew, was making it harder for him to settle.

"*Non parlare,*" Miri said. Don't speak.

Gradually, Cipriano's shallow breathing eased. But his glittering gaze was still on her, and she waited patiently for him.

"I see," the old man said, when he had saved up the breath. "You want it for *yourself.* Not by the cigarettes. *You* want to do the killing."

They stared at each other for a long time. In these minutes of patient, expressionless eye contact, Miri wondered what went through Cipriano's mind. Was it just *the mad Contessa, the mad Contessa*? Did he dare to see the camps, the scenes Miri herself was trying to drill into his brain? Did he see Vittorio, did he see his hated ones, Piero and Rosanna?

His brief but loud, hoarse breaths, each one taken so carefully, so mindfully, made Miri conscious of the freedom of every deep breath she took. Breath had become the sound of time passing, as Cipriano's audible sips of air measured out the minutes and the hours in the small, shadowy room. Light came and went through the shutters as clouds hid the sun, turning the room dark, and then released the sunshine again, thin beams of warm light leaping up as if a searchlight had been turned on the house, catching the motes of dust revolving slowly like tiny galaxies.

The bees hummed steadily, the sound rising and falling a little, it seemed to Miri, with the return and disappearance again of the light. Now and again a louder rattling noise announced the arrival of a bird, heedless of the bees.

Cipriano's eyes were rarely on her. Mostly his gaze rested on Giacomina, and at other times, his face went slack, the mouth fell open, and his gaze, directed entirely inward, nonetheless projected agony – an all but involuntary projection, Miri knew – in the direction of an open door or a source of light that the room entirely lacked. There came a dreadful moment when Miri recognised that almost accidental look of mute, helpless appeal. It belonged to

San Sebastiano, to the head on the baroque altarpiece in the little chapel; and Miri wondered, to distract herself from the connection she was making, whether the painter had seen and derived his inspiration from the faces of those on the verge of the hereafter.

And all the while the old man wanted to speak to her, Miri knew, and could not, for fear of another attack and the pain it brought.

Was he also afraid each time that it would kill him? Miri wondered whether he knew that in all likelihood it would not, and that he would die in his sleep. If he didn't know it already, did he deserve this consolation? Should she tell him? Surely all men on the point of death deserved consolation – didn't all religions, and even humanism itself, preach that?

Telling him not to reply, but simply listen, she explained the probabilities.

He didn't seem to be listening. All his energy was going into his furious gaze.

"Let me live a little," he said at last. "Then you can have me."

Miri nodded, exasperated, feeling her anger return. Yes, why not? Let the demon live on. Why shouldn't he suffer more days like this?

But something in his gaze, unexpiated, told her she hadn't understood what he was trying to say. His eyes went to the girl standing beside the door, in the shadows, and then back to Miri, and now the tears that surged into Cipriano's eyes infuriated her. How dare he feel so much for this child and have felt so little for hers?

"Giacomina," he said, as if to say, I live only for her. *You understand*, said his pleading gaze.

"I understand, signor Cipriano. Who could understand better than I do? You know that."

His eyes had returned to Giacomina.

Was it time to ask him? Must everything, Miri wondered, be said?

"How could you take my child from me?" she said at last. "You, of all people?"

Cipriano turned his head away.

Once more the minutes passed, and she sensed that she would get no answer. Was there one? Or was it simply too harsh to speak – was it that it was precisely because Cipriano knew better than most what Vittorio had meant to Miri that he had to take him from her? Was it precisely because Miri had loved the boy so much that Cipriano, knowing what that love was, could revel in the prospect?

Finally, when he spoke, his head still facing away from her towards the wall, it was softly that she barely he caught his words.

"They took my life."

Was that what he had said? *They*, yes, *they*. Not "*You*", not Miri. Neither she nor her forebears had taken one iota of his life. Why had Cipriano made *her* pay? Why had he taken *her* life in exchange? Just because she cared more than anyone else, because she was vulnerable? That had singled her out. Her love of Vittorio, not Piero's, was what had offered Cipriano a naked breast, a sword-thrust deep enough to slake his need.

And had it? she wanted to ask. Had it?

"I know," she heard herself say. A life for a life. The other Miri, inside, still cried, What had I done to *you*?

Yet she knew the answer: what had he, Cipriano, done to Piero's father to deserve betrayal? Nothing. He had been as innocent as she. A life for a life: an innocent for an innocent.

Marshalling his forces, Cipriano turned from the wall, gazing ahead at Giacomina, who had stepped forward, sensing the renewed tension in the room.

"They took my life, and left me Giacomina. I had only Paola in all the world. And when she died, when she died and left me Giacomina," he paused, and couldn't finish.

Breath failed him, and with terrible caution he let it return, head back on the pillow, eyes on the ceiling as he concentrated on the interior struggle.

She knew the rest of it. He'd had to watch, yes, watch Miri and Vittorio, growing up. But was that enough, was that an excuse, an exculpation? It couldn't serve to forgive him what had already been done, long before Piero's marriage. *You slept with your sister.* Miri repeated it in her mind, unable to feel repulsion, or reanimate in her soul the shock she had felt, deducing it from Rosanna's journal. *And in order to keep her pregnancy a secret, you sacrificed her life.* God knows it was shocking, and yet – here on this windblown, deserted promontory, a thousand steps above the sea, amid shattered lives, it seemed barely even surprising. Was it that it was all so long ago, or did normal standards not apply on the Vessinaro, as if the wistaria that had crawled from house to rooftop, to neighbouring rooftop, were a horribly well-disguised disease, like the blossoming flush on a dying face?

As she looked from Cipriano to Giacomina, and back to the old man, she felt a start, felt her body react anew with the very shock that a moment ago had seemed so distant and irrelevant.

Had the jolting of her body alerted Cipriano, or had he, in the wordless electricity that connected the three of them for hour after hour in the silent room, intuited her question? His face was turned to Miri's now. Had he slept with his daughter too?

No. The word was barely spoken, only mouthed, with the faintest shake of the head. The eyes were appalled, imploring.

He was crying now, no longer looking at her. Miri knew he was crying for his lost sister, his lost love. The distress was impossible to see without sharing it. As if she were stretching a hand across time, from one world to another, from the living to the dead – as if, in fact, she were reaching through the veil of appearances to touch Vittorio himself – she extended her hand to the old man's wet cheek. She could not stroke his skin, or move her hand once it had touched his face. Her head swam with the craziness of it. Ordinary, sad, elderly skin, belonging to a man in pain, who had caused others so much pain. The burden of time and knowledge was too much to bear, in the moment. Miri couldn't move her hand. But if the demon were to turn his face and touch her palm with his lips, she felt she would die of it.

Miri became aware of Giacomina watching, her eyes on the juncture of Miri's hands and Cipriano's face, intent, still wary, a cat ready to spring.

"*Bicchiere d'acqua, Giacomina*" A glass of water. Had the girl understood? Miri repeated it, and at last Giacomina backed away, before turning and leaving the room, to return with a small glass filled, not with water but a dark, amber liquid. She handed it to Miri.

"*Vino?*"

Giacomina nodded solemnly.

Cipriano's eyes were closed, his wet face resting on Miri's hand, which was pressed into the pillow by his cheek. Suddenly a cough racked his chest, and a groaning effort to replace the expelled breath brought him sitting upright, eyes wide in terror.

Miri put down the glass and quickly brought the inhaler to his lips.

"*Acqua*," she insisted, sharply, to Giacomina, and this time the girl brought water.

As Cipriano eased back onto the pillow, Miri changed the cold compress and applied it to his forehead. After a while, she took the inhaler away and offered the old man a sip of water, which he took.

His eyes were no longer on Miri, but gazed ahead, into the shadows.

"*Forse dormerà.*" Perhaps he'll sleep, Miri said. Her eyes returned to the glass Giacomina had brought her first, in place of water. She raised it, and sipped, meeting Giacomina's gaze. As Miri had suspected from its colour and the way it pooled in the glass, it was *vinsanto*, fortified communion wine. It had been a favourite of Piero's, as it was of many who rarely or no longer attended church. When they drank it, Miri often wondered, did Catholics secretly like to imagine they were raiding sanctity, sipping Christ's as yet unconsecrated blood, the bare material stuff of faith before the miracle of transubstantiation? Did they picture priests taking a swig in the vestry, between services?

Miri saw that Giacomina was staring at her, and read the purpose in the girl's eyes. She took the glass to Cipriano's lips, which parted at the smell of the *vinsanto*, and poured a few drops into his mouth.

The shocking absurdity of the scene came home to her in a rush, and she couldn't keep from her mind the single thought: Vittorio's blood.

And what shall I do for a wafer? came a shamed and caustic voice inside her head. How shall I go home now, or ever again? Better to step next door, take the service revolver from the desk drawer and turn it on myself.

Cipriano's eyes were still closed, his breathing so soft it showed no sign, if he was breathing at all. Miri reached quickly for his pulse.

Don't you die on me now, damn you, she muttered aloud under her breath, trying to replace the thought of the blessing she had just administered.

The pulse was faint but present. Miri met Giacomina's gaze and nodded in reassurance. The girl came to the bed, on the other side from Miri.

Miri could only watch as Giacomina knelt and bowed her head onto the blanket, kissing Cipriano's motionless, bluish hand, like the wrinkled claw of some strange tropical lizard.

IN THE DAYS and weeks that followed, Giacomina let Miri in each morning, fetched her food and water, and *vinsanto*, and watched from the shadows of Cipriano's shuttered bedroom, as Miri tended to the old man.

At Miri's request I fetched her oxygen from Genoa, in cylinders, and accompanied her, carrying the heavy things up to Olimpio's – this was as far as she would let me come. The Vessinaro was hers, hers alone to share with Cipriano and Giacomina, though by now, as Miri must have known, the town had a pretty good idea (especially with the arrival of the oxygen) of what was going on.

Or thought they did.

Letters came for Miri from Signorelli, the lawyer, describing the tortuous windings of the law, or more precisely of connections pursued and favours called in, hoping to establish not only an acceptable basis for prosecution but alliances which would guide their very strong case, as he continued to insist, through the political labyrinth. Had Miri received his first letter? He needed her help; he needed all the detail only she could provide, in order to fill out their case. Was she receiving his letters?

Miri left them unanswered on her desk.

She was living, I believe she would have said, in a different reality, compared to which courts of law could only seem like hollow pomp.

It was the reality of the confessional, a court of the spirit that Miri would herself have anatomized, until now, as a specious, empty formality.

Forgive me, Father. No such words were spoken. Few were spoken at all in the final weeks, and when they were, it was on a subject Miri would never have imagined that she would one day broach with *dottore*

Cipriano, the demon. They spoke of love. More precisely, they allowed each other to speak, in turn, of those they had loved. And in the other's silence, listening, was a forgiveness no Hail Marys could surpass.

In halting sentences, Cipriano spoke of Rosanna when she was young, of her beauty and how he had loved her from the day his sister brought her schoolfriend home. As a teenager he had seized the duty – everyone knew why – of taking to the *biancheria* any shirts that needed starching (as his father's always did), and collecting them again, for a glimpse of Rosanna. He spoke of his love for Piero's father too, who had been, like Piero in his turn, a magnet for the town, its figurehead. He had loved Vittorio like an idealized elder brother. One smile from that proud, fine-featured face could keep you going for a day.

How gracious he had been, Piero's father, in victory, Cipriano said bitterly, and how easy it must be to be gracious when you are the victor. Miri knew that when he said this, the old man was thinking of Piero too. But old Vittorio's had not been a clean or fair victory. He had courted Rosanna behind Cipriano's back. To Cipriano, that was everything. By the fierce code Cipriano's father had taught him, honour was all. If Vittorio *senior* had come to Cipriano and confessed his love for Rosanna, before doing anything, then at least he, Cipriano, could have given Rosanna a choice. At least, if she had chosen the *Conte*-to-be, Cipriano could have been given the dignity of surrendering her voluntarily, instead of becoming a laughing-stock along with Vittorio's catalogue of cuckolds in the town. Vittorio had deprived him not only of Rosanna and the life he had been building for himself, but also of the name he had been building for himself in the town, a name which would now forever be inseparable from his defeat.

Ashamed, Cipriano spoke to Miri of Piero himself, whom he had watched grow up. Perhaps, Miri thought, the dying man was a little giddy from the oxygen. The subject of Piero's youth seemed to reanimate parts of the old man – expressions, minutely to be gauged on the exhausted flesh of his face, but unmistakable, that she had never seen before – from earlier strata of his life.

As a child, Piero had been a fine, beautiful boy, Cipriano said. Miri studied the old man warily. There wasn't even the faintest hint of rancour in *il demonio*'s voice. What kind of trap was this?

Young Piero had been, perhaps, a little too much protected by his mother, Cipriano continued in the same tone. *Dolce* was the only word for the sweetness in his voice. A sweet demon, oxygen-buoyed? Miri could scarcely keep the astonishment off her face, as the old man spoke of Piero's youthful defects. Beautiful but, naturally, spoilt, like all his kind. He said it tolerantly, gazing into Miri's face in perfect unawareness, it seemed, that she might refer his remark to her own protectiveness as a mother.

Piero – Piero – the old man seemed, to her amazement, to be unable to stop saying the name in the same caressing tone. Piero had suffered from too much admiration, that was Cipriano's opinion – and yet, yes, he had grown to be a fine boy. He was a fine boy now. Was he not?

A fine boy *now*? If Cipriano, as he said this, imagined Piero to be still alive, Miri wondered whether he had any idea where they were, and what had happened over the years. Or was he already in another place and another time?

The old man was still gazing at her questioningly. Was Piero, Cipriano now asked in an innocent, tender tone Miri had never heard from him, a fine husband?

THE QUESTION SEEMED to Miri to come from Cipriano as though she had planted it in his head herself, or as though, on the verge of the hereafter, he was able to see into her thoughts and take his cue from her.

It had only been in the past few weeks that Piero had started coming to her in her bed, under the mosquito net. She had wondered whether the memories of their love-making had been banished forever by the intervening events – by what she felt to have been his rejection of her. Had it not been the most violent of rejections, to abandon their child and stalk off to die on the battlefield?

He had sworn not to leave Vittorio unprotected.

And he had been a fine boy, as Cipriano said – this ancient, dreamy Cipriano who now gazed at her as though he had done nothing to be ashamed of in her eyes, as though they shared nothing but their loving, albeit fondly scolding, admiration of *il Conte.*

The Piero who came to her lay face down in the pillow, weeping as she had never seen him weep.

His face was averted, and she knew he would not look at her until she forgave him.

And to forgive him, she had to acknowledge that his loneliness had begun while they were married, long before she left for England.

She had not meant it to be so. Until Piero, she had been content to be herself, the stranger in the world that she had always felt herself to be, who had somehow won a prince's love (he had to be mistaken in his choice, but why argue?) and held him, glowing and golden, in their bed. It had been wonderful, a miracle, more than sufficient to exceed all her hopes and dreams. But then what happened could simply never have been anticipated, that into her life came herself in another body, in her own body of course at first but then apparently (yet not really) separate, not merely a lovable child or a compatible personality but herself entirely, as even the dearest children surely were not. This was not – how could she ever have said this to Piero? – an offspring. This was a recurrence, a hole in time. She was there again, in another heart. Ah, how could she have *not* said this to Piero? But she said it now, as he lay and wept, turned away from her.

Would it not make it worse for him? Piero's tears seemed not to be abating, as she watched her golden love shake with the pain of it. But if she could make him understand that he had had no rival, that he could never have had a rival if Miri had lived a thousand years. No lover and no husband could have been preferred to him. No love, either, because what bound her and Vittorio never fitted the word. Love was between two distinct creatures whose pieces of the puzzle fitted. She and Vittorio were the same piece, with exactly the same contours – they could never be placed side to side and attached to each other, because they were, the two of them, only one piece. Or, to see if differently, in the world's jigsaw, her set (and his) had been issued with two identical pieces of sky, to fit the same space. And it wasn't only Piero to whom she had been unable to say this. It was everybody. They understood, or thought they did, at once

– ah, a mother's love! But it had nothing to do with a mother's love. Had he not been Vittorio, Miri had often reflected, she might have found no mother's love, no maternal instinct in herself at all, when her child was born. Because Vittorio called forth no such love, no guiding, sheltering, obsessive spirit. Whether she even possessed such a capacity, Miri believed she would now never know. Vittorio had merely allowed her to be herself, from the days of his infancy until the day she left him, in a way that she had never experienced or expected, simply because he *was* her. They had even discussed it. She was afraid he might feel threatened by her utter identification with him, more claustrophobic, potentially, than any mothering love. But he had acknowledged it as the utterly obvious, known to him since before he could remember. It wasn't 'closeness' as other people (you too, Piero, my darling) termed and conceived it. They were the same person.

I never left you, she implored as she felt Piero grow quiet, his sobs turning to hiccupping sighs. I could never have left you in my heart. I was there twice, that's all, in myself and in our son, and in him I drank at a fountain neither you nor anyone in the world could provide, a fountain of selfhood. You had all my love. Believe me, you had all my love.

It was almost enough, but not quite. She knew she had to say it, and it was the hardest thing she would ever say in her life.

Piero, I understand why you did it, why you left. I am to blame, too. I drank from him too greedily. Forgive me, my love.

HE WAS NO longer the demon.

And somehow there was no longer any point in seeing in Renzo Cipriano someone he no longer was. These days, as soon as she reached the bedside and sat down, he took her hand as if to say, At last, I've been expecting you.

Once taken, she could no longer relinquish his hand. At first, she had been conscious of Giacomina's watching, expressionless eyes. No longer, now. Not for weeks. It was grotesque, but there was no avoiding the sense that they were a family.

More and more dependent on the oxygen, Cipriano spoke little.

One day, to Miri's alarm, a puzzled look of desperation entered his eyes as he woke from sleep, and he seemed all too completely to have reinhabited the present.

As he struggled against it, Miri pressed his hand harder, until at last he calmed, staring at her.

After a time his brow furrowed in the effort to speak, and the word that emerged might have been hard to make out if Miri hadn't know the syllables so well, and hadn't anticipated what they would be.

"Giacomina."

It was not said to the girl, but to Miri, and there was no mistaking what he meant.

Yes, but would she come? Would Giacomina come?

Giacomina at the Casa Rosa. Miri had thought about many it times, and recognized that what she felt for the girl went back to her earliest visits to the Vessinaro, when Vittorio could barely walk. Giacomina, three years older than her son, had been their silent partner and playmate, a witness to their joy as she peeped through the laurel hedge. Had she resented or envied them, motherless as she was? Or had Cipriano perhaps been all her world, and Miri and Vittorio no more than visitors from another planet?

It would be a gift of life to her house. A child again in her house. And it had not escaped Miri, while reading Rosanna's journal, that the year that Giacomina had been born was the same year that Miri had met Piero on the little beach, that it was from that very year, the year of Giacomina's birth, that Miri's life had belonged to the town. They were of an age, twinned, the motherless child and the childless mother.

Miri nodded, and called to the girl.

It took several requests, and Cipriano's pleading eyes, to bring Giacomina to Miri's side of the bed.

They had never embraced, and when Miri took Giacomina's hands the girl trembled so violently that Miri was afraid she would have a fit of some kind.

Giacomina's eyes were on the old man all the time, even as Miri kissed her on the forehead.

Now they were all crying, and a part of Miri stood aside and watched in incredulity. Was this a true bill, a true ceremony sealed in love, or a delusion, a grotesque charade in which Cipriano's final trick was to write the script for her life, to the end? She had come to kill him, and was she now adopting his child? But it was Vittorio in her mind's eye who calmed her, little Vittorio sitting playing on the sandy orange path and ignoring Giacomina's watching eyes until he thought his mother wasn't looking. Then he would shoot a brief keen glance at the laurel hedge, as if to say, You're watching, aren't you? Keep watching. I'll make something for you one day, wait and see – proud and unabashed, as if he were the *prigionniera's* future bridegroom.

Vittorio was guiding her, and as the idea took root in her heart, it was all Miri could do not to start preparing a room for Giacomina that very day, and dropping hints that would cushion the shock for Serafina, Leandro and Pina.

They would adjust. They would understand, in time, that this was the mad *Contessa's* new child, her adopted daughter. Serafina would find her tasks. They would all continue to eat together in the kitchen, and the frightened animal that Giacomina would be at first – how would Miri even get her down the hill? – would slowly adapt to her new lair. (Miri pictured herself carrying a writhing, struggling little Giacomina downhill in a sack, like a captured wildcat.) Even once transplanted, Giacomina would not stray far, of that Miri was sure. She would become as much a part of the Casa Rosa as Miri herself, as intrinsic to it as its very walls. The girl would come to depend on Miri, mute as Giacomina was, to interpret her moods and needs. Her eyes would follow Miri, and await Miri's return when Miri went into the town, as she would rarely do. Why bother? She had all she wanted. She would open the Casa Rosa to her old friends, to the Berlins, to the Baldinis, and they would come over often. In time, she would introduce Giacomina to them.

No, wait – was this really possible? Was she indulging in a heedless fantasy, thinking to make her life whole when nothing could ever be whole again? *La pazza!* Was she really going mad at last? But the vision had grabbed hold of her, consuming her.

It would not be long before this new life would begin. The day would come, soon, when a trembling Giacomina would be listening for her footfalls on the clifftop Vessinaro path in the morning – where exactly would the girl be? In the house, weeping at Cipriano's bedside? Or hidden somewhere in a corner, convulsed? Or at the front door, eyes turned up to the sandy ridge and the path she knew would bring Miri, any moment?

Or might she even, in her anxiety, walk up the nine or ten paces to the pathway itself, where she could look along the ridge and see Miri coming half a mile away, picking her way between the green of the thorny scrub and the blue of the aniseed plants and the little low volcanic boulders that forced the path to twist and turn?

It was possible that Giacomina had never been out of the house in her life, that she had never penetrated the all-enveloping twice-blossoming wistaria vine – *Chinese* wistaria, Cipriano had murmured hoarsely, in a fond whisper Miri would remember all her life, when he saw Miri's gaze go to the window – that girded the house, with its garrison of guardian bees. What death-defying courage might it need, to emerge from the house and its vine, into the terrible openness of day?

And yet – mightn't Giacomina be there on that day, to see Miri early and to let herself be seen? Mightn't she be there on the path, rather than hiding in the house, to announce what they both knew had been coming? For surely Giacomina did know it was coming, and knew it would be peaceful, if she had grasped what Miri had told her. Miri had repeated it to her many times, that it would happen *quando dorme*, in her father's sleep. And Giacomina would know it. She would know it had been peaceful, from Cipriano's face.

More than for any other reason, mightn't Giacomina then brave all the terror in the world to be there awaiting Miri on the sandy path, standing out there precisely to tell Miri that she dared to be there, that she was capable, now that her long vigil was over, of doing what she had never done during all those years when Miri had beckoned her to come and join her and Vittorio in their play and their *pinoli*-feast? Mightn't she be out there in the promontory wind, under the umbrella pines, to tell Miri that she was coming to them now, at last?

Brooklyn, New York
October 2012

ACKNOWLEDGMENTS

My thanks go to Puny and Vanna Miroli of Portofino, to Pina and Leandro Lanfranconi of Santa Margherita, the flames of whose respective lives have burned in my spirit for over 60 years. They, and the dear departed, have helped to animate a landscape which is always before me, and is often more vivid than the world I wake to every morning. My thanks go, too, to my mother, whose devotion to her work, both as painter and novelist, gave me more than an example: a vessel into which to pour my own working life. Her love for the landscape inhabited by *Justice* was a constant presence in the unfolding of this tale – in which she does not appear as a character but, in my heart, as the guardian spirit of the hills where the characters walk. No person I ever met or heard of sat for the main characters, but I thank those friends and acquaintances who, living in this world or only in my memories, sat for the minor ones. Finally I bless my daughter Chiara for being the miracle that inspired this book: for teaching me what it is to be reborn in another; two bodies, one person.

ABOUT THE AUTHOR

Carey Harrison was born in London, during the Blitz, to actor parents Rex Harrison and Lilli Palmer, and was brought to America as soon as World War II ended. Since then he has spent half his life in the United States and half in Britain and other parts of the world. He has won numerous literary prizes with his novels and his plays, and is Professor of English at the City University of New York. Details of his work and life can be found on his website, *iwontbiteyou.com*. Carey Harrison lives in Woodstock, New York, with his wife, the artist Claire Lambe.

Alessandro Clemenza